Totally Bound Publishing books by Aliyah Burke

Single Books
Through The Fire
Seducing Damian

Code of Honour
A Marriage of Convenience
The Lieutenant's Ex-Wife
A Man Like No Other
When Stars Collide

In Aeternum
Casanova in Training
Harbour of Refuge
Protected by Shadows
Polar Opposites

Theta Corps
Restitution
Contrition
Vindication

Interludes
Temporary Home
Alone With You
Till We Ain't Strangers Anymore

The Edge
Called Home to The Edge
Straying to The Edge
Returning to The Edge
Cuffed at The Edge

The Monroe Sisters
Need You Now
Let Me Go
I Won't Say Goodbye

Keeper of the Stars
Part One
Part Two
Part Three
Part Four
Part Five

Astral Guardians
Chasing the Storm
Highlands at Dawn
Fields of Thunder
Branded by Frost
Driven by Night
Moon of Fire

What's her Secret?
Preconception

Heart's Compass
The Princess and the Marquess

With Taige Crenshaw

Single Title
Unbreakable Bonds

Kemet Uncovered
Talios
Devi
Linc
Saffron
Taber
Ashia

Heart's Compass

THE PRINCESS AND THE MARQUESS

ALIYAH BURKE

The Princess and the Marquess
ISBN # 978-1-83943-847-9

Interior text design by Claire Siemaszkiewicz
Totally Bound Publishing

Published in 2020 by Totally Bound Publishing, United Kingdom.

Totally Bound Publishing is an imprint of Totally Entwined Group Limited.

THE PRINCESS AND THE MARQUESS

Dedication

Thank you to Totally Bound for coming with me on this journey as I get to play in the past. To my readers, I know, I know, not enough historicals, but here is another for you. DH—love you. As always, my heartfelt thanks to the men and women of the Armed Forces who sacrifice so much.

Chapter One

The intense weather fell harsh and unforgiving, offering the inhabitants a preview of what was to come in the frigid months that loomed ahead. Thunder rumbled as lightning flashed through the mountains. A winter storm. The winds howled as if they were straight from the bowels of hell, intent on ripping everything in their path to pieces. No living person, sane person, would be caught out in this.

Twenty-four-year-old Ciara Malika McKay swore to herself as she fought and strained against the winds that whipped through the mountains. Every single step she struggled to take, their strength knocked her back five. *What am I doing out on a night like this?*

In her defense, she'd needed more herbs and when she had left her cabin this morning the weather hadn't been like this at all. Of course, she could have returned earlier when she had experienced the air change with the impending storm. But when had she ever done anything the easy way?

The life she led was hard, but she wouldn't change it for anything. For all intents and purposes, she was alone on this mountain with only animals to befriend her. She did not often venture down into the town that was at the base of a neighboring mountain because she disliked the crowds. Especially after that *one* incident.

Ciara preferred to keep her interaction with people confined to the elderly women who lived at the outskirts of the town. Even then she kept her visits short. She visited them only because they were the final link to her parents she had left.

* * * *

Paradise Cove was nestled at the foot of a mountain. It was a town composed of outcasts. All were welcome there, regardless of race or religion or any other determining factor in most places. The numerous occupants comprised escaped slaves, Indians and whites who had ventured in and chosen to stay. The residents had a close network. Despite their differences, they protected, defended and supported each other. It was a prosperous spot.

Regardless of the good they presented, Ciara chose to live high up in the mountains, keeping to herself. All the townspeople knew of her and yet few could call her friend.

She was legend, a myth. A young woman who lived by herself up there. Those who sought her out never found her. Not a trace of her or her cabin. She was like the mist.

How she came and went depended on her mood. There were those few adventurous men who declared they would be the one to find this elusive wood sprite. But when they made it back to civilization all they had were faint memories of a hooded figure who had stood over them and carried them to the base of the mountain.

* * * *

She cursed again as the wind ripped her hood off her head. Ciara jerked it back up as she squinted through the pelting rain. Her herbs were safe at her waist and, as she sank into some mud, she growled to herself. A shape materialized out from the rain itself before her and she smiled despite her current situation as she laid her eyes on her friend, Faolan.

He was a large wolf, blacker than the darkest night and just as dangerous. She had saved him from a trap years ago and he had never left. Silent, he stood gazing upon her with amber eyes before turning and melting back into pitch black. She followed with the knowledge that he would lead her safely through. Ciara groaned with relief as she saw her cabin outlined in the flashes of lightning, so she hastened, eager to be out of this weather.

A push opened the door and she stood dripping on her wooden floor as Faolan streaked past her to shake and lay himself by the stove. Taking off her sodden cloak, she shivered as she hung it, then made her way to start a fire. When the room heated, she stripped and put on some dry clothes with haste. Then, turning her attention to the herbs she had gathered, she laid them out to dry as well.

Warm, dry and safe from the storm, Ciara set to her next task. Food. She enjoyed a simple meal of soup and bread and remembering the past as she cleaned up from that.

Closing her eyes against the onslaught of pain at the memory of her parents, she banked her fire and climbed into her bed to fall asleep, ignoring the tears on her face, alone except for the wolf in her two-room cabin.

* * * *

Lucien St. Martin, the eighth Marquess of Heartstone, smothered a groan as he looked out of the window at the endless miles of dust, dirt and anything far from clean. This country was vast and not at all where he wanted to be. However, being that he was unable to tell his father, Sebastian St. Martin, Duke of Stokley, no, here he was, traveling in this godforsaken continent to acquire a horse.

Turning to his companion, Blake Trent, he asked, "How much longer? I wish to get out and get cleaned up."

The man in the carriage looked him in the eye as he answered, "We are almost there. The town will have a place for you to stay and then in the morning you can speak to the ones who can tell you how to get the horse."

"Not until morning." His words were laced with disgust. "I have had enough of this rustic crap. I wish to get the horse and leave. I thought that this was understood."

"With respect, sir, this is a rather large place and these horses are very worth the wait."

Arching an aristocratic brow, Lucien looked down his nose at the man across from him. "I realize that this is a big place. The country is larger than my own, no doubt filled with thieves and scoundrels of the worst kind.

However, I was promised that the horse would be here for me."

The carriage jolted to a stop and Blake jumped down. "You are the one two weeks late. The horse was here on time. We had to go have the horse brought back."

Lucien watched in silence as the man disappeared into the dusk. He climbed down out of the carriage and had to keep his temper so as not to blow the sale of the horse. The town was clean but small, the streets well-lit, and as he looked, there was an imposing picture of the mountains behind the town being covered like a veil by rolling dark clouds. He straightened his clothes, to once again regain his impeccable look, then turned and headed into the building the carriage had stopped beside. *Momma Marie's.*

He swung open the door, then stepped inside. Behind the counter stood a tall, distinguished black man.

"Good eve, sir. Were you looking for a room to rent?"

A brusque nod answered the question. He strode to the counter and slapped his leather gloves down on it. He gazed around and took in the surroundings. A few patrons sat at the tables through a walkway as they ate dinner in the dining area, but otherwise it was very quiet.

"For how long will you be staying, sir?"

"Not sure. Where can I find M. Thomson?" In an instant, the man's eyes shuttered.

What is going on here?

"I can have someone show you. Your key, sir, you are in room four. It's upstairs and to the left. Dinner is at six. I will send someone to your room to escort you to the Thomson residence."

"My bags?"

"They are already in your room. Paul shall be to your room shortly."

"Good evening, sir. I am Paul. I will be taking you to the Thomson place."

Gritting his teeth to keep his automatic response contained, he nodded as he followed the boy down the stairs. As they stepped out onto the street, he noticed the clouds rolling over the mountains in the distance. The wind picked up and plucked at his cloak like a young debutante plucking the petals off a flower.

"This way, my lord."

Arching his brow, he looked at the lad. "How is it you know my title?"

"Everyone knows. It's not often that anyone with a title comes through. Just that titles don't mean much here. We are all equals."

Lucien hid his surprise at that statement. As he looked around, he noticed many different shades of skin color on the people in the town, from the palest white to mahogany to a deep coal black. No one but him seemed to notice any difference. Children played together in the increasing winds and adults spoke to each other regardless of sex and color. The attitude was much more lackadaisical than anything he would run into back in England.

Lucian noticed how people automatically got out of his way. He doubted it was because he was a titled marquess from England, he wasn't sure they knew, but because his presence and sheer size made them move to the side.

By the time the sun had set, Paul was leading him up some stairs to a small house on the edge of town. On his estate, it would be considered a crofter's hut.

He waited with impatience while Paul knocked. Lucien followed Paul into the house and stopped in shock when he saw two ladies sitting in chairs smiling at him. One of them spoke.

"I'm M. Thomson. Please come in and sit down."

After his large frame had settled in a chair that appeared too fragile to hold his body, he gazed at the women and asked, "Where is the one with whom I was corresponding?"

The little lady with the gray hair smiled at him. She reminded him of someone he had not thought about in a long time, his own grandmother. "I am the one who you need to deal with. About the stallion. We expected you earlier and for that reason the horse is not here today. But we can have him here tomorrow."

"How is it that I was dealing with you and not your husband?"

"Mind your tongue, boy. This may not be England, but you can still show some respect," she snapped at him.

"My apologies. I am just anxious to get the horse and leave."

"Very well." With a wave of her hand, she sent Paul on his way. "You are dealing with me, because my husband is dead. Not that it is any of your business. The stallion will be here in the morning and then you can leave. Now we need to discuss payment."

"Payment will come after I inspect the horse." His response fell right away.

This was an area that he could handle. He wasn't going to pay that much for an animal that may very well be worthless. He had been against this from the beginning and the only reason that he was the one to go was because his father had ordered it. Who heard of traveling across the seas to get a horse when the finest cattle were to be found in England anyway?

Humph. "You will want the horse, although you may not be able to handle him."

"Madam," he groused, his tone imperious, "I have yet to meet a horse that I cannot handle."

"Temper yourself, boy. You English sure are touchy. By the way, my name is Marie and this one here is Angelique. She is deaf but not blind so smile at her."

Colonials. They would be the death of him. This wasn't even in the colonies but in the untamed west. Worse. They were dreadful and wild. And still, he did as she bade him and smiled at the one named Angelique.

"I shall bid you good night then and will see you in the morning." Lucien sketched a bow to both of them and let himself out of the house. Striding up the street back to the hotel, he looked down as he saw Paul running up to him.

"Sir, what are the seas like?"

Childish inquisition was something Lucien was not prepared at all to handle. He was not a man used to dealing with children—rather he felt that they should be seen little and heard even less. Paul was gazing at him with some kind of worshiping eyes as he waited for the answer to his question.

"Wet," Lucien snapped and strode on.

He had zero remorse for biting at the boy but he had no experience in dealing with children. His own father had not wanted to deal with him and now it was only to issue foolhardy commands such as this one. He looked back and saw that the boy had stopped and scuffed the toe of his boot in the dirt.

The memories of wishing that his own father would show any interest in what he had done came back with a vengeance to haunt him. The pain of rejection made him reevaluate his manner.

"Come here. Paul, was it? What do you wish to know about the sea?"

Grinning so wide his face must be about to split, the boy ran back up to him. "Everything. I want to go to sea so bad but I can't. Have to take care of me Ma."

"Have you eaten?"

"No, sir. It is about dinnertime but I haven't eaten yet."

"Come with me and I will speak with you while we eat." The glow that crossed Paul's face made him further upset for the way he had treated him earlier.

By the time Lucien St. Martin had finished his dinner, there sat four boys and two girls around him as they listened to him tell tales of his travels from England to here. He had purchased food for all of them and they ate and grinned from ear to ear.

Chapter Two

One of the boys asked when he had finished eating, "Are you getting that big bay stallion that runs these mountains?"

"What do you know of this stallion?" Lucien asked, wondering if he would have to deal with people trying to steal the animal from him.

"Everyone knows about him. His sire is the best horse around, but since there is no way you could have him, it is easy to guess you would be after the son."

"His sire? There is another stallion?" Yet one additional blow about him not being able to handle a horse—this was getting old. And yet he was intrigued because the sire of this horse could be his ticket to the racing circles in England.

Paul broke in. "You may as well forget the sire. You will have enough trouble with the bay. You couldn't handle the black."

Insulted beyond words, Lucien bit back a retort and as he asked his next question the steel underlay to his tone hinting at his displeasure. "Why do you say that?"

One of the girls spoke. "Paul don't mean no harm by it. It's just a fact. No one but *her* could handle a horse like that. Besides, he isn't around on this mountain anymore so it don't matter anyway." This little woman was mouthy, something his own sister was anything but. She was glowing and full of life as she talked to him, looking him straight in the eyes.

"Who is *she*?" The words slipped out before he could catch them.

"Children, enough." The black man who had been at the counter of the hotel interrupted them with a stern voice. "There is no need to bother him with stories. Especially ones that are none of his concern." His eyes sent a silent message to the children. "He will get his horse in the morn and be gone. Y'all need to get home before that storm hits here."

None of the children argued. It was as if someone had removed every one of their tongues. All of them nodded at him as they disappeared out through the door into the night after thanking him for dinner.

"What were they talking about, a black stallion?" Lucien asked the unsmiling man.

"Nothin', sir. Children like to tell stories. That is all. Nothing more, nothin' less. Your horse is here and you can see him in the morning. Will there be anything else that I can get for you tonight?"

"No. Thank you. That will be all."

"Goodnight then." The man departed as silent as the children had, leaving Lucien to digest it all. The kitchen maid came and took his dishes and before long he was the only one still in the room.

He went up to his small room. The bed was big enough for him, but just. This was a strange town. It was as if they had a secret to protect. Secrets had always intrigued Lucien and his juices were flowing. They were hiding something.

He paused at the footsteps coming down the hall, and whispers. He listened.

"They spoke of the black stallion. He wanted to know more. The children also mentioned her. I know when a man is curious. Should we warn her?" The black man's voice reached Lucien through the thin walls.

"She can handle herself. She is a special girl. Besides, she isn't over here. She is on her mountain. My guess is the black will be over there. I don't think this one will try to go and find the 'heart of the mountain.' You stopped the kids before they could say anything else." This time it was a woman who spoke.

Heart of the mountain? What are they speaking about? Her mountain?

"Besides, once he sees the bay he will leave. The money from the horse will help out for the families coming in. She will make sure that Marie will see to that. Don't worry so, Abe. Come to bed." The voice seemed a bit strained.

"Yes, dear. It's just that she is all alone and I worry about her."

"She is better protected than we are here in town and you know it."

The voices faded as a door shut.

Something was going on. Lucien lay on the bed as his mind whirled about what he had heard and he fell asleep with thoughts racing through his head about this *heart of the mountain*. Whatever that was. Who was she and why was she better protected than they were in town?

* * * *

The next morning, Lucien, anxious to see this horse, ate a fast breakfast and headed once again down the main street of town. Paul was there to lead him to his destination and, before he thought about it, Lucien asked, "Whom were you speaking about last night? The *her* that you mentioned, who is it?"

Even though the tone he had was the one that made most people just do his bidding, it didn't work.

Paul didn't look at him, instead squared his shoulders and kept walking. "Nobody. We were talking. That's all. The livery is over there. Good luck. I gotta go." He ran off before Lucien could blink. All traces of being in awe over a man who had sailed the seas were gone.

After he entered the livery, Lucien saw a large man bent over as he pounded on iron in the back of the building. The noise ended when he loudly cleared his throat a few times. The man stood upright, and for once in his life, Lucien found himself looking up at another man.

He was huge, about a head above Lucien, who was a big man. This man had coal-black skin and sweat poured down his face even at this early and cool time of the day. The man turned to wipe his face and slip on his shirt. As he did, Lucien saw crisscross marks all over his back. There was no doubt what they were from. A whip.

Turning around, the man smiled and held out his hand. "Morning, my lord. You must be here to see the bay. I just brought him in last night. Follow me. He is out in the corral."

Aside from the American accent, the man could have been in a drawing room in England with his speech. Lucien shook the offered hand then followed the man out to the corral.

The bay shocked him. His coat gleamed in the morning sun. Small defined head, powerful hindquarters and a deep chest. Lucien walked up to the fence and smiled. He would indeed be hard pressed to find cattle like this at Tattersall's on a good day. There looked to be some Arabian in him but he wasn't sure.

The horse screamed speed, endurance and all that he knew his father would want. His father had one of the top stables in England and the duke was always looking for ways to increase his stock. The only reason he wanted this stallion was because he'd heard he was fast, amazingly so, and since he knew that Lucien wanted to have a racing stable he bought him before his son could.

To add insult to injury, he had ordered Lucien to fetch the horse for him. Anger pooled in his gut as he looked at the horse and thought of what his father had done.

"He's a beaut, isn't he? He knows it too."

"Yes. I would look at him closer."

The large man nodded as he picked up a rope and sent it sailing over the neck of the stallion. Murmuring in low, soft tones, he approached him and, when the horse was secure, the man led him over to Lucien.

The horse was every bit the arrogant stallion he had been promised. Excited at the prospect of being on the back of such an animal was a shock to the man who rarely got that way about anything. Even his trips to his mistress were done in a cool and calculated way, no emotions allowed. He wasn't referred to as The Black Marquess for nothing.

"I would ride him."

If the blacksmith was surprised by that declaration, he showed no signs of being so. Saddling the horse, he stepped back and looked at the man.

Lucien stared at the saddle. It was not what he was used to, that was for sure. He grabbed the reins and swung up into the unexpectedly comfortable seat. The stallion tensed as Lucien's cloak settled over his haunches but made no other notice of it.

As he swung open the gate, the blacksmith looked at him and spoke before he stepped out of the way. "Stick to the paths, my lord. We don't want you to become lost."

Lucien bit his tongue to keep his retort in his mouth. He was no milksop. He did not know this place as well but he did not need anyone to babysit him. The stallion below him was prancing and anxious to be off. The breath from his nostrils could be seen in the cool morning air. The contained power beneath him was obvious as he moved the horse forward.

Lucien took the street out of town and found himself looking out onto a field of green flowing grass. Without a second thought, he touched his heels to the horse and they shot away. The horse had speed, and as they flew across the ground Lucien couldn't help but be at peace. He lost himself in the ride and the fluidity of the animal between his legs.

Pulling the horse to a stop, he looked around him. The view was unbelievable. The grass that flowed in the breeze, the wildflowers, and the stream sparkled beneath the morning sun as it ran along the edge of the field toward another mountain covered in snow. There were no signs of human life anywhere and he felt as if he were the only person in the world. A snort made him look in the direction of the stallion's gaze. What he saw took his breath away.

On the side of the mountain, next to the one the town was under was a horse the color of ebony. He gleamed in the sun as he stood and surveyed his domain. He could have been a statue carved out of black marble for he was so still. His ears forward, neck arched, mane and tail the only thing moving. What he spied presented such a gorgeous view that it took Lucien a moment to realize what he was seeing was not fake but flesh and blood. This must be the black stallion they had been talking about at the hotel.

The horse beneath him started to prance and blow. Automatically, Lucien brought him under control. Lucien watched as the free horse in the next second pinned back his ears and let out a squeal that chilled him to the bone. His horse reacted as if he had been shot. He reared up and screamed a challenge back at him.

The one on the ridge tossed his head, then, as if he had wings, turned and ran from view. As he struggled to keep control over the horse, Lucien failed to notice the clouds rolling in. Fast, dark and ominous.

His mount sidestepped and almost tossed him. In the time it took him to regain his seat, the stallion had grabbed the bit and headed up the other mountain in hot pursuit of the black horse. Lucien settled in for the ride, knowing his best chance was to hang on.

Higher and higher the stallion took him. When the rain came, he didn't slow or even stop. They had taken so many turns that Lucien was not sure at all where he was. Lightheaded—he was lightheaded from the thin air. As man and horse burst into a clearing he saw the black horse at the other side. His stallion's sides were heaving from exhaustion, but the bay still issued a challenge to the other horse.

Lucien wrested control back from the irate equine and as he sat there, what had begun as rain turned to snow. The temperature dropped even further, and he contained a shiver, grateful for what little protection his cloak offered. He was in real trouble. His mount had a desire to fight another horse and he didn't have a clue as to where he was.

A crash through the trees followed a low lumbering growl. His horse was no longer fixed on the black across from him, but the thing headed at them. An angry bear came thundering into view. It stood and roared at them all. Lucien's horse spun and lunged away as the bear dropped and headed for them.

As his mount ran from the enraged bear, Lucien prayed he would get out of this. The air rushed by him as the ground rose to meet him. He had been thrown. The bear, after taking a swipe at the horse, turned his attention to Lucien. For the first time in a long time, since he had first entered the army, he experienced pure fear.

The last conscious thought he had was that he was going to die in this bloody country. No one would know where he was and his father would probably say only "such a bloody shame he didn't bring me the horse." He smelled the foul breath as the bear ripped at him with its teeth and claws.

Chapter Three

Ciara shivered as the cold wind blew around her. *I should have worn my heavier coat.* Dressed in her buckskins, she did a final check on her winter wood supply. It should last. Her father had made a shed right outside the cabin and she had spent the past few months ensuring it was stocked full. It was. Her food larders were full also. A grin split her face as she gazed over at the valley below her. She took a slow, deep breath of the crisp air and turned to Faolan, who was stretched out on the ground fast asleep. Snow was coming—she could smell it in the air and see it in the clouds.

"Get up, old man. We have one more stop to make."

At her voice, Faolan rose to stand beside her. His head was higher than her hip and he was a sinister-looking wolf. He leaned on her and Ciara knew that the wolf could push her over if he wanted to. Ciara pulled on his ear with affection before she headed off.

With a quick stop-off at the cabin she picked up her cloak and herb pouch. The rain had started and she knew that by this evening there would be snow on the ground. Ciara started a fire to make sure her cabin would be nice and warm when they returned. After closing the door behind her, she stopped to fix her cloak.

The thickness was one reason she wore it—the hood helped. The main reason was, however, it was a special cloak. She had made it to suit her needs. It had the ability to cover her from head to ankle to wrap her in a cocoon if she wished or had to sleep on the ground, keeping her warm, but it also could be formed to fit her body like a second skin.

There was a row of buttons on the back that she could undo so the cloak would split, which enabled her to secure each half to each leg. The part by her waist could be pulled in for a snug fit. She could go from a woman enveloped by a thick cloak to a woman who looked like she wore heavy clothing.

When she needed to move quickly or carry a kill, she would secure the cloak to her body so there was no loose material. She did so now, not wanting to repeat the drenching experience of last night. Once ready, she set off on her jog she always took through the woods, Faolan by her side.

When the rain switched to snow, she stopped gathering herbs. She rose and turned to head back to the cabin when she heard it.

Faolan hackled and faced toward a deeper part of the woods. It was the growling of a bear. *Strange, they should all be sleeping now.* Ciara moved forward swiftly, albeit without noise, as she headed for the sound, scanning the ground for signs. The ones she saw didn't bode well for the object the bear had in its clutches because she noticed the prints of a smaller cub too.

Something came between a mama and her cub.

She heard another noise in there as well. A cry. A moan. A scream. The closer she got, the more uncertain she became. A scrap of cloth caught her attention. It was from a cloak. A person. The bear had a person in its clutches.

Without conscious thought for her own safety, she ran into the small clearing where a bear mauled a man, making him look like a rag doll she'd had as a kid. She screamed at the creature.

"Get away from him! Get out of here!"

Faolan jumped in, drawing the bear's attention from the man. Faolan kept the bear moving backward to avoid the attack of the large wolf that held no fear. Every time the bear turned to make a circle back to the man, the canine was there to hold him at bay. When Faolan and the bear were clear of the human on the ground, Ciara ran to him. He was alive, but not by much, and unconscious.

She worked fast to make a paste from some of the herbs and falling snow to help staunch the flow of blood. When she had ripped his cloak, what was left of it, off she sucked in her breath.

Thick, silky black hair was plastered to his head. His skin was pale from blood loss, but she knew that it would be a golden tan when he was healthy. Ciara shook her head to regain her wits. He would never make the night here.

Ciara hefted him to an upright position, unfastened her cloak and put it over the shoulders of the man slumped against the tree. The cloak barely fit him.

While she scanned for any signs of the bear or Faolan, she bit her lip in concentration when she realized what she had to do for this man to survive. Ciara crouched down in front of him then put her shoulder into his stomach, as she pulled him so he toppled into her.

She rose slowly as she adjusted the large man who hung over her shoulders, her legs staggering under his weight. When he was secure, she headed off to her cabin. He was carried just like she would carry a kill she made.

However, he wasn't like any kill she'd made before. Even in as good shape as she was in, she breathed harsh as she entered the copse where her cabin resided. As she approached the cabin, Faolan came from out of the trees unharmed and hit the latch with his head and let himself in before her.

Ciara unceremoniously dumped the man on the bed nearest to the fireplace, the one she'd used when her parents had been alive and they had occupied the only bedroom. She shut the door against the increasing flakes and cold. First, she built up the fire even more, then she prepared some more pastes to heal those wounds and draw out any poison from the bear's claw marks.

While the paste cooled, she stripped the man on the bed. His chest was broad and covered with a dusting of dark hair. Even with his given wounds she saw he was not a lazy man. He was in good shape so she hoped he would heal without delay, which she told herself was the only reason she looked.

She bathed his chest and applied the paste where necessary, covering his injuries with bandages to keep the plaster in place. There were three wounds that concerned her, but from the way the bear had sounded and acted, she was worried there might be more.

His upper body done, she covered him with a quilt, and after a short struggle to get his breeches off because they were wet with blood, snow and mud, she muttered and slit them with a knife.

She cleaned his scratches and checked for broken bones. His arm had been fractured and she splinted it. His legs seemed to be fine aside from the scores and abrasions. She rolled him over and checked his back, and backside. Other than the three deep gashes that went across his ribs and onto his back, he was clean from any major wounds.

Sure there were no more wounds that needed to be tended, she covered him with thick quilts to keep him warm then saw to herself. She changed into a dry pair of buckskins. She hung his clothes over a chair by the fire then made herself something to eat, but she still checked on her patient every once in a while.

She made some willow bark tea and dribbled it into his mouth, knowing if a fever did hit him, it wouldn't be good. He seemed to be in a peaceful slumber as she headed for her own bed, the door left open so she could hear him in the night.

"No! Get off me. Damn it, I don't want to die here." In a voice that almost broke her heart, he asked the elusive person in his dream, "Why couldn't you just love me? Why did you hate me so?" Even filled with so much tormented pain, his voice was deep and smooth.

Ciara jumped out of bed at the masculine voice that resonated through her cabin. She flew out to the bed where her stranger lay and noticed that he was thrashing around, covered in sweat. He had a fever.

Chapter Four

For the next two and a half weeks, Ciara battled his fever as she watched her mountain become buried under more snow than she had seen in many years.

She stretched as she heated some stew on the range. Exhaustion had begun to own her. She looked over at the man lying prone on the bed. She fed herself and went to check on him.

He was cool to the touch. She had done it. His fever was gone. Ciara grinned in relief at a successful job. She rose to go get him more willow bark tea and after she dribbled most of the cup into his mouth, she offered up a prayer of thanks. She took the cup over to her table and set it down. She changed into her warm bedclothes. She wore an old shirt of her father's. It was linen and hung down to mid-thigh on her.

Before she left to get some much needed and deserved sleep, she checked on her patient one more time. She brushed her hand over his face that now sported a beard, grateful to discover he was still cool.

Briefly she closed her eyes, nodded her relief and withdrew her hand.

She found it clasped in a grip that was tight despite the weakness the man himself had.

"Don't leave me. So soft, so sweet. Stay the night with me," he mumbled, tugging her closer.

Ciara allowed him to pull her closer, ignoring the low growl that came from Faolan. Her stranger's hand moved upward and tangled itself in her unbound hair. His mouth brushed over hers, which caused her heart to beat wildly. He moaned against her lips as he slid his tongue along them, then slipped it inside her waiting mouth.

"So soft, like silk. You are so beautiful, everything I could ever want in a woman. Beautiful skin, the color of rich cream, hair like golden wheat."

Realization hit her like ice water. He was dreaming of someone. For some reason that hurt. She tried to pull back but he tugged her down so she was sprawled over him, not even wincing from the pain of her on his wounds. He edged over a little without relinquishing his hold on her.

She settled in beside him, for what did it matter where she slept as long as she finally got some sleep? Her last thought before she drifted into a much welcome oblivion was that she was warm and safe in this man's arms.

* * * *

Lucien came awake a bit at a time and wished he hadn't when the pain hit him. His whole body was sore. He tried to open his eyes, but it was just too much. His body was on fire. He tried to move but there was something on his arm. As he turned his head, he noticed a head on his shoulder. He breathed in a scent that was unlike one he had smelled before. It was clean, fresh and pure. The skin against his bare shoulder was soft like silk. It felt right, was what he thought before sleep claimed him again.

* * * *

Ciara woke to a chill in the air of the cabin. However, she was comfortable and warm. And she found out why, because she lay draped over this man like a common whore. Her nightshirt had ridden up and her legs straddled one of his. She was flush up against him and yet she was thankful he still slept.

She slid out of bed, covered him and went to dress. She came back into the room much more comfortable and she built up the fire. Ciara ruffled Faolan's ears as she put on her cloak to go outside for a bit.

* * * *

His eyes opened. His head was pounding and his body was still in tons of pain. He couldn't make sense of where he was. He remembered a bear, his stallion running off and the subtle smell of something that made him hard with desire. A woman. He couldn't remember her face, only her scent. It was next to him, where she was supposed to be. *Where is she? Where am I? Who is she?*

He glanced to the door when it opened. A hooded figure came in followed by the biggest, blackest dog he had ever seen. The cold air that blew in with them made him suck in his breath even though he was under all those quilts. At his gasp, the figure turned toward him.

The person set down the wood it carried and made sure the door was shut tight against the howling winds. With a wordless gesture it sent the black canine to go lie down.

"Who are you?" His voice was raspy, dry. "Where am I?"

The figure took off the cloak and what he saw made his jaw drop. It was a woman. She had on pants that fit her like a second skin. Black hair that looked to be very short. She had full lips and a petite nose on a face graced with the most beautiful eyes he had ever seen set above high-placed cheekbones. Amber. Not just any amber, but one that reminded him of a rich whiskey. They were hauntingly beautiful. Potent.

Her bronze skin glowed from the cold and it was not long before he realized he had begun to stiffen under her direct gaze. She looked like no one he had seen before. The women he had known and loved from England to Egypt vanished from his thoughts. He groaned.

Right away, she moved to the stove and made him a cup of something. She didn't move like most women he knew either. Hers was a natural grace and not one that had been trained to look that way in attempts to snare a rich husband. As his vision stopped beside the bed, she held the cup toward him.

"Would you like to sit up?" Her voice, low and melodious, made his member twitch.

"Yes." He struggled to do so but, to his immense embarrassment, he couldn't do it.

Without any comment, she set down the cup and lifted him as if he weighed nothing. She placed him up against some cushions and when he was settled, she handed him the cup. "Drink it all."

He drank with small sips as his eyes followed her about the cabin. Another very small building. He rested on a pallet of some kind in an alcove. As the warmth sank into him, he looked around the cabin, noticing Celtic artifacts and some that appeared to be African as well. Lucien slanted a look at her as he wondered what her story was. His hand shook with exhaustion by the time he finished his drink.

After, he gazed down at his bare chest. He looked up at her heading over with some fresh bandages.

"I will check your wounds, then if you wish something to eat, let me know."

She was so direct Lucien didn't know how to respond. Still, he wanted to keep her talking. Had to find out information. "Where is my horse?"

Surprise flitted across her features. "What horse?"

"You didn't see one? Maybe he made it back to the village." He tried not to be affected by her nearness as he recognized her scent from the one that had been next to him in his dreams.

She sat on a chair beside him and proceeded to check his bare chest like it was something she did every day. "Paradise Cove? You are the man, the Englishman who was coming for Nyama and Cloud's son." It was not a question but a statement. "The bay stallion."

He responded as he sat forward. "Yes. Damn it. Now I don't know where he is. This whole trip will be for nothing. Who are Nuamama and Cloud?"

He stumbled over the pronunciation of the words. Lucien flopped back against the cushions while he panted for breath. As she applied more paste to his scars and put new bandages on him, her subtle scent flowed over his senses, making him respond in ways he should not have. Ways that he had no energy to even think about.

"Nyama and Cloud. They are the sire and dam of the bay you came for." She stood, and before he could stop her, she flipped back the quilts covering his lower half, which had kept hidden his substantial erection he had as a result of her closeness to him. Lucien flushed with embarrassment, but as he tried to protest he noticed she didn't even seem to be fazed by it. She only doctored his wounds and that was all.

Chapter Five

Ciara was fazed. It took every bit of her inner strength to keep all emotion off her face. She had no idea he would look like this. His rod jutted out from a thick nest of black hair. It quivered as if it had a life all its own. There was a tiny drop of dewiness at the very top. She wanted to touch it, to see if it was as soft as she imagined. She finished as fast as possible without circumventing any of his wounds. She stood as she flicked the quilts back over him with a dismissive glance.

"Would you like to eat? I have some stew that you should be able to handle."

"Have you no shame or are you so used to looking at men in that state?"

She ground her jaw and took a deep breath to remain calm.

"I have no time for modesty. I have been taking care of you for the past two weeks, since I was merely concerned with keeping you alive. I did not mean to embarrass you. If you think you can handle me looking upon you, I will help you to dress in your pants."

"No, I am sorry. Have I really been here for two weeks?" He readjusted the quilt over his lower body. "My name is Lucien St. Martin, Marquess of Heartstone. You can call me Saint. What is your name? And yes, I would like at least my pants."

Men. Always trying to impress a woman. "Ciara." She pronounced it *kee-ar-ra* with a slight rolling of the 'r'. She turned her back on him and went to the stove to get him a bowl of soup. He needed to stay in bed for a bit yet and keeping his clothes from him seemed to be the best way.

"That's it? Nothing else to your name?"

She settled herself back on the chair by his pallet and offered him the bowl. "Ciara Malika McKay. What about you, anything else to your name? Can you eat on your own or would you like some help? Eat first, clothes second."

Regardless of the fact that he shook with exhaustion, he snapped, "Lucien Brenden Remington St. Martin. I can feed myself." He took the bowl and set it on his lap, but the first spoonful he spilled most of on his chest. His face flamed with anger or embarrassment, maybe both.

Ciara said not one word, just rose and got a cloth to wipe his chest clean. She took the bowl and fed him little by little.

Once he'd eaten and drunk everything, she set it to the side. "Do you need to relieve yourself?"

"Help me up. I will go outside."

"I don't think so." She rose and got a pot. It was placed on his lap and she said to him, "I will be back in a few minutes." Ciara swung on her cloak, and flipped the hood up as she and her canine disappeared into the swirling snow.

Upon her return, she noticed how he almost knocked the pot over when he got back into bed, dressed in woolen pants her father had worn.

Not saying anything, she came and removed the pot and took it outside. She was gone for about fifteen minutes. When she returned, she carried more wood along with the pot, cleaned out.

Ciara set down the wood and hung her cloak. As she stoked the fire she turned to look at her 'guest', watching him fight exhaustion as he struggled to pull the heavy quilts up over him. When her hands were warm she walked over there, lifted the blankets and made sure he was tucked in.

When he would have said something she interrupted, "Stop fighting it. The more you rest, the sooner you will recover. Remember you were attacked by a bear. You will be up in no time. Rest now."

"Will you stay and talk with me?"

"Aye. If you wish it. I will return." She left to her room.

She had changed into dry buckskin breeches and fuzzy moccasin slippers. She sat in the large rocking chair by the fire as she absently stroked the head of her massive pet.

"Where did you get your dog?" As Lucien struggled to sit up she tensed, ready to jump up to assist if needed.

"Faolan is no dog. He is a wolf. I saved him from a trap and he has decided to stay with me."

"Faolan, what does that mean? Why are you here? Why don't you live in the town?"

"My business is my business, Wolf. Please do not ask me to speak of such things for I will not do so."

"Wolf? Why do you call me that?"

"It suits you, like Faolan. You should rest. Lie back." She liked his voice but that could prove to be problematic, she didn't need to get involved in anything with this man.

"Why do you not come lie with me? You have before, for your scent was over the pillows."

Without so much as a smile, she stood. "Of course they smell like me. This is my place and those are my blankets. I am sorry if they offend."

"Are you saying that you were not sleeping with me?"

"I have my own bed. Call me if you need anything. Goodnight, Wolf." She nodded her head and walked out of the room.

Ciara lay in her bed and trembled as she tried to get hold of herself. Having seen his aroused, naked body had shattered her composure and she was having a hard time getting it back. She thought of what he had said. *'Skin the color of rich cream and hair like golden wheat.'*

That in itself was enough to square her resolve. She just had to make sure he survived because it appeared someone waited for him. For a single selfish moment she wondered what it would be like to have a man such as him waiting for her. She fell asleep with that thought.

* * * *

A low growl woke her a few nights later. Awake in an instant, she had a knife in her hand even before her feet had hit the floor. A tall figure lurched unsteadily in front of the fire. Faolan had woken her but he stayed by her. Taking a deep breath, she put the knife down and slipped on her moccasins.

Ciara stood in the doorway and watched as he struggled to get strength back in his limbs. The fire cast a golden glow over his body that was healing fast. He would have scars, but he would survive. As she watched him in the firelight he pitched forward.

He muffled a curse as he hit the floor. Within seconds there was a pair of surprisingly strong arms around him lifting, yes lifting him up, helping him back to the bed.

Ciara laid him on the bed. "I have to make sure you didn't open your wounds." She did a quick and thorough exam before she covered him back up.

Anger at himself for being here, being injured, being so weak, all rushed to the surface and he grabbed her arm and squeezed.

"What? You aren't going to tell me that I shouldn't have been walking yet? I'm too weak? Why don't you say something? Anything?"

He was shouting by this time and Faolan had risen to stand next to his mistress. The wolf did not even hackle but Lucien couldn't mistake the menace as it rolled off him in waves.

Her calm, lilting voice broke through his fog. "If you value your life, remove your hand from my arm." He realized it had been a huge mistake to touch her in anger with the wolf around.

"You are brave with the wolf to hide behind," he sneered. He did release her arm.

"No harm done. What good would I do if I told you those things? Your body is weak, not your mind. I don't need to tell you things like that. I couldn't know what your body is capable of more than you could. You are a man. I figure you would like to be up and able to take care of yourself soon. You didn't hurt yourself so there was no harm done."

She didn't even touch the fact that she had a wolf to defend her.

When she put it that way, he could find nothing to argue with. At least she had noticed he was a man. She spoke a word to Faolan and he went to lie down on the rug by the fire. It was a word he didn't understand.

"What did you say to him?"

"Not important. Can I get you something to drink?"

"No. Thank you." He reached up to touch her face, and when he did, she stiffened but her eyes stayed on his, clear and guileless. She was beautiful. Achingly so. He wanted to kiss those full lips. He wanted to run his tongue over them and nibble on them.

"I will see you in the morning, then." She straightened and spoke one word to Faolan and he followed her into her room. She made no mention of his treatment to her and the fact that she was silent and not upset by his words or actions had a greater effect than if she had yelled at him for it.

Come morning, he was a bit stronger as he ate the breakfast she set before him. She was dressed as before in buckskins. When the meal was done he looked at her.

"How did I get here?" His memory was sketchy except for seeing the bear charge him.

"I brought you here."

"How?"

"I carried you." She took the dishes and washed them with water that had been heating on the stove.

Lucien snorted in disbelief. She was a female. "You mean you had someone help you carry me?"

"No. I carried you. There is no one usually on this mountain. You are far from Paradise Cove. It is dangerous for you to be out without a guide. Why was there no one with you?"

"I don't need someone to babysit me. I am a marquess. If you must know, I was taking the stallion for a ride. Before that damn horse spooked because of the bear." His temper rose with indignation and his voice was laden with scorn. He knew it was not fair to blame the horse for running but he had to blame someone or something and it sure wasn't going to be himself.

The dish dropped and she spun on him, eyes flashing golden fire. "You! You were a fool. You alone are to blame. Not the horse, you. I know in town they told you not to go off the path. Bears are only *one* of the things you would have to worry about in this area. While it is not a battlefield, neither is it a path through your self-absorbed, pigheaded and conceited society of the *haut ton*. As for the stallion, I hope that no harm came to that splendid creature because of your arrogance and stupidity."

Her entire body trembled. "Apparently you did and still do need someone to babysit you because if you did not, you would not have been one mountain over from where you started and I would not have had to carry you and nurse you back to health and...and now be stuck with you until spring." She spun, dishes forgotten, ripped on her gloves and put on her cloak as she exited the cabin in a blaze of glory.

He sat there in stunned silence. There were few who would speak to him in that tone. Here all winter. This was news to him. How did she know about the *ton*?

Perhaps he had been a bit arrogant in his decision but surely she was exaggerating. Females always did so when they wanted men to feel sorry for them. Damn but she was spectacular in her rage and he knew that her responses to lovemaking would be just as passionate. To his lovemaking. He had a goal—he would seduce her. She was good-looking, all right she was stunning, and he had been a while without a woman, so it would work for them both. Satisfied that his life would be getting back on track, he smiled. He with deliberate purpose forgot her accusations.

Lucien waited for her to come back into the cabin. After thirty minutes he walked a bit then sat on the bed to regain his breath. When an hour had passed, he got worried. Still no sign of her so he struggled up again and stumbled to the window by the door and pushed aside the heavy curtain. As he cleared the frost away, he looked out.

His gaze took her in as she played tag with that wolf of hers. The snow still fell and it was about up to her knees. She smiled as the animal would pounce at her and knock her down. He watched her for about fifteen minutes before she turned and loaded herself up with some wood and headed toward the cabin.

He had just made it back on the bed before she came in the door. The silence was strained as she put more wood on the fire and removed her cloak and gloves.

Taking a breath, Ciara looked at him. "I must go out for a while. Would you like to have a bath?"

A bath? It would be wonderful. "Yes, I would like one. Where do you bathe?"

"I will bring in a tub and heat the water for you. If you are sure you can handle it yourself."

His groin stirred at her words but as he looked at her face, he realized she was not being coy with her wording. Just straightforward. It was like she didn't know how to flirt and that alone made the words she spoke all the more provocative.

"I will be fine. Besides," he added, flashing a grin that was known to make women melt into his arms, "I have to get up and moving around or I will not get better at all."

"Very well." No blushes. No sighs. For all intents and purposes she was not affected by his grin at all. Lucien frowned to himself. This was going to make seduction even harder, but victory all the sweeter. The Black Marquess did not fail when it came to women. There was not one he couldn't get into his bed.

Ciara dragged in a huge metal tub. She set water to boil on the fire while the tub warmed beside it, then left him alone for a while.

After a bit, she poured the water in, laid some soap and a drying cloth on a chair next to the tub. After, she walked over to him and took off his bandages. "I believe that they can stay uncovered now. Do you require any assistance?"

The devil in him made him want to say yes, but he needed to do this on his own. "No, I will manage."

Ciara spun and went into her room and when she came back out she placed some shaving tools on the chair as well and, at his look, she added, "I did not know if you wished to shave."

Nothing more was said until she was by the door. "There is a clean shirt and your pants are there as well. You may wish to keep wearing the wool ones since yours were ripped. The fire should be fine and there is stew on the stove. Will you be okay for the day?"

The day? *Where is she going?* "Where are you going?" The question came unbidden from his lips. "It is dangerous out there. You should stay here."

"I have things to do. Will you be fine here?" She waited for his nod, then slipped out of the door, Faolan at her side.

Chapter Six

Lucien St. Martin had never been so confused. This woman must not be right in the head. Determined to forget her, he allowed the warmth of the bath to soak in. He picked up the soap she'd left and was pleased it was not a flowery scent but a more masculine one. At the same time he wondered why she had soap like this.

He shaved first so he was sure to have the energy and was better right away, having never liked beards. He stayed in the water until it started to chill before he got out and dried off by the fire. Later, after he slid back into the wool pants and socks, he looked for the shirt that she had mentioned. It was a heavy flannel that was a little tight in the shoulders but would suffice to keep him warm.

Better, he wandered around the room with little steps as he regained his strength. The items were a mix of African and Celtic heritage. The two blended together in a fashion that made the cabin look more like a home than his ancestral mansion did. His place was large and screamed wealth where her little cabin screamed love. His chest tightened when he realized this was what he needed in his life. Love.

He knew that when he returned to England he was going to look for the appropriate woman to be his marchioness, get her with an heir and go seek his pleasure with a mistress, as did most of the peers. There was no way one woman could keep his attention for the rest of his life and he would not be a cuckold. For some reason, though, the thought of living the rest of one's life with love held some appeal.

His father had treated his stepmother badly and she in turn had done the same to him. Theirs was a cold, icy relationship, different from his memories of his mother who had died birthing his sister. His father and stepmother had each carried on discreet affairs after they had married. While they lived in the same house, they slept in different rooms and barely said any civil words to one another. Not what he was looking for in a wife.

He walked to her bedroom and pushed open the door. It was barren. Well, not barren, but compared to the women's rooms he had seen it was. Most of the room was decorated the same. Bright colored cloths on the walls, her bed covered by the same type of quilts he had. There was a shelf along the wall that had some dried herbs on it, making the room smell different. Her scent, however, filled the room. He couldn't place it. It was a blend of honey and something. Something sweet, like a berry of some kind. Under the herbs were some books. There were no knickknacks aside from a carved rearing horse, a running wolf and a soaring bird. On the wall beside the mirror she had there was a painting, faded with age but still striking.

A tall redheaded man with the same color eyes as Ciara. He stood beside and stared down upon a stunning woman with skin a bit darker than Ciara's. His hand under her chin as he tipped her face up toward him. The woman had her hand on his chest and her eyes were full of love, life and laughter as they gazed up at the man beside her. Whoever had painted it had caught that with incredible fashion. At the bottom it said, Cormac Aiden and Kerry Jahzara McKay. Her parents? Whoever they were, he had never seen a couple look like that, so in love. He could feel the love coming off the painting. He left the room uncomfortable with the feeling he got.

Lucien made himself eat a bowl of the stew. It was good despite the fact that he had no idea what he had eaten. She had left some bread out for him as well and he ate that. His energy spent, he lay down for a nap.

* * * *

As she headed back to the cabin, Ciara smiled. It had been a productive day. She had located her missing herbs, even though she'd had to dig through the snow to get to them. It was fortunate she had found them for they were almost no good. She had also discovered a small mountain lion kitten next to the body of his dead mother. Not such a nice part, but it all worked out. Faolan was being its surrogate mother whether he wished to or not and it pleased her to watch as the young kitten tried to keep up with him through the deep snow. Her wolf was used to creatures coming and going in the cabin.

She had a deer slung over her shoulders. She had food but fresh meat was always welcome, especially with this growing kitten to feed as well as the very large man in her cabin. She had two rabbits hanging from her waist. Her cloak was split to fit her and as she strode toward her cabin she had a smile on her face.

For the first time since her parents died she would have someone to talk to throughout the winter, even though he was an arrogant man. As they entered the small clearing in front of the cabin, she laughed as the kitten tackled Faolan with his teeth, which caused the large wolf to howl in pain.

The sound of an animal yelp woke Lucien and he sat up slow as he cursed his weakened condition. As fast as he was healing, it was not fast enough for him. He. He despised weakness, a lesson his father had taught him and one he would never forget. He moved toward the window and pulled back the curtain. He observed Faolan as he chased what looked to be a kitten around the yard through the deep snow. He looked past them and saw a hooded figure striding up with a deer over its shoulders.

Ciara? No way. The person turned and headed for a small building to the side and dumped the animal in the snow. Then it came toward the cabin. Not sure what to do, Lucien figured that as long as the wolf didn't have a problem then it couldn't be someone bad. The door swung open and a wet wolf led in a figure in black.

After the snow was stomped off the boots, the hood was pushed back.

"You? You were the one carrying that deer?" *What kind of world did I land in?*

"Yes. How are you doing?" She leaned over and placed the tiny kitten on the floor where it looked at

Lucien, arched its back and hissed. Ciara headed to the fire and added more wood, before she began to drag out the tub.

"Wait. What are you doing?" Lucien sputtered.

Ciara returned to the cabin after a brief time while he watched warily as the kitten tried to attack the hanging quilt.

"It won't hurt you. He is only a few months old."

"Where did you get him? What is he?"

"His mom was dead. Since I couldn't leave him, I brought him back. It is a cougar kitten."

"A what kitten? What are you wearing? And what were you doing carrying a deer?"

"A mountain lion, cougar, wildcat, I don't know what you know them as. I am wearing my cloak like I always do. I thought fresh meat would be good. Especially with the little one here. I have to go and fix the meat. You stay here with the baby." At the door she paused, looked at him and smiled, completely open and unreserved, filled with humor and good cheer.

His heart stopped for a second before it started again at twice the speed. Blessed hell, she was gorgeous when she smiled like that. "Play with him, it will help you get your strength back." She slipped out through the door with Faolan.

The little creature ran to the door mewling and crying. When it couldn't get out, it made its way back over toward Lucien. The males sat and looked at each other. They sized each other up, not sure what to do. The little tan spotted furball was kind of cute.

Lucien rose with caution before he headed for the chair near the flames. The kitten followed him and rubbed against him, purring. He picked up the little thing and before long both males, wolf and lion in their own right, were fast asleep by the fire.

* * * *

Ciara came in with fresh meat for pies and stew. After the door shut, she looked and found the two weakened males asleep by the fire in the chair. Her weakened males. She put the meat down and unfastened her cloak. The kitten opened its eyes but didn't move from his warm place on Lucien's lap.

She moved in silence even as she made them some dinner. After it was in the oven cooking, she opened the door to go back out when the kitten appeared by her side. Ciara snuck a glance at the man in the chair but he was still dead to the world. Soft snores escaped his mouth. A quick glimpse at the fireplace told her that it was fine so she, Faolan and the kitten she had dubbed Kosse headed out to play in the snow that fell in fat flakes.

Lucien woke to the rich smells of cooked food. His stomach growled as he sat up in the chair and looked down at his lap. Empty. He was alone in the cabin yet again. He rose to put more wood on the fire then snuck a peek into the oven.

There was a thick roast surrounded by gravy with biscuits. His mouth watered. He listened for any sound of Ciara and smiled when her husky laugh filtered in from outside. He peered out of the window and saw her with her cloak billowing around her, as she stood between and petting two horses. One was that big black that he had seen before the bear and the other was a bay like the stallion he had ridden the day he was thrown.

Faolan and the kitten romped in the snow and the horses did not seem to be concerned by them at all. This was a strange place and she was a different kind of woman. The wind picked up speed, enough to blow her hood off her head, enabling him a clear view of her face. As he watched, the big black pawed at the falling snow and tossed his head.

Ciara grabbed his mane and swung up onto his back. He gave a halfhearted buck before he trotted around the small clearing. The mare fell into step beside him and as he watched, while in midstride, she leapt from one horse to the next. She rode the mare for a bit then hopped down before the mare even stopped.

Lucien's heart jumped up to his mouth. Anger seethed through him that she would risk herself like that. He was almost to the door to yell at her when he realized what his situation was.

He was a titled man, set to inherit a dukedom. He was trapped in a cabin, unchaperoned, with a female of marriageable age. If they were in England he would be forced to marry, well maybe not since she was not in any way what one would expect for a wife of the elite. Instead of her trying to trap him, she appeared to be almost indifferent to him. She treated his wounds and took care of him, but was much more comfortable with the animals that surrounded her for when she was with them she was completely unreserved with her emotions.

Here was a chance for him to find himself. Maybe discover that one part of him that had always been kept down before because of who he was and who he was to become. There was no society here that could slander him. No parents to show their displeasure at his activities. He could do as he wished and no one would know or care. Perhaps he would get a *friend.* He didn't have many friends, in fact he had two, but he had many acquaintances.

The company he kept obviously did not care about his title so there would be no mindless prattle to try to get in his good graces. What would they think if he came back with a wife in addition to the horse his father had ordered him bring? Shocking his parents was something he did well. What better way than to come back with a wife who was not of 'good breeding.' One who was not a blueblood. That bore further thoughts.

Ciara gave a short whistle and Faolan came to her, with Kosse in tow. She made sure that there was some grain for the horses out and she headed back into the cabin. Lucien sat at the table, his gaze predatory. In an instant she was on guard.

"Are those your horses?"

"No." Her answer came too quick to suit him. She hung her cloak and put some food down for Kosse. She let Faolan out to go hunt his own food.

"Whom do they belong to?"

"They are wild. They belong only to themselves." She set the table for dinner and, for once, she would not meet his gaze.

"Why did you help me?"

Ciara paused, confused. He was after something. "You were injured. Nothing more, nothing less."

"Thank you for that. I will repay your kindness." His voice was smooth as if he soothed a savage beast.

"I did not ask for payment, and therefore require none." She pulled the roast out of the oven and set it on the table. The aroma filled the cabin and she served him then herself. She gave him some coffee and herself some water.

"I always repay my debts." His voice showed his displeasure at her for having turned him down.

"Eat. It will get cold if you don't." Ciara closed her eyes and offered up a prayer before she began to eat.

"Do you pray?"

"Yes."

"Why did you not do so out loud?"

"I don't know your beliefs and did not wish to make you feel uncomfortable."

"Tell me about you," he commanded as he watched her eat.

Ciara looked up from eating. "Why do you wish to know about me? What interest can you have in me aside from the obvious fancy of one who is different from you? I am merely a passing interest, nothing more. I am not on display for you."

He wiped his mouth. "Tell me about Faolan."

"I already did."

Ciara understood what he was after. He wanted answers but she wasn't up to giving him any right now. So they ate in silence, even though he watched her with an astuteness that bothered.

When Faolan's low woof alerted her to his return, she got up to let him inside.

Kosse pounced at the black wolf and when Faolan ignored him and went to the fire to lie down, the kitten followed and curled up beside him. Ciara smiled as she got a pie from the back of the stove. She took a piece and set the rest by him.

She blinked and spoke. "Would you like some whiskey? I believe that I still have some."

"That would be great. Thank you."

She had to find some common ground or the rest of the winter was going to be long and horrible.

Chapter Seven

She walked away from the table before she set a bottle in front of him. It was Irish whiskey. Lucien looked up at her, his face bunched in confusion. "Where did you get this?"

"It was my father's."

"Was? Where is your father? Where are your parents?"

"Dead." She offered nothing else.

Damn it. He wanted some sort of conversation from her. Some kind of emotion. Happiness, anger, sadness. Anything. Something. Not this indifference. He was used to being the cold one who shut people out. People tried to get him to open up, not the other way. They wanted to be the one to 'tame' The Black Marquess, the one who broke through the wall that surrounded his heart.

"How did they die?"

Her eyes deepened with grief as she searched for the right word. "Heartache."

She rose from the table and picked up her cloak. "I will be back later. Can I leave Kosse here with you?"

"Kosse? Who's Kosse?" He was lost—the conversation had been taken from him again.

"The kitten. Kosse."

"Sure. No problem." Lucien kept his own counsel. He might be a rake and a harsh man but even he knew when someone needed to get away. Heartache? What did that mean? He conceded this round to her.

"Faolan." The word was spoken so soft he wasn't sure he'd even heard it. The wolf did. He rose and padded over to her side and followed her out into the increasing darkness.

Lucien sat at the table as he stroked the kitten that seemed as confused by the abrupt exit as he was, as he thought about his woman. His woman. There was something about her that made him want to gather her in his arms and protect her, to shield her from the memories that she ran so hard from. He put the dishes in the sink and heated some water. While he was still weak, he found that his strength was rapidly returning to him. She had done a wonderful job of healing him.

Despite the fact that Kosse dodged his footsteps, he did the dishes. He put more water on for some tea. Maybe she would have some more of the one she gave him when he was sick for he would not deny he was a little achy.

Lucien looked at the door and noticed a large pair of boots. They were heavy and the insides were fur lined. He put them on, and while they were a tight fit, they would keep his feet warmer than his riding boots. He noticed his cloak, what was left of it anyway, hanging on a peg as well. It was shredded and he cursed as he realized how close he had been to dying.

There was a man's heavy coat by the door and he slipped it on. It was again a little snug, but it would work. As he went to open the door, he noticed a cane resting there. It was a deep red color, smooth with figures of running wolves carved on it. The craftsmanship amazed him. He took it just in case he needed some extra help. A gun would have been nice.

As he opened the door, Kosse burst out in front of him and tumbled off the porch into the deep snow. He made the slow journey to take care of his needs. When he was done he spied Kosse who still played in the snow. Kosse lifted his head and bounded off in the opposite direction. Lucien had no choice but to follow.

He struggled through the snow as he wished he were healed all the way, wishing that there were a clear path. It was snowing and he was having a hard time following where Kosse was. In the trees, he realized that he'd lost him. "Damn cat."

The hairs on the back of his neck stood up and he turned his gaze, not in a rushed movement, getting a better grip on the cane, because that was his only weapon. It was Faolan. He relaxed a little. The wolf looked at him and trotted past him and headed off again. Before he was out of sight he angled his head and stared at him with those amber eyes as if to say, *Are you coming or not*?

Lucien followed the wolf. Faolan went at a pace that made him never disappear out of sight. He came to the clearing of a large meadow. He saw a figure in black as they kneeled in the snow by a headstone.

It was her parents' grave. He knew it just as he knew his own name. Before he got to her, he cleared his throat so she would know he was there. He noticed Kosse romped beside her.

Ciara rose when he cleared his throat. "I see you found the cane. Good. Come, we should get back. There is a storm coming."

"Do you think that we could rest for a minute? I wore myself out following that cat of yours." He gave her a crooked grin to try to lighten her spirits and the somber mood.

She gave a slight one in response. "Fine. Not long, though. I wish to be back before the storm hits. It is going to be a big one. We are going to get a lot of snow."

"How do you know?" he asked as he collapsed on the ground and tried unsuccessfully to push Kosse off his chest. Although still a kitten, Kosse was strong.

"I have lived here most of my life. I know the weather. It smells differently when there is going to be a big storm like this."

He sniffed deep and only hurt his lungs. *Nope, can't smell anything except cold.* "Is that why you said that I would be here until spring?"

"Yes. In the winter the trek to Paradise Cove would take close to a week. It is too much of a risk, with storms that come up so fast. You could be stranded right by a cabin and die not knowing how close you were to survival. Look at you now, you probably think that you walked a good distance to get here when the cabin is not very far at all. Just with the snow and cold winds, it takes a lot out of you."

"I feel like I walked a good distance." Kosse was busy and occupied as the kitten pounced at the cane. He teased the kitten. Lucien pulled it away and dropped it just out of his reach.

"No doubt you do. That is only because you are still weak from all your blood loss." Ciara approached and held out her hand to him. "We need to go now. Come, I will help you up."

The devil in Lucien twitched to life. He reached up to take her hand with the full intent to yank her down into the snow with him when she narrowed her eyes and braced herself. "How did you know what I was going to do?" He sounded like a petulant child.

"It was all over your face. You get this devilish glint in your eye." She pulled him without effort to his feet.

"Saint's woman, you are strong." *Saint's woman, my name is Saint and she should be my woman.*

"Aye, I am. And it's a good thing that is so or you would be still lying on the ground." She turned, gave him his cane and proceeded to walk away. Ciara left him to follow.

Lucien saw she was right, that Kosse had taken a long way to get to her, as the cabin was not that far away. By the time they got there, though, he was exhausted. Ciara looked back over her shoulder at him and flicked her gaze over his body in obvious perusal, making him just about groan aloud with desire.

"Do you wish some assistance?" Her voice came to him.

"Yes."

She walked back over to him and ducked under his arm. "Lean on me. You won't crush me."

He gave her most of his weight and, true to her word, she didn't fall—she did not really even stumble. As they got to the door he began to pull away so she could open it when she said, "Faolan, door." By god if the wolf didn't hit the latch with his muzzle and the door swung open.

She helped him inside to sit on the chair by the fire. She closed the door, and after making sure that Kosse had not gone back out, she took off her cloak and hung it on the hook.

Lucien liked the intimacy this gave him. He removed his boots and set them by the fire to dry out. Faolan lay down and Kosse flopped down next to him. Lucien looked up to see Ciara holding out a cup for him.

"Tea," she said to his raised eyebrow. "You looked like you were in some pain, so hopefully this will help."

"Thank you." He drank the warm brew and enjoyed it, much to his surprise. Before he would not dare drink tea. Hated it. Every time his stepmother wished him to drink it he would have a brandy or something.

She pulled up a cut log and set it between them then brought over another chair. She propped her feet, snug in warm moccasins, up onto the log and gestured for him to do the same. As she took a drink from her tea she spoke. "Tell me about your family."

The question startled him. Lucien swallowed hard as all the old resentment came up at the mention of his lands, holdings and such. He started with the stuff that had been drilled into his head to say when asked about his status.

"I am the eighth Marquess of Heartstone and will be the—"

"No," she interrupted with an unexpected wave of her hand. "I don't want to hear title stuff. Tell me *about* your family. Not what you are worth."

"My family and I don't get along. We are estranged. My parents, father and stepmother, rarely speak to each other and have affairs with other people. My brother—my stepbrother—despises me because I am to become the duke when our father passes on. He is four years younger than I. Nothing I do is good enough for my stepmother who seems to hate me with every breath she takes." Lucien didn't ignore the bitterness in his voice but for once it just was nice to get it off his chest. He glanced at her to see if there was pity in her gaze. There was nothing of the sort. Nothing but assessment.

"My stepmother is a cold, vain woman who wishes me to marry someone like her. A cold, heartless bitch. But one I suppose she can control. I spend my days doing things that will shock them and am usually found in the middle of a scandal. I have a sister but she is different. Her name is Devonna, she is eight years my junior, the one family member that I like but she doesn't acknowledge me. She spends her days sitting while she stares out of a window, not smiling or laughing. Our mother died when she was born. Of course, in our houses there is not much cause for laughter. I'd say that about sums it up. What about your family?" He looked to see if his language shocked her, but she sat there and listened to him without judgment.

"Well?" he prodded. "Your family?"

A wistful look came across her face. "My father was a farmer and bought my mother as a slave in Ireland. When they fell in love, he freed her and married her. They headed here for America to start over, where I was born. Why they left Ireland, I'll never know. I do know he wished to return some day.

"My father was a tall man, not as big as you, but close. He had bright red hair and I remember him having a booming laugh. He was a strong man, but gentle. So gentle. My mother had skin the color of mahogany. Her hair was black like ink, but soft as silk. She was tall as well and muscular. Very strong for a woman. I remember teasing Dad that she could beat him up if she wanted to. He would just laugh and say it was only because he could never raise his hand against the most beautiful woman he had ever seen.

"He taught me how to hunt, carve and speak his native Gaelic, which is where I get my accent at times. His name was Cormac, Cormac Aiden. My mother claimed that she was an African princess and Dad never argued with her, just said it was probably true. She knew medicines and taught me how to use herbs to help heal the sick.

"She was also one of the gentlest people ever. Never said a bad word about anyone. Unless they badmouthed my dad. Her name was Kerry Jahzara. She taught me to speak in her tongue and so I learned that along with English too. I am sure every now and then I sound like Mama did when she was vexed with Dad." Her words were not meant to brag, she stated what she knew.

Lucien watched as her face grew soft with love for these people she spoke of.

"We would spend our days outdoors. They helped to found Paradise Cove. But one day we moved away." Her tone grew sharp, then, as if she remembered herself, she calmed down. "Dad built this all on his own and made several trips to the town to get the things. No one knows where it is. You are the first person to be here.

"Anyway, we weren't rich but we had love. I learned to be strong and fend for myself. I have many happy memories with my parents." Ciara got up for another cup of tea. She brought more for Lucien as well.

"I think that is enough about my family."

Lucien experienced a pang of something, wistfulness perhaps, as he listened to her go on about her family. The love and happiness was something he didn't know much about. It was no wonder that most of London referred to him as the black sheep. He was a loner because that was what they made him. His parents never had time for him, never showed him love and so as an adult he was the same way. Heartless. Cold. Empty. He didn't like that revelation.

After he settled back, Lucien rubbed Kosse with his foot. The wind picked up and hammered the side of the cabin with increasing force. It was cozy and warm inside the walls, however, and he was glad to be there. They sat in comfortable silence as she sewed his cloak back up. She brought him more clothes from her father and put them on the bed.

After a while she stood and looked at him from under her lashes. "I will bid you goodnight."

She got to the door of her room when he stood and spoke. "Wait."

Ciara turned to face him. She was tall and yet she came only to his shoulder. He stroked one lean finger along the side of her face and lifted her chin to meet his gaze.

When she had said goodnight, Lucien knew he couldn't let her go just yet. He rose and bade her wait. When she turned he could no longer resist the urge to touch her. He needed to have the silkiness of her skin against his own. Lucien stared into her eyes, eyes the color of whiskey, and he could not stop himself from tasting her.

Their lips met, soft. Gentle. It was a featherlike touch but there was no denying the jolt all the way to their souls. Although he wished for more, Lucien backed off her mouth but stayed that close to her as he whispered, "Goodnight, my lady."

Ciara backed into her room.

Lucien sat by the fire and tried to control his lust. He had never been so close to taking a woman with a need like this. His breaths became ragged and he banked the fire for the night and climbed into his bed, lying there for a long while before he surrendered to dreams ruled by a bronze-skinned woman who smelled of honey and something else.

* * * *

Lucien woke late warm and toasty under his quilts. The cabin was empty but there was a note on the table for him.

Breakfast in the oven. Kosse's with us.

He ate alone and afterward he got dressed to go outside. After he opened the door to the cabin, he found a difficult time maneuvering on the porch. The snow was up to his knees there. He saw a shoveled path leading to the outhouse and one to the woodhouse. With the wind, the porch stayed covered as if she had not been there at all with the shovel.

Lucien swore under his breath about the fact that she'd had to do this instead of him while he walked to where the shoveled path ended. Her footsteps were visible in the snow that led to where she had been yesterday. He gripped his cane and plowed after her.

The closer he got, the more he could have sworn he heard voices.

"Easy there," a voice crooned, husky and making the hairs on his body stand. That was Ciara's voice. "Easy, boy. That's right. You are a handsome one, aren't ya? You know me. Easy now. Let me take care of you. Just a little more, a little harder and then we're done. That's my boy. You are fine now. Easy now, don't fight me. You know me, I won't hurt you."

His blood ran hot. What the hell was going on out here? He stumbled around the last tree and into the clearing, his body tense and ready to fight. She was talking to a horse. His stallion. The bay. She worked on his side.

"Ciara. Move away from the horse."

"Good morning to you too, Wolf. How are you feeling?" She stayed right where she was. Ciara calmed the stallion with a few words when he started to fidget at Lucien's presence but never once did she look up from her task.

"That horse could injure you. Move away from him." Fear made his voice sharp.

"This horse was injured." She patted him on the neck as she spoke to Lucien then the magnificent stallion headed off. She turned her gaze to Lucien. "He will be back, worry not. You will have him by spring. If he makes it through the winter." She looked at Lucien. Really looked.

Chapter Eight

Gold met brown. Eyes met and held. Kosse broke the spell when he attacked Lucien's ankle. When he tumbled into the snow, the cat was all over him. Before long, Lucien was actually enjoying himself.

Ciara allowed herself a smile. He was so handsome it made her ache to watch him. She just watched as he rolled the kitten away and as it came back for more he obliged him until they both panted with exhaustion.

A quick glance at the sky told her all she needed to know. "We must get back now. It is going to get very cold."

Lucien didn't argue, just reached up a hand for her to pull. When she placed her palm to his, he tugged and she fell on top of him. Her face was scant inches away from his. Their breath mingled and he inhaled her fresh scent along with that of horse on her cloak. Her body was plastered to his. Her legs were inside his muscular thighs and lean hips.

Ciara's hands were on either side of his neck as she licked her lips and lowered her head unable to keep her lips from his. She groaned as their lips met. Or Lucien groaned. Maybe they both did. His tongue slipped between her lips and invaded her warm, silky mouth. Lucien's hands were on her arms from when he had pulled her but he moved them to her back and pressed her closer to him. Her curves against his hard body inflamed his passion even more.

He was oblivious, as was she, to the cold. He wasn't, however, oblivious to the cold that was making its way down his collar. His eyes flew open and he saw into Ciara's laughter-filled gaze. The snow she pushed had passed the coat and was headed down his shirt.

Ciara pulled back and jumped up. She was trying to keep in her laughter as she watched him try to get the snow out of his shirt. Kosse was not making it any easier for he was jumping on him and adding more snow from his massive paws.

"I will get you for that, woman." He growled his promise. He took her hand when she held it out this time and they made their way back to the cabin.

The temperature had dropped by about ten degrees when they reached the cabin. Ciara turned to him and said, "You go and add to the fire in there and I will bring in some more wood. I think we will need a lot for the night."

One dark eyebrow quirked at her while he commented, "I know better ways to keep warm at night than that."

Humph. "Get going. I want the place to be warm soon." She strode to the woodhouse while he went in to do as she bade.

She made three more trips before she was content that they were sufficiently stocked. Then she went out and brought more to the porch so it was stacked high there as well. She took a rope and tied a line from the cabin to the other structures. By the time she had finished, the sky had turned black and snow fell so hard she had to use the rope to get back to the cabin.

As she entered the cabin, she shook off her cloak, now white instead of black. It was warm in the cabin and she tried without success to repress a shiver. She headed for her room to get into some warm dry clothes. When she came back, Lucien feasted his eyes on her with an intensity that made her repress a completely different kind of shiver.

"It's getting bad out there, isn't it?"

"Yes. My guess is we will be stuck in this cabin for a few days. I tied ropes from the porch to the woodhouse and to the outhouse. If you do go out, use them."

"What about food?"

"The larder is stocked. Since we have been eating fresh meat, I haven't touched what is in there."

"You don't have enough for the two of us for all winter, do you?"

"Don't worry. On days that it's not snowing like this I will get fresh meat. Faolan hunts for himself, unless the weather gets too bad. But he usually gorges himself so if he misses a day it is fine. Since I wasn't expecting Kosse here, I would have been doing extra hunting anyway."

"I will pay you back for this."

"Very well then. I would have your word on something."

"What?"

"Your word that no harm will come to the bay stallion by your hands."

"You have it. I am getting the horse for my father, the duke, but as long as he is with me I will not allow harm to befall him. Anymore."

"Do you race horses in England?"

"I am too big. I like to wager and watch races. I have wondered what it would be like to have a horse that would beat one my father had. His thoroughbreds are amazing. For being a mean old man, he does have good horses."

"Why don't you open your own stables? I assume that, being a marquess you would have the money."

Lucien thought a moment before he answered. "I have mulled it over. But if I ever showed interest in a horse, he would offer the person twice what I did just so I wouldn't be able to get him. That is what he did with this one. Rumors of the bay reached him from sailors who had been to Baltimore and so he asked, no, *ordered* me to get him for his own collection. Since I had shown interest in the horse, he claimed it first.

"I would have the money, I just would not get any horses. I would have to start from scratch."

"What's wrong with that? I would think that you would jump at the idea to do that. I mean to have something that is yours alone. Not because you were born to it, but because you made it what it was. Something your father could not take from you."

Ciara shrugged as she stuck dinner in the oven then joined him by the fire.

"Look, I don't know your situation…"

"No. You don't." The tone sharp. The meaning clear.

"However," she continued, one hundred percent dismissing his veiled threat as inconsequential, "I do know when someone is trying to live up to someone else's expectations. I look at you and see a handsome, a very handsome man. You are lost, you have no direction. You are still under your father's rule and will be until you do something for yourself and not something with the sole purpose of it being to shock your parents."

"Handsome? You think I am handsome? What else do you think of me?"

"Nothing. Stop changing the subject. You have enough arrogance without needing to add me to bolster your ego. Maybe in England it is good to have that cloud of arrogance but I am the only one here. Stop trying to impress me. I don't like your attitude. All it shows me is rudeness and that you believe you are better than someone because you were born into something. You did nothing to earn it except being born.

"You probably don't even mean to flirt. I am guessing it's a second nature to you and you don't know you're doing it. I have no use for flirting or anything similar. To me it's petty. I don't find it attractive. I have seen something in you that I like, but when I think you will let that person out you shove him away, and become cold, hard. Soulless. I much prefer honesty versus sweet-sounding words that have less meaning than the air you wasted saying them." She rose to check on dinner.

Lucien was shocked. Shocked. Astounded. Enraged. Furious. Embarrassed. Was that how people saw him? She was closer than she knew on her observations of him. He was all of those things. For him, to flirt was as natural as breathing. He didn't think of the women he slept with, for they were nothing more than a brief distraction. Servants and nonmembers of the peerage were not worth a second glance.

His nanny and schoolteachers had drilled, no, *beaten* all that into him from the time he was a baby with their whips and rulers. She was right. He was a veritable jackass. Until now he just hadn't cared what everyone else thought.

The anger deep within him that had festered, stewed and grown since he was a boy boiled over at her words. His eyes narrowed in challenge at her turned back as she put the dinner in the oven once more. "Honesty," he sneered. "You wish me to be honest? Very well. Let me tell you.

"I want to take you to your bed and strip off all your clothes. I want to run my tongue all over your body, delving into each and every crevice to find out what you taste like. I want to fill you with my hardness and spill myself into your depths." He rose and stalked her. He knew she listened but she wouldn't turn to face him. She stayed and faced the window after she'd put the rabbit back in the oven.

"What I want is you. You. You have bewitched me. You with your bronze skin, golden eyes, lush lips and intoxicating scent—that I have yet to identify—I want to take a lifetime getting to know you and then, when I am done, I would wish to begin again. You with your body that you keep covered by male clothing yet there is nothing masculine about you. You who don't lose your composure. You spurn my advances and I want to break that. I want to break you, tame you, make you *mine.*"

His strong hands gripped her shoulders as he spun her around to face him, his voice deep and resonating. He forced her to look at him, not physically but with the allure and velvet heat of his words.

"I want to hear you moaning my name. Not Saint, not Wolf, not my lord. Just Lucien. Lucien. I want you to call me Lucien as I come deep within you. I want to spend days learning your body, your likes and dislikes. I want to show you things that I learned in my travels. I want to brand you as mine. You will belong to me. I will have you."

Her eyes flashed dangerously.

He quirked a brow and added, "I want you to dream of me. I want to know that the very thought of me makes you wet and wanting me. Is that honest enough for you? Or would you like me to go into more explicit detail of what I *honestly* want?"

His hands cupped her face, his thumbs caressing her lips as his eyes bore deep.

Ciara's eyes narrowed in response.

"Thank you for proving my point. You are rude. You try to sweet-talk me and when that doesn't work you try to shock me. I find it a shame that you English can't just talk to someone. Just because I have breasts doesn't make me an idiot. I am good for more than just spreading my legs for you to find some relief and bearing children as a wife."

"Who said I wanted to marry you?" His scorn scathed her. His anger made him foolish with his words.

She continued on with no response to his ridicule. "But I guess that is what happens when you all marry into the family. It was called incest way back when and over here it is still called that today.

"I suggest that you come to terms with the fact that I am not going to simper over you just because you are a beautiful man. We have all winter to spend here and I am not going to do this every day. If you wish to rant and rave some more, go ahead. I will stand here and take it but when dinner is ready, you are done. This attitude of yours will cease. If not, you can leave. You can leave and fend for yourself."

The impact of her words poured over him like ice. He realized he would never have done that in England. He had never been so rude—regardless of her status in the world, she was still a woman and deserved some respect. Not even to his stepmother had he ever behaved in such a manner. She just made him so angry. She didn't seem upset by it—she felt sorry for him. That struck him deeper than her hurt ever could. He turned away from her and went back to the fire. After tossing on more wood, he sat and played with Kosse.

* * * *

Lucien saw her leave the room, and as Faolan followed her and Kosse followed Faolan, he found himself alone. Just like in England. He had two friends in the world and this woman. This remarkable woman was offering him a chance to find out who he really was and all he did was hurt her.

He gripped the cane and when he felt the carvings he took the time to look at it. Its detail staggered. It was made of cedar and the wolves ran up the side. The top was a wolf silhouette that had been lacquered over to keep it smooth to the touch. A cane like this would be very hard to acquire for cheap in England.

Lucien rose and set the table for the two of them. He placed a candle that he had found in the center and lit it. Since he didn't know how long the food needed to be in the oven, he just headed for the doorway of her room.

He knocked on the doorframe and received a growl in response. He stuck his head in and saw her on her bed as she stared off into space. "Ciara?"

Eyes that shimmered with unshed tears looked at him. "Dinner will be ready in a few minutes. Sorry." She slid off her bed and walked to the door. He didn't move.

"That isn't what I came to say. I came to apologize." She kept her head down as Faolan and Kosse slipped past them to the main part of the cabin.

Hesitating a bit, he reached out a hand and tipped up her chin. She met his gaze straight on. No hesitation, no false tears, no cry for sympathy. Just a direct gaze that hit him smack in the heart. Even in her own room she wouldn't allow tears to fall. She was so proud. His princess had a will of iron. His.

"I want, no, I *need* to apologize to you. You were right about what you said." A grin flashed across his face as he tried to lighten the mood. "Except about that incest thing. I have a request to make of you. Will you help me plan a stable?"

"I don't know that much about stables. I have ideas, but I am no expert on it."

"Please. Help me."

She searched his eyes. "I will offer what I can."

"Thank you." A grin, huge, spread across his face. He drew one finger up her jaw and his gaze became hesitant like he remembered something. "I set the table and even found a candle." He turned away from her and hurried back to the chair by the fire as if he didn't trust himself with her that close.

After grace had been given, he waited for her to look at him once more.

"Will you serve, Wolf?"

"'Twould be my honor."

He cut off a chunk of the succulent rabbit and placed it on her plate before he served himself some. There was thick gravy that swam with vegetables. She had made some biscuits that released steam when opened. They were so warm and fluffy when he broke them open.

He nearly groaned with pleasure as he ate. She did wonderful things with food—even though it was plain fare, the spices were outstanding. It was not like home where it was creamed peas and other rich food, like pheasant, served on gilded plates. This food was for people who worked hard during the day and needed something to sustain them. Not for the life of dancing until the wee hours of the morning and sleeping until dusk.

She brought him a cobbler of some sort for dessert and he had coffee with it. Full and content, he helped her clean up and wash the dishes. When they were finished, he took her by the hand and asked, "Do you have some paper I can have?"

Without a word, she went to get one of her father's empty ledgers and a pencil. He settled in at the table and was working on sketches and long-term plans in no time. Ciara grabbed another item of his clothing that she was still fixing and sat in a chair by the fire as she sewed.

Chapter Nine

They sat in a companionable silence for over an hour. Lucien glanced up and found his gaze straying to the woman by the fire. She sewed something that resembled his breeches. She worked tirelessly and when she was done, she rose silently and let the two animals outside for a bit.

The wind howled and she grabbed the oversized jacket. She slipped her feet into the boots he had worn and went out with them. She looked like the bear that attacked him. Lucien put down the pencil then started some water on to heat for tea. He smiled as he gazed over at his sketches and plans.

It was good. He had something he wanted to do. She was right. It would be his, not his father's. He made her some tea and went to the door. When it opened, a snowy wolf ran in, trailed by a small snow-dusted kitten. A snow-covered woman who was shivering followed both of them.

He held out the tea to her as he took her coat. "Here. Drink this."

"Th-th-thank you. It is cold out there."

"Looks that way. Come sit here, I want to show you what I have so far." He herded her toward the table.

"Bring it to the fire. I'm cold."

Lucien picked up the papers as he followed her to the thick animal pelt that was on the floor before the fire. Ciara flopped down on her belly on the fur. Lucien swallowed as her firm butt was exposed to his rakish gaze. He laid himself next to her, allowing his leg to press against her firm one. He spread out the papers he had been working on.

Ciara held on to her tea as she looked over his ideas for stables. She pointed out some that she liked and others she didn't. As she perused the drawings, she spoke. "Thank you for the tea. It hit the spot."

Lucien grinned as if he had been named a hero for saving her life. He found that he craved her praise, her words of encouragement. The earlier incident was over. She had not held a grudge against what he had said and things were once again friendly between them. If that had happened in London, he would have had to spend money to soothe an irate mistress's feathers.

"I like this, this and that one." She moved them closer to him. "All seem good ideas to me and good if one is starting out small. I like the designs of the barns and the training areas. The others are good, but I don't see you in them. They seem to be colder. I envision your father when I look at these based on how you spoke of him."

She pushed herself up and stood. "I have some other things that need my attention. Can I get you anything while I am up? Coffee? Tea?"

When he rose after her and headed to the table, he muttered, "Coffee." He was already absorbed back into his plans. She grinned as she made him a cup and set it in the middle of the table so he wouldn't knock it over.

Ciara went to her room and checked on her drying herbs. She put them into containers and pouches before she picked up more things that needed to be sewed. She had almost finished a quilt for Marie. It was a slow process but she was almost done. All she needed to do was tie it. That could be finished tonight. She carried the heavy quilt out to the room and settled herself back down in the chair.

Three hours later, Ciara found herself exhausted. The quilt had been tied off, after months of work. She was still not caught up on the sleep she had lost from when she had nursed him back to health. She turned her head to glance at the object of her thoughts. He remained bent over the table making slash marks with the pencil as he worked on his ideas.

He was on the mend. His hair shone with health instead of hanging listless and dull. His skin was back to the golden color she knew it would be. He was not tired and his fracture seemed to have healed just fine. He was a strong man. He was not lean and wiry. He was big and muscular. His shoulders were broad, arms were well-defined as was his chest and stomach. His waist was narrow. He was a very good-looking man.

He had full lips, which as she knew were very nice to kiss. His eyes were piercing and she often found herself drowning in them when he looked at her. Thick lashes, that seemed a sin to be on a man, framed those eyes. His nose was slightly bent, as if it had been broken in a fight. His hands were large with long fingers that she knew could be gentle or, if provoked, cause serious damage.

"Like what you see?" The amused voice broke into her perusal of his body.

Her eyes snapped up to meet his, full of male arrogance. He was beautiful and he knew it—and knew that she knew it. "Yes." She spoke plain and honest while she hoped she was not blushing.

The animals made a quick trip and she was back in no time. "Goodnight, Wolf."

"Goodnight, princess."

* * * *

The storm woke Lucien in the middle of the night. He got up to put more wood on the fire when he heard it. Whimpers. Thinking maybe Kosse needed to go out, he lit the lantern. Kosse was nowhere to be seen.

The whimper came again. He carried the lantern and headed for the room where Ciara slept. As he stopped in the doorway, light reflected off the eyes of Faolan who watched his every move.

Lucien held up the lantern as he peered into the room. Ciara cried in her sleep while she tossed and turned. He stepped in but kept one eye on Faolan who stared at him with an intensity that was unnerving. Still the wolf did not stop his entrance into the room.

He set the lantern on the dresser in the room and sat down on the edge of the bed. "Ciara. Ciara, wake up." She moaned some more and began to whimper. Lucien snuck one last look at the wolf and he saw that he had put his head down on his paws, but those eyes were still watchful, ever vigilant.

He reached out to touch her shoulder. Only his lightning-quick reflexes saved him. One second she was dead to the world, lost in the throes of a nightmare, and the next she had knocked him off the bed and was lying on top of him with a knife that moved smoothly into his neck.

"Ciara." He gasped as the tip slide farther into the flesh under his chin.

Recognition poured in. She retreated and dropped the knife. "Oh my god! What have I done? I am so sorry. Sorry. So sorry. Are you all right?"

"Do you think you could get off me? Normally I would love to have you on top of me but right now I think we need to talk." He struggled to keep his voice even, but he shook with untold emotions. A near-death experience was never a good thing. She moved like the wind.

She slid off his body and stood. When she offered her hand down to him, he ignored it and rose on his own. He knew she felt the slight but she did not say anything. When he regained his feet she said, "By the fire."

He went first, Kosse next, followed by an ever-watchful Faolan. He had taken a seat by the fire when she came out of her room. She wore a gown of bright colors like the hangings in the cabin. It was form-fitting and worn thin from so many washings. He groaned as he shifted in the chair to hide his arousal as he traded one pain for another.

She walked toward him, heedless of how she affected him. He noticed her hair was down. It cascaded down her back and framed her face like a lover's hands.

"What was that all about?" His tone was firm—it was the tone he used to give orders and have them followed to the letter.

"Sorry. Can I see to the wound?"

"Later. Tell me now. What happened that you would react so strongly like that?"

He was angry, and he knew she picked up on it. "I have always had a knife when I sleep, since we moved here. I am not used to having someone sleep in this cabin so when you touched me… Well, you were there, you know what I did."

"That is not an answer."

"Why did you come into my room?"

"You were crying in your sleep. I thought to wake you from your nightmare."

"Thank you for that at least." She rose and got a cloth to put on his neck. He sat completely still as she moved to be sandwiched between his thighs to administer to his wound. "I am sorry. It won't happen again."

He gripped her hand and applied pressure until she raised her eyes to meet his gaze. "It was a nightmare. It may happen again. It is nothing to be ashamed of. Tell me what it was about."

Her eyes, which had been so full of remorse for what she had done, hardened. "No." It wasn't a 'please ask again and I will tell you' type no—it was a flat refusal. "I would ask for your forgiveness for my actions, but I will not speak of it. Not to anyone."

Lucien slid a glance to the wolf on the floor that watched him. His free hand tipped her face to his as he spoke in hushed tones. "I will forgive you. I do forgive you. I would ask for but a kiss in return."

"You don't forgive someone and then ask them to give you something." Ciara pulled away from him.

He stood as well. His eyes were hooded as he stared at her. "I don't ask because I gave you my forgiveness. I ask because I want to taste you." His voice lowered. "I wish a kiss, Ciara. Nothing more. Just a kiss."

Lucien did not take his eyes off her. His body thrummed with need. He had to touch her. Taste the sweetness he knew she contained in her dusky rose lips. He wanted her to touch him of her own accord. He took a step toward her and heard a low growl.

It was Faolan. Lucien stopped. He didn't look at the wolf but kept his eyes solely on Ciara. "The kiss? I am asking. Will you kiss me? Your wolf will not let me closer to you. The choice is entirely yours, Ciara."

Ciara stepped toward him. When she was in front of him, he stood tall so as not to touch her. His hands clenched into fists to keep them from delving into her thick tresses that tantalized his senses with every movement she made. She looked up at him. He was too tall. "You are too tall."

"Kiss me." His soft command pulsed through the air. She reached up and put her hand behind his head and tugged. He bent, but as soon as she paused he stopped moving.

She pulled his head down so she could reach his mouth. When his lips were a breath away from hers she pressed them together. Briefly. It lasted only seconds. It was nothing more than a chaste kiss, but she did it on her own. It was a small victory in his eyes.

Ciara released his head and stepped back. He straightened, never once breaking eye contact with her. He blinked and gave a small, secretive smile before he spoke. "Goodnight, princess."

Lucien sat back on his bed after she had disappeared into her room. His body was wound so tight that even if he went out into the cold he didn't think it would cool his ardor for the embodiment of perfection that slept in the next room.

* * * *

When Lucien woke the next morning it was still dark. The fire blazed and there was the smell of food in the air. He looked for Kosse or Faolan. When he didn't see either, he rose and dressed. He went to her room and saw Kosse asleep on the floor but there was no sign of Faolan or Ciara.

Lucien muttered as he looked to the door. Her cloak was gone. The wind strained against the cabin and he shuddered to think of her out there. He pulled on the boots and coat to go to take care of his morning ablutions as Kosse followed in his wake. The chill took his breath away as he held on to the rope. He cursed the weather. This was why she had said she wouldn't be going anywhere till spring. The weather turned with the drop of a hat.

On the way back, he noticed Faolan was on the porch. The wolf entered in front of him and headed for the fire, Kosse trotting underneath his belly, protected from the precipitation that came down. As he closed the door behind him, he heard a voice say, "Don't close the door."

He watched as Ciara stumbled into the cabin, covered in the snow and rain mix that was falling. He had to push against the door to shut it, the wind was so strong. Ciara had gone to stand by the fire as she stripped from her cloak.

He removed his things and joined her by the fire. "Morning."

"Good morning, Wolf." Ciara looked into his gaze and gave him a small nod. "I will have breakfast ready soon. Just give me a few seconds to warm up."

"Whenever. Is there anything I can do to help?"

Was this him? A marquess who offered to help with the making of food? No one back home would believe it.

"You could set the table. That, and get some water on for coffee. I am freezing."

Lucien did as she'd asked. He liked this feeling of comfort, closeness. When he had been in England, his family harbored the opinion that servants were nothing. That all they cared about was money. They were beneath his notice. As he set the table he realized this was what it must feel like to be part of a real family.

Breakfast, a simple affair, still filled him up full. After, as Ciara cleaned up, Lucien went back to work on his plans.

Chapter Ten

"Ciara? How did the reputation of the bay get out? This place is very remote so how did people find out about him?"

"Baltimore."

"Baltimore?"

"Baltimore. He used to be a racehorse there. Someone stole him from the farm where he was kept and released him out here. None of those dandies from the city can get close to him. When he raced no horse could touch him. A legend in his time."

"How did he get here? Do you know who took him?" Lucien wondered what sort of troubles this would cause him.

"I don't know who took him. I never wanted to know. I suspect he fell in with a wild herd."

"When were you in Baltimore? I thought you said you lived here the whole time." He grew cold at the thought that she had a man back east.

"I did. I never said I lived there. I said that is where his name was made," Ciara mumbled, deliberately obtuse.

"Tell me the whole story. There are some dark rumors surrounding that horse, are they true?"

"The ones about him being a man killer? Aye. Those are true."

"How do you know so much about him?"

"I was there when he was born. He was born out here and taken to Baltimore by a man who was determined to turn him into a racer after he had been seen running free across the plains. Once he started racing, his name became legendary for no horse could touch him. I am sure you know all that." She stopped her sewing and took a deep breath, holding his gaze.

"Anyway. His jockey was a mean bastard. He loved to saw on the reins and take a whip to him. During what turned out to be his final race, he was winning, but apparently not fast enough to suit the jockey. The jockey took his whip to him for no reason. Everyone agreed that there was no way any of the other horses would catch up to him."

Lucien could hear the disgust in her tone.

"What happened next, or rather why, is really anyone's guess. The jockey was thrown. Instead of running off, Colonial Star—that was the stallion's name—charged him, trampled him to death under his hooves." She fiddled with her hands.

"Everyone knows that the track is no place for a killer, so they were going to kill him. That night someone stole him and took him away. I guess that even though he is a killer they figured that as long as he wasn't there it was all right for him to still be alive."

Ciara looked at him with assuredness in her gaze that smacked hard. She knew what she talked about on a personal level. "He has been here, running free. I don't know how you got sent in this direction to get him. I don't want to know. Don't get me wrong. With the right trainer he will be once again the legend he was before. I have known of only one horse that was faster than—" She broke off as if she had said too much.

Lucien sat as he digested her information. It sounded like the perfect horse for his father. Mean. No problem for he handled being under a saddle, maybe it was just other horses that bothered him. He had been well-behaved on his ride, up until the other horse appeared, and of course the bear incident. But one can't really hold that against a horse. What horse wouldn't run from a bear?

Then it hit him what she had said—*one that was faster. Who was faster?* In town they had mentioned the same thing. "Which horse was faster than he was? Tell me? If there is a horse that you say can beat him I could take him for my stable."

Whiskey eyes glinted with a hard vigilance he had not seen before. "No. You will not take him. I will not let you."

"Who is it?" He ignored her protest. His tone once again belonged to the haughty marquess who did not believe there were those who would dare disobey his command.

"His sire. Nyama. The black." Resignation tinged her voice.

"Why are you so sure that he is faster? Maybe you are just saying that to get me to leave the bay."

In an instant a change came over her. She did not raise her voice but even an idiot could tell that she was beyond angry. Livid. Her words were sharp and had a hint of a brogue in them. "I am sure because I was there. I was riding the black when we beat his son. That is how I know. By all rights, the bay is mine. I agreed to the sale, for the sake of the town. Unlike you and your damn society, I don't lie. I wouldn't make a deal and then go back on it.

"Besides, anyone who knows horses would know that while the son is fast, he is merely a combination of what his parents were. The black—his father, Nyama—was brought here from the Barbary Coast. He is nothing but speed and endurance. Combine that with the heartiness of the dam, a mustang, and you get the son. Nyama can beat his son any day of the week carrying me while his son carries none.

"I know that most of the horses in England are of the Byerley Turk and such lines but they are more weakened lines than those of the Arabians which they date back to. The Barbs may not be as old as the Arab but they are still just as pure. Colonial Star is of mixed descent and he is not as fast, but the mare was not the best either. I may be a female, but I am an intelligent one. Don't ever question my loyalties, my honor or my word again."

Lucien sat still as he stared at her. How come she knew so much about horses? He was not sure how to proceed and so he mistakenly did so in the arrogant way he would handle someone who tweaked his anger at home, with sarcasm and menace. He fixed her with the most autocratic look he had.

"How did *you* get a horse that was from the Barbary Coast? Whose horse is it?"

Ciara's Irish overpowered her tenuous hold on her temper. She set down her sewing and rose from the chair. "Listen to me and listen well for I will say this to you only one more time. Nyama is mine. Given to me by my father and my mother. The day you take that horse from me will be the day that I draw my last breath. Are we clear on that? Nyama is mine. Mine." She trembled she was so angry. Faolan had risen beside her and had leaned against her leg to offer quiet support while Kosse sat by Faolan, copying his seriousness. Lucien would have laughed at the kitten if the situation hadn't been so precarious.

Unrelenting, he continued to badger her. "Where did they get him? You said yourself that your mom was a slave and your father a poor Irish farmer. How would they be able to afford a bloody horse like that?" His tone was snide. He wanted answers and she swore he believed that she, this little person, an upstart colonial at that, wasn't going to stand in his way. At least that was his thought.

"Listen, you condescending bastard." Venom dripped off each word. "You have no right to speak of my parents in that tone of voice. I never said my father was a *poor* farmer. I said he was a farmer. The fact that my mother was a slave holds no bearing on this whatsoever. I suppose that to most men of your station anyone with dark skin is considered to be inferior.

"I mean even you have said as much. 'Skin the color of rich cream and hair like golden wheat,' those were your own words to me after you grabbed me—not that I look like that—and kissed me. My parents knew a love that went beyond skin color. The love they had was real. Something I am sure you know nothing about.

But that is not what you wished to know, is it? Fine. I will tell you.

"On the way here from Ireland they stopped off in Africa in Côte d'Ivoire. Don't know why, for I wasn't born. Anyway, that is where they got Nyama. They proceeded to land somewhere, maybe Baltimore, I am not sure. By the time I was born, they were out here. We went from Paradise Cove to Baltimore with Colonial Star but Mom and I came back out here while Dad stayed there.

"One day he showed up here in Paradise Cove. He had a bunch of other people with him and that is when the town really began. There was an incident in town and he moved us out of there. We came to this spot and helped build this cabin. The trek always takes a couple days because he didn't want anyone to know where we were.

"Two people other than you know of the cabin's location. They took that secret with them to their grave." At the look on Lucien's face, she continued on in a tone that was sharp enough to cut him but devoid of any emotional feeling in the words she was saying. "Not enough for you? What, would you like me to tell you how my parents died?

"How I found them? My mother, cut, bleeding from having been raped and tortured. My father tied to a tree with his lids sewn open forcing him to watch as they raped and tortured my mother—the love of his life—before they finally killed her, releasing her from her pain? What more do you want me to tell you? Would you like to know what they did to my father, what they cut off of his body? More details for you? Or is that enough to satisfy your curiosity?

"Nyama is mine. I agreed to sell his son. Don't make me regret that decision any more than I already do." Ciara still quivered with anger and sadness as she left the room to go lie on her bed, Faolan and Kosse with her. She curled up in a thick quilt, and as her body was racked by sobs, she cried herself to sleep.

Lucien felt like he had been hit upside the head with a tree branch while he rode a horse at top speed. The wind had been knocked out of him and he tried without success to find his bearings. The conversation was not supposed to take that kind of turn. She was just supposed to bend to his will like the others of his acquaintance. He was a marquess, he demanded respect.

She was nothing like the people he knew. She was real. She didn't put on airs, or try to be someone she wasn't. She was Ciara. And he was the ass that made her cry. Not only that but he was the one that had made her relive the horror that happened to her parents.

His head dropped into his palms as he sat in the empty room and groaned aloud. He'd messed this up. She would never trust him. All thoughts of seducing her vanished. It was not important to make her another one of his many conquests—all that was important was getting her to forgive him.

Not being close to his parents, Lucien couldn't even begin imagining what she'd felt when she had lost her parents. Now that he realized how she'd found them, it made his guilt even heavier. This was not something that could be fixed in his usual way, by buying some meaningless bauble for the offended party, because she wasn't like that. Not to mention he had no way of buying her anything stuck up here on the mountain.

And this high-handed way just cost someone more pain than he had ever wanted to deal with. Lucien did not remember saying anything to her about 'skin the color of rich cream' or 'hair like golden wheat' at any time. He had hurt people before—and not cared—but this was more. He had slandered the memory of her parents for no good reason.

Even now he wished to know what had caused them to leave Paradise Cove and move out here. Was it connected to the ones who had killed her parents? Lucien realized he *needed* to protect her.

She was right. She was different. Her skin was darker, and that only made her all the more beautiful to him. She was alive and not afraid to be outside, a place Lucien loved to be instead of in the city. She was so full of life, so unconventional and refreshing. It was like inhaling a breath of fresh air around her. Ciara loved life and it showed in everything she did.

A woman like this didn't come along every day. He realized that was what her father must have seen in her mother. A woman full of passion, life, adventure and love that waited for just the right man to enter into her life. Lucien wanted to be 'the right man'—hell, he wanted to be the only man.

He could see himself with her by his side. Children—their children—playing at his home, Heartstone. A warmth in his home that was not there now. Maybe even she could make his sister open up. If she had managed to make him realize what an ass he was, there was hope for anyone, and that included his sister.

Which brought him back to the original problem. How to acquire her forgiveness. Lucien fell asleep by the fire and woke when it got chilly.

He put more wood on the fire and wondered what to do about something to eat. A glance at the door showed her cloak so he was sure she was still indoors. He moved to the door of her room and was met by silent bared teeth as Faolan blocked his entry to the room. She lay prone on the bed, wrapped in quilts, silent.

Shame cascaded through his body as he turned and went back to his bed. He dallied with his stable plans but his heart wasn't in it. He made sure the cabin was toasty warm so the heat would make it to her room. Lucien sat and faced the flames as he stroked the cane.

A noise behind him made him look around. Ciara had put on her cloak to take the animals outside. She didn't even look at him. When they came back in from the cold, Kosse bounded over to him and stretched up to be scratched. He obliged him.

Chapter Eleven

Ciara awoke in slow increments. She was still tired, emotional and physical, but she was hungrier. She looked out of the small window in the cabin, pleased that snow no longer fell. The skies were clear so she should be able to get some hunting done. She rose and dressed fast for the room was icy.

Faolan came to her side while she put on her cloak and headed off to run her trap line. She knew she should have yesterday but she just couldn't. Kosse followed them out. She set out across the dark yard. No matter what the weather, she loved to be outside.

Throughout the time Kosse and Faolan ran free, she checked her traps. Most were empty—there were a few rabbits that would work for Kosse's food. She strapped them to her waist.

She went to her parents' grave and cleared away the snow from the marker she had carved for them. Ciara wept on the inside for the loss of her only family. After a while, she rose and headed back to get some grain to set out for the horses. She hoped they were all right.

The scene Ciara came back upon showed Lucien working like a man possessed. He had shoveled a path that followed the rope to the woodshed. There was one to the outhouse and even the porch was cleared. Kosse, seeing flying snow, decided to attack it and took Lucien down with a grunt.

Ciara turned her back on the scene and went to her smaller building. A bit later he swung open the door to the shed, allowing a small shaft of natural light to enter and add to the lantern glow. Ciara leaned over a table and didn't acknowledge him at all. She tossed the bloody chunks of meat into a bucket. Silence stretched between them as she scraped the furs clean and put them on a rack.

When she was finished with the three rabbits she washed off the knife with some snow that was in another bucket. She picked up the lantern and both buckets and turned toward him. Her eyes flicked over him as she passed him—her body, however, pressed up against him.

Even covered with animal parts, this woman was able to arouse him. She slid past his sweaty body and out of the door where she set down the buckets. She blew out the lantern, making sure there was no chance of remaining heat from it, and set it back inside the shed.

She took the buckets to where the animals were. When they realized what was in them they followed her to the edge of the copse. She dumped the one with the meat on the ground for Kosse. The one that had the bloody snow she gave to Faolan. She made sure to wash out both buckets well with snow before she took them back to the shed and placed them inside the door.

Finished, she headed for the cabin. "Good morning, Ciara."

The gaze that settled on him was detached. "Morning, Wolf." She disappeared into the cabin.

Well, that didn't go well.

Lucien wanted to follow her. He had to talk to her, touch her. His blood burned for her. With the wolf outside, maybe he could at least get within a foot of her.

After a slight hesitation, he followed her inside and shut the door behind him as he entered the cabin. The smell of pancakes and frying ham hit him and made his mouth water. He hung up his coat next to hers. *Everything about us looks good together,* he realized.

"Ciara. We… I need to talk to you. You don't have to say anything, just listen." He didn't say please but the word was there. Implied even if not spoken.

She stopped her work and looked at him. She waited. Silent.

He sat down at the table. Lucien gestured to a chair and asked, "Will you sit?"

Ciara crossed her arms over her chest and leaned back against the counter where she kept one amber eye on the cooking breakfast.

"Fine. We'll do it your way." His hands threaded through his hair as he searched for the right words. She was retreating more and more from his grasp.

He turned a beseeching gaze to her only to find she countered it with a bland stare. This wasn't going to be easy at all. He heard a yelp from one of the animals and knew his time alone with her was just about over.

Lucien jumped up, acting on an instinct he didn't know he had—protecting and holding on to what he thought was his. He had never wanted anything like this before—his chair screeched across the floor planks as it was shoved back. He strode over to her, cupped her face with his calloused hands and kissed her. Inhaled her.

He tugged on her lips with his own. He coaxed her mouth open with his tongue before he plundered its depths. His body tingled. He couldn't get enough of her. Couldn't get close enough to her.

Ciara slid her arms up and wrapped her hands in his hair. Their tongues met, dueled, parried and made love to each other.

Both of them panted and desired more when the door swung open and they were shocked back to the present. Current time, current problems. Lucien dragged his mouth—a huge effort—off hers. He couldn't relinquish his hold as he turned his head and looked at Faolan and Kosse as they tumbled, wet and snow-covered, into the cabin.

He stared at her, a promise in his gaze. A promise to finish what was started. His eyes were narrowed, his body quaked as it shook with need he was more—much more—than ready to comply with. His breaths were convoluted as he tried to control the fire that had consumed him in its entirety. Lucien clenched his hands into fists he took deep breaths but could not look away from her.

She was magnificent. Her skin flushed, her eyes smoldered with barely restrained passion that would take only a spark to set off, and releasing what he knew would be nothing short of volcanic in reaction. He had aroused the sensuous woman who had lain untapped beneath the surface.

That knowledge was an aphrodisiac in itself. He wanted her. The other women were faceless, not even a memory. He left them and they left his recollection. Women experienced in the art of seduction could take lessons from her. Ever since the kiss in the snow—and yet perhaps before then—she had been the only one present in his mind.

Ciara stood by the door as she watched Lucien. By all that was holy, the man could kiss. Her body desired, craved, yearned for more of his touch. She sucked on her bottom lip to savor his taste. Even from where she was, she could see his sharp intake of breath at her action.

She approached him with caution. Eyes locked on one another, sparks jumping between them. She passed by his hardened body to the counter. Lucien didn't make a move to touch her—nevertheless, he moved with her as he kept eye contact. It was as if they both knew what would happen should they touch again.

Breakfast was a tense affair. Neither of them attempted to speak and they kept their gazes lowered. It was very awkward. After a spell, Ciara looked up at him and spoke.

"What did you have to say to me?"

"What? I wanted to apologize for my disrespectfulness yesterday. You were right—I have no right to speak of your parents in any way. Very poorly done of me. I also agree that I have no right to question you on where you got your animals. As a marquess, I know that I get aggressive even when it is not in the best taste. I always have.

"I can only hope that you will give me another chance to become your friend. I am not used to having a woman as a friend, but I do truly value your opinion and hope that what has transpired between us will not overtly affect our relationship."

Ciara stared intently at the man across from her at the table. She was drawn to him like a bee to a flower. She schooled her face into a bland expression. "The winter will be too long if we can't get along. We both were out of line and I also apologize. I could have handled it better, but I lost my temper."

"So. What do we do now?" He voiced the question that neither one knew the answer to.

"Since we are likely to have only a few more hours of nice weather, I am going to go outside. I can show you around if you wish."

"This is nice weather?"

She nodded and he dropped it.

They cleared the dishes and as they got ready to go out she looked at him. "I am going to wash some clothes today as well."

"Good. I think I have worn out my welcome in these." His words fell on deaf ears as she pictured him naked. "Ciara? Is everything all right?"

Ciara blinked and cleared her throat. "Fine. Are you ready?" She reached for her cloak, as did he.

He held the door and they all paraded outside. Faolan, Kosse, Ciara and he brought up the rear. They had made sure that the fire had been fed so it would be warm when they returned.

Ciara led him to a ridge that overlooked a lake down in the basin. "I used to hide around up here from my parents. They always pretended they couldn't find me. Even if I was sitting in plain sight, which was often the case, I was never really good at hiding. I learned how to swim in that lake. I built a raft and when I was in the middle of the lake, it sank. Well, it felt like the middle. I seriously doubt I made it very far.

"My dad and mom laughed so hard, causing me to cry even harder. Dad just smiled saying, 'A raft is more than two pieces of wood.' I hadn't even tied them together. Just thought it should work. That was the first and last of my deep-sea adventures. That was, however, when Dad had decided to teach me about woodworking, carving and such.

"The lake in the spring turns a beautiful rich blue. Mom was forever saying how she wished she could get that color to come out in her dyes. It was never how she wanted it, too dark or too bright. Never that exact shade she wanted." *The same shade as your eyes, Lucien St. Martin.*

Chapter Twelve

They walked farther. When they entered a clearing, he stopped as he saw a herd of horses. It was Nyama's herd. His bay was there as well. It was as if they had banded together for the winter. All the horses were in their winter coats and it couldn't take away from their beauty.

Ciara walked out to the edge of the clearing and released a low whistle. The black, Nyama, tossed up his head and came up. She spoke to him in a language Lucien couldn't understand but knew that the horse did.

As she spoke to the horse, he took the time to look him over. He was interesting—not ugly but not as beautiful as he had been from afar. He was smaller than the thoroughbreds and had a distinctive face. The head was elongated and the quarters were sloped. The tail set was low.

He could see raw power in that horse, though. She was right—he moved with a grace that one wouldn't expect if they stared at him.

With a smile that would rival the heavens, she asked, "Would you like to go for a ride?" When Lucien just looked at her with a blank stare, she tried again as she swung up on the horse.

"Would you like to take a quick ride? We can ride back to the cabin." Her voice urged him to accept her proposition.

The thought of riding behind her was too good an opportunity to pass up. Titled or no, rich or no, he was not a man who had ridden bareback much. A frown crossed his face. How would this work? Pride dictated that he do it, but he didn't want her to know that he had not done so before.

"Sure." Arrogant male won out over logical person. "I will ride behind you."

"No. Do you think you can handle the bay?"

"A stallion? With nothing on him? Are you sure that would be wise?" He didn't care that the question was way less than a manly response.

Ciara quirked a brow in perfect imitation of him as she swung down from Nyama. She gave another low whistle and a mare came up. She was a beautiful brown color with a white rump that had spots on it. Looked kind of like she had snow falling on her hindquarters.

"This is Epona. She is my favorite mare. I got her from some of the Indians. She is something else. This is whom I want to breed Nyama to. I think that their combined endurance and speed will be amazing. You can ride her."

Lucien looked at Epona. "What does her name mean? Epona?" He moved in and rubbed the mare's nose. She was large—almost larger than the stallion—and solid.

"Epona was a Celtic goddess. Of horses. Besides, I couldn't pronounce her name when I got her, so I changed it. Go on. Get on."

Ciara swung back up on Nyama and waited for Lucien to mount. He did so, his action a bit clumsy but she made no mention of it.

As they rode through the quiet forest, Lucien gained a new appreciation for her and her horses. The mare he rode was calm and very strong. She walked along and responded to his legs. He stole a glance at Ciara and saw one of her rare, unreserved and wholehearted smiles that rocked him to the core.

They approached another small clearing when he heard Ciara whisper to him. Epona stopped and he looked at Ciara. "What?" he asked in a whisper as well, not sure if there would be trouble.

"Wolf, look." She pointed to the trees. It was a bunch of bunnies that ran around on top of the snow, completely enjoying the sun and mild day. Their antics were funny and cute.

They sat and watched the bunnies until an overzealous kitten came into the picture. The sight of Kosse as he slid across the smooth surface of the snow, trying without success to catch a bunny, made Ciara peal out in laughter.

Lucien felt his heart stop. It was like the first time he'd enjoyed her laughter. It was not a little twitter meant to attract a man's attention, but it did. It was a full laugh, husky and seductive, without intention of being so, but still seductive.

With a gaze slanted at her, he saw her head tipped toward the sun. Her teeth shone bright against her dark skin, that sexy throat moving as the laugh erupted. Her eyes sparkled with joy. It was unrehearsed. It was pure. It was life. It was what he had missed. Joy.

Ciara looked over at Lucien as he watched her. She smiled as she watched him try to contain a smile of his own. He just didn't realize it yet that she was good for him. He needed to find happiness in his life. She was determined to help him find it. Even if it was for only the short time they were together. Everyone deserved to know what pure euphoria was like. No hidden agendas, no plans to get something back.

It was a way to honor her parents' memory and the reason they had started Paradise Cove. To give people a place to start over, no matter where you came from or how you looked. If you were willing to accept others on those same terms, you were welcome to stay. Everyone was equal. Everyone deserved a chance to be happy.

Lucien seemed to have missed a vital part of life. He was rich, yes. He was titled, yes. On the outside he appeared to have everything, but the more Ciara watched him, the surer she was that he was far from being complete. His childhood had not been good, and now people didn't want him as a friend, they wanted the benefits that came with knowing a marquess. That was something Ciara had no use for. What did she need? Her life was pretty much near perfect in her eyes.

Since she had grown up with nothing but love, it was hard for Ciara to imagine what it was like for him. A cold, bleak world. Money was important, but nothing, *nothing,* was more important than love and family. What good is all the money in the world if you have no one to love, no one to share your life with? It seemed that he was short on both.

"Go ahead and smile, Wolf. I won't tell anyone," she teased.

His eyes snapped to her face as she grinned.

"See, that wasn't so hard, was it? You should smile more. You appear very—how do you say it in England? Suave? Debonair? I don't know. I do know that it makes you very, very handsome. Come, we need to go back. The weather will change soon." She nudged Nyama on with her knees and he followed suit with Epona.

"What does Faolan mean?" Lucien asked as Epona drew up alongside Nyama.

"It is a Gaelic word for wolf. Pretty inventive, don't you think?"

"Well, why do you call me Wolf? It's not even part of my name."

"Does it bother you?"

"No. But that doesn't explain why you do it." He could listen to her talk all day.

"Why do people call you Saint?"

"Part of my name. Besides only certain ones do that."

"Let me guess, certain ones that you see at the functions you attend. Right?"

"Yes. That's right. My friends call me Luc. My parents call me Saint as well."

"Sort of a formal title for you. Well, I call you Wolf because you remind me of Faolan. When we were first together, he didn't trust me and was overly cautious around me and yet at the same time he was full of himself. When I would get close to him he would hackle up and bare his teeth, to try to scare me. I knew he was just full of bluster. He was more scared than anything, and while he knew I was no threat, he still had to act tough. That is why I call you Wolf."

"What about Kosse? What does that mean, lion?"

"Actually it does. In the language of my mother. What can I say when it comes to names? I am not very clever."

"I think you are very clever." The words made her stomach go all quivery. "Will you let Kosse go?"

"When he is old enough to fend for himself, the choice will be his. Faolan will teach him to hunt. He just never would have made it through the winter alone without his momma."

"Amazing. And you didn't think of the meat that he would need to survive? How that could affect you?"

"Not everything is about what you have. If I went through life like that, I would have left you in the bear's clutches. It's what I do. I help things that are sick. And when they are better, they can go. If not, well, then I just have another mouth to feed on occasion.

"Sometimes when Faolan brings down a deer, he brings me to it and we split it. We share and we survive. It is the only way up here."

"Amazing."

They rode into the area before the cabin. She swung down with grace as he slid off Epona, not as nice as she had. The mare stood there next to him and nudged him. "She wants some grain. I will bring it out," Ciara said before she disappeared into the woodhouse and came back out with two buckets of grain.

The horses made short work of it, then with final pats from both humans they disappeared back into the trees. The clouds rolled in and snow started to fly. Both of them loaded up on wood from the woodhouse and headed into the cabin with the four-legged members of the group.

Lucien built up the fire as Ciara began making dinner. They had missed lunch since they had been away from the cabin so they were both hungry. By the time she got the dinner on the table the winds howled and the snow was so thick she couldn't see past the porch.

Dinner was relaxed and easygoing. Afterward, since they had stayed out later than she had first believed, she said she would do laundry in the morning. Ciara changed into dry clothes and found some clean, dry ones of her father's for Lucien to wear. He changed in her room and when he came out she was making up his bed pallet.

He groaned as he saw her bent over to pull up the blankets, her butt encased in tight buckskins that hugged her small waist and firm legs. Her hair was braided down her back in a thick, black rope. Whoever said that women should not wear pants was absolutely right, but not for the reason he believed that they stated that. They would drive men crazy if they all wore those kind of things. It had to be a sin to look like that.

He made himself some coffee and sat at the table to work on his plans. He couldn't concentrate. His eyes kept straying to the woman bent over across the room. She moved a chair to beneath a shelf. He put down his pencil and watched as she stood on the chair and reached up to grab a small trinket off the shelf. She was crazy. Utterly and totally adorable, but crazy.

As he stared at her, it gave way. He was moving even before it registered what happened. "Damn it, woman! What in the blue blazes were you doing? You could have killed yourself. I would have gotten that for you if you had asked. Don't ever do that again. Promise me.

You just took ten years off my life with that stunt." Words came in a rush as Lucien tried to slow his heart that, to him, sounded like war drums.

Now that she was in his arms, though, he didn't wish to let her go. Seeing her fall toward the fire was too hard on the slim control on his nerves.

"Why didn't you ask me to get that for you? That chair was not meant to be stood on." His voice, once again calm, belied his true terror.

"I am not used to having someone here with me. I had hoped that the chair would hold." Ciara wasn't fighting to be let down.

His voice, deepened by desire, asked, "What was it you were getting from the shelf?"

She blinked like an owl, staring at him until he tapped her cheek with a finger. Then he repeated the question.

Lucien smiled as he saw what her reaction to him was. No matter how cool, calm and collected she appeared on the outside, he rattled her. He had to repeat his question twice before she answered him.

"The…the box. The carved one. Please."

Seconds after he stepped away from her, Lucien felt empty. He took down the carved box and handed it to her. He observed her in silence as she sat on his pallet and ran her fingers in a loving manner over the box.

Ciara held the carved box in her hands. It was made of maple and, on the top, her name was carved into the wood.

On two of the sides, opposite ones, were a string of Celtic knots that led up to the top. The other two sides had African designs leading up. She ran her fingers over the knots and pressed a hidden button. The lid flicked open.

The gold and gems that were there were ignored. She instead looked to the underside of the lid where her father had engraved a saying for her.

Our dearest daughter,
We were blessed the day you came into our lives
This is your legacy. You are our legacy.
No matter what, we are proud of you.
We love you.

Lucien glanced over her shoulder. His jaw almost dropped as he saw the gold and gems inside the box. When he read the saying, he sat down beside her and took the box away from her and pulled her into his arms.

When she was settled on his lap, he just held her. He was not sure how to offer support but what he was doing seemed to be working. He rubbed a hand in circular motions on her back as her body shuddered with silent sobs.

They sat like that for a bit. Lucien froze when Faolan jumped up onto the bed and settled himself by them. The wolf did nothing more than nose Ciara and lie next to Lucien's leg. Kosse, after a struggle, pulled himself up and was on the other side of Lucien.

What a picture they made. An English marquess holding an American colonial flanked by a black wolf on one side and a mountain lion kitten on the other.

A sense of security flowed into Lucien as time passed. When he realized that she no longer sobbed, he leaned her back and looked down at her. She met his gaze and he saw the unshed tears.

"I am sorry. I take it down only once a year. Will you put it back up there please?"

"Sure." He wanted to ask her about the money and gems but now wasn't the time.

Ciara got off his lap and the pallet. As the lid closed, she whispered, "Goodbye, Papa. Goodbye, Momma. I love you." She caressed the lid as he took the box from her.

* * * *

It was late when Lucien took his attention from the papers. He was done. He had come up with a plan for how he wished his stables to look and the training area. Excited, he glanced around for Ciara. She wasn't there. He banked the fire.

He saw Kosse come out of her room and when he looked outside he realized just how late it was. Damn, he had wanted to share this with her. He still did. His foot tapped the floor and he acted before he could realize that what he was about to do was dumb.

Lucien entered her room, held the lantern up and watched her sleep. She looked peaceful. She lay on her stomach, head under a pillow, one brown hand tangled in Faolan's coat. The wolf looked at him and bared his teeth.

"Just go away. I am not going to hurt her. Can't you see that?" Great, now he was talking to a wolf. If his jaw hadn't been attached, it would have hit the floor when Faolan rose and left the bed, to curl up away from them.

"Ciara. Ciara, wake up." More than a bit unsure of whether to touch her based on what happened last time, he spoke a little louder. "Ciara. Wake up."

"What is it? Is something wrong?" Her voice, heavy with sleep, came from the pillow.

"No. I finished. I want you to see. I'm done."

She pushed up from the bed. Ciara rolled over. Lucien gaped at the vision before him. Delectable. Her hair was free and looked rumpled. She looked as if she had just been pleasured, and pleasured well.

His groin hardened. Her tongue slipped out to wet her lips. He groaned. Lucien inhaled as he watched her nightgown slide off to bear one shoulder to his lecherous gaze. Her skin shone like bronze silk in the muted light from the lantern.

She patted the bed. "Let's see them. Come sit. It's cold out there and I am not getting out of bed."

He moved to join her, once the light was set on a table beside the bed. It was difficult to swallow when she flipped back the blankets for him to get under them with her. He slid in to be immediately surrounded by her scent of honey—how she got that he had no idea—and a faint smell of drying herbs.

She took the papers from him and spread them out in front of them. As if it were nothing to have him in her bed. Their hips were flush and their legs were pressed against each other. It was not a huge bed.

Lucien's vision swam as he pictured making slow love to her in this bed. The sight of her naked body as it was exposed to his gaze. The feel of her skin on his. He blinked a few times to clear his mind as soon as he realized that she had spoken to him.

"What? Can you say that again? I didn't catch it."

"I said, I thought they were good. Very good." She gathered them up into a pile as she spoke. She set them on the table on her side of the bed and snuggled down into the quilts.

"That's it? Nothing more to say about them? What are you doing?"

"It's the middle of the night. I am going back to sleep." She snuggled up against him and he thought he heard her say, "So warm. This is nice."

Why not? He blew out the lantern and as he slid down next to her, he half expected her to demand that he leave her bed at once. Nothing. Well, not nothing. She curled up even more and flopped over onto her stomach. She put one leg over his and placed her hand on his chest, over his heart. It was like they had been sleeping together for years.

The last thing she said was "Faolan." The wolf bounded up on the bed and curled up next to her. Kosse, the cat scrambled to get up as well. Before long it was quiet except for her soft breaths into his neck.

It was going to be a long night.

They slept in. Ciara awoke first. Her hand was still on his chest and her leg was, well, it was up against something rigid. Waking had never been so nice. She felt the chill in the cabin, and as she moved out of his embrace he groaned and tightened his grip.

Ciara wished she could stay there but she slid out of his arms and made sure he stayed covered by the quilts before she headed for the fire. She fed it and let the animals out as she heated a bunch of water.

She slipped on his coat and boots before going out onto the porch to drag in the tub. She set it close to the fire so it would warm. With Faolan and Kosse outside still, she snuck back to her room and found some clean buckskins. She brought them, along with a drying cloth and her honey and berry soap, out to a chair by the tub.

Once all was ready, she sank into the hot water. She groaned in ecstasy as she let the water ease her stiffness away. She washed her hair then, as she rose out of the tub, she heard, "Oh my god."

Chapter Thirteen

Lucien awoke alone. It took him a minute to place where he was. The room was very colorful, he was in her bedroom, and it suited her. She was gone, the animals were gone, and he was alone. He was hard. He willed himself under control and slipped from the bed to head for the main part of the cabin.

What he saw when he got there nothing in all of his twenty-six years could have prepared him for. He had seen naked women plenty. Not like this. Not even close. Even the famed statue of Aphrodite rising from the foam had nothing on the vision before him.

She remained motionless in the tub at the same time as water ran down her body. The light from the fire transformed the water on her skin to diamonds and topaz. Her hair was down the middle of her back and ended at the curve of her waist.

Her breasts were full and high. Her stomach flat, muscular. Her legs were toned and firm. He ogled at flawlessness. "Oh my god." The groan slipped past his lips.

Ciara turned at his voice. Before she could say or do anything, he strode across the cabin. Lucien plucked her out of the tub as if she weighed no more than a feather. Compared to him, she didn't.

He set her down in front of the fire and picked up the drying cloth. He looked at her, asking the unspoken question. Could he dry her off?

She smiled shyly at him, which gave him the answer he wanted, craved. He worked at a snail's pace as though to savor every moment. He started at her neck. When the skin was dry, he flicked his tongue in the spots of the water droplets. He stroked down each arm, as he followed the towel with his lips.

"Gorgeous." He placed little kisses along her belly. Her body shuddered.

He dried off her legs, lifted each foot and kissed the instep on both. When she was dry, she was still shivering. He didn't believe it was from cold. It had come time for him to make good on his promise. He swept her up in his arms and laid her on the pallet.

"You are so beautiful." He moved up and inhaled her clean scent. He skimmed his hands along her body, making it tremble where he touched. "So wild, so untamed."

He ran his calloused hand over her breast and swallowed her gasp as he plundered her mouth with his. Her nipple hardened in his palm. Her reaction was like a jolt to his system.

She arched her back to press herself more and more into him. He lay over her, dressed. Ciara inched her hands under his shirt.

"Off. Take it off, I want to feel you."

He didn't know he could get any harder. Lucien reared up and ripped off the shirt, not caring where it landed. "I always thought you were beautiful, even when I first brought you here bleeding. These scars only add to it. You are beautiful." Her words made him feel like the only man in the world.

He kissed her quiet. She pulled on the waistband of his pants. Her meaning was clear. He shucked off the rest of his clothes. Within seconds he stood before her completely naked and watched her reaction.

Lust. Raw hunger filled her gaze, as she looked him over.

"I want you."

Those three words hit him and he almost jumped on her right there.

"Slowly. We need to go slow." Lucien prayed he had the control to go slow.

"No." She looked up at him. "Now. I have dreamed about this since you arrived."

"My god, woman," he groaned as he fell on top of her. His hands were everywhere. They touched. They caressed. He slipped one hand between her legs and dipped his finger, one long finger, between her sable curls.

She was right, she was ready. She was wet. So wet. He almost spilled himself right there. Lucien moved over her and put the tip of his cock at the juncture of her thighs.

Ciara spread wider to accommodate him and she whimpered when he just ran the head along her slit. She raised her legs and wrapped them around his hips.

"God, that's right, wrap them around my waist, princess."

Lucien didn't want to hurt her. Didn't want to appear like a rutting bastard, but he had just about lost control. Her musky scent filled his nostrils, making him want to plunge deep within her and claim her as his own.

In the end, Ciara made the decision for him. Her legs, strengthened by years of traversing throughout the mountains, yanked him toward her. He slammed inside her to the hilt.

Both of them groaned at the sensation. In the back of his mind, Lucien realized there was no barrier that he broke through. It didn't matter. She was tight, so tight. She fit him like a velvet glove. She caressed him.

Lucien lost control. Primal feelings, the likes of which he had never felt before, dominated his slim hold on his restraint. With a low growl that would have done Faolan proud, he pounded into her like a man obsessed.

She met each one of his thrusts with undulations of her hips, drawing him in deeper, farther, harder and faster into her soul. Lucien felt her body tighten so he slipped his hand between them and rubbed her core. Her back arched as she let loose a cry of uncontrolled and unrehearsed feeling as her lithe body shook with the aftershocks of her ardent release.

Concurrently, her dampness gripped him, milked him, and he couldn't hold back any more than he could stop the rise and fall of the tide. The tendons on his neck stood out as he withdrew then plunged into her deeper than he had been. He was one with her as his head fell back, and he roared his fulfillment to the cabin and the mountains that surrounded them as he spent himself deep within her. He couldn't move. He didn't want to move. Lucien dropped his face into the softness of her neck as he fought to slow his erratic breathing. He was exhausted. They lay there, limbs entwined, each gasping for breath.

Lucien was mortified. He had had countless women and never before had he lost control like that. Before, he had always maintained a distance from the women. It was only a matter of physical release and that enabled him to always withdraw before he spilled his seed inside them. He had no wish to father any bastards.

He couldn't have pulled out of Ciara if an army had swarmed the cabin. He had lost all rational thought. His only necessity was to ravage the woman beneath him and fill her to capacity with his seed. For a man who had just acted like a primitive heathen, he wanted to make it up to her.

In his defense he didn't hear any complaints from her. "Are you all right?"

"Aye. Never better." When he made to move off, she gripped him and said, "No. Stay. I like the feel of your weight."

"I'm too heavy. I want to hold you." He slid out of her, moved behind her and pulled her into his chest, so they rested together like spoons.

Ciara reached to the end of the pallet and swung an extra quilt over them. They fell asleep like that.

* * * *

Ciara awoke later as waves of pleasure throbbed through her. Lucien lay between her spread legs and licked her pussy. Her legs were draped over his broad shoulders to hold her open with his fingers and teased her with his tongue.

She dug her fingers into his scalp grinding herself into him. It was scandalous yet she couldn't help it. He drove her wild. While his tongue laved attention on her clit, his fingers teased the entrance before they slid within her, right away for she was slick with her own juices. He paid her worship in ways she had never dreamed about.

First only one finger was inside, then that was soon joined by another. He used one muscled forearm to anchor her writhing body in place as he slipped yet another finger deep within her. Her moans were coming louder and more constant in time with him as he moved his fingers in tandem with his tongue. Lucien brought her to the verge of pleasure. He retreated just before she could find that elusive release. He teased her again and again as she writhed above him. She begged, pleaded with her moans, because she couldn't form any coherent words, for him to allow her to reach the pinnacle she sought.

Ciara arched and screamed as she was allowed to find her release. Lucien stayed with his arm across her hips continuing to pay homage to her as she came harder and harder. While she still quivered with tremors, he rose above her and plunged deep within her in one smooth stroke. He filled her to entirety.

Lucien lowered his mouth and kissed her. Ciara tasted him and her both as he moved within her. She pressed her body closer to him, determined to take whatever it was he was willing to give her. His body responded to hers like brandy and cigars, so his own release arrived moments later as he moaned her name into her mouth.

They lay there for a moment before Ciara pushed onto his shoulder. He picked up his head to glance down at her. He questioned with his eyes as he kissed her again, not able to get enough of her taste. "I have to get up. The fire is going low and the animals are still outside."

"You don't have to go anywhere. The animals are fine and personally I think the fire is nowhere near going out." He waggled his eyebrows at her.

"Arrogant male."

"Uh-huh. I have every right to be. I earned the right."

"Aye. That you do and you did. But I really have to get up." She rolled him off her and rose gracefully from the bed.

She felt his gaze on her as she walked nude to the chair that held her clothes. She hesitated before she headed for her bedroom. She needed to take another bath now before dressing into clean clothes.

She put on her dirty clothes and lugged the tub outside. When she brought it back in and started to warm more water, Lucien got up. "What are you doing?"

"I am going to clean myself and then do some laundry. Why? Did you wish to bathe?"

"Only if you join me."

"Thanks but I am fine for now." Her enchanting flush betrayed her true feelings on the matter.

Lucien cleaned himself off along with her. He put on some clean clothes and gathered more snow to melt for water to do laundry. He helped her with the wash, then, when all the clothes were done, spread out on chairs by the fire and hung on a rope he strung up, he dragged the tub outside for her.

While he emptied it, she started to shovel the porch. Lucien came up behind her and made a grab for her. She screeched and ran down the steps while he gave chase. He tackled her to the ground and covered her with kisses.

Faolan and Kosse jumped in to join the fun and before long all four of them were involved in a huge snow fight. The animals would hit them in the knees and run before they could get up. Lucien and Ciara threw snowballs at each other and at the animals.

Tired, cold and wet, they all stomped back into the cabin to get something to eat and dry off. While Ciara made some food, Lucien made a nuisance of himself as he nibbled on her neck and constantly touched her, distracting her.

It was as if that morning had changed their whole friendship and the next month was full of joy and cheer.

Chapter Fourteen

As he watched the woman across the table from him eat stew a few nights later, he realized that he wanted her to be his for all time. "Come back to England with me."

Ciara's head shot up. Something flickered in her eyes but was gone before he could identify what it was. She offered him a grin and he knew it was forced. "No. I don't belong in your world."

"I want you with me," he persisted.

"No."

"Why not?"

"I just told you. I don't belong in your world. It is not for me."

"You would fit. You fit with me. I could offer you things you never dreamed of. Bedrooms bigger than your whole cabin. Silk sheets. Servants at your beck and call. Rooms full of gowns made by the best modiste in town. I would dress you in the finest clothes, you would be the envy of all London. I would make love to you on beds covered in rose petals, what do you think?"

As her eyes flared, he realized that he'd erred. Grievously.

She responded with a sad chuckle. "That was a very sweet thing to say, no matter that it is not true." At his questioning stare, she continued. "Don't you see, Wolf? I don't need that kind of thing to be happy. Silk sheets, dresses, all of what you offer comes at too high a price for me."

"What do you mean?" She was the only woman he knew who would turn down the chance to be a marchioness, or to be the mistress of a marquess.

"If I were to take those things, I would have to give up the thing that means most to me." At his confused look, she pressed on, "My freedom. I would be bound and confined by your rules and your society's dictates. I love the smell of the country—I would not last in a city. Within these mountains, my heart beats the strongest.

"Besides, I can't be your mistress. I won't be."

Pain lanced through his heart at the thought of her left behind when he returned to England. *But would you be my wife?* "What do you call what you are being now?"

"I call myself your friend. What I give you is just that. Something from me to you. I want none of the things you bestow on your mistresses. You will leave soon. I want you to find happiness. For once in your life, have someone like you for who you are, not because of what you own. My lying with you is just that. A gift, something that I love sharing with you. I harbor no illusions of what will happen. I am living for the now. I am happy.

"Also, I don't think that Faolan would do well in your country, much less Kosse." She rose and sat on his lap, her arms looped around his neck to bring them nose to nose. "There is something inside you, Wolf, that is very special. All I want from you is *you*. For once, forget all your wealth and privileges and just live your life. That will be enough for me. Have fun while you are here." She kissed his lips then stood and cleared the table, leaving him alone with his thoughts.

Lucien looked at this woman. She was mind-boggling. She went against everything he had been taught about women. The way she answered him didn't even allow him to be angry with her. As long as he walked the earth, he knew he would never find another like her.

Ciara kept her own counsel as she cleared the table.

Lucien reached down to scratch Kosse and wondered if he would ever get her to change her mind. He realized who the 'heart of the mountain' was. It was Ciara. She thrived here. In an environment that would kill off most, she lived, survived and prospered. If she ever left, it would be to follow her heart, not because he asked her to.

"Ciara? Would you consider selling me a horse? I would like a son of Nyama and Epona."

"And how am I to get this son to you? Are you going to come back to Paradise Cove to get him?"

If that's what it takes to see you again.

"I was thinking that you could send him by ship to my country estate, Heartstone. I would leave you the address and payment in advance so all you would have to do is put him on the ship."

"Why would I want to do that?"

"Because I asked for one."

"A son? There is no telling when that could be. Why would you wish to do that?"

"Like you said before. If you give your word, you don't go back on it. I would be content to wait for one. Yes?"

"Deal. You will leave payment with Marie. And when there is a son, I will send him to Heartstone." The price she quoted him was a fair price and he agreed.

"Good, now come here, woman. If I am to have fun, I wish to have it with you." He swung her up into his arms, holding her before he placed her back on the floor.

"Good." Her eyes grew dark with desire and expectation as she tugged his head down for a kiss.

* * * *

Lucien ran her trap line with her. He was getting into shape as he trekked beside her in the mountain snow. She had taught him how to skin the food and stretch the hides so they could be sold.

Lucien learned how to have fun. He was smiling more and more as the days passed. He felt better than he ever had before. For not having gaming halls and places to drink, he found that he was even happier.

He found himself watching Ciara when she didn't think he could see her. Although she smiled, it was rare for her to grace him with an honest, open smile. Her smiles normally could make his heart race. When she gifted him with one that was without reservation, it could bring him to his knees.

If they were in the cabin she would wear loose-fitting clothes that she said were African. They were bright-colored and only enhanced her beauty. Usually they were pants and a long shirt that would go to her knees, but she also had some dresses. Dresses were too cold to wear during the winter, she claimed.

* * * *

He carried her to the bedroom, set her down then removed her clothes. When she tried to sit up, he pushed her back. "This is my gift to you. Let me worship you."

Christmas had come upon them and he'd seemed pleased with the hand-carved statue she'd given him after they ate.

At his words, she tingled all over. As she watched him with a heady gaze, her body was already wet and ready for him. He took off his clothing and stretched out beside her. She reached for him.

"No. I want to look. I want to remember how you look right now, forever." He stroked a hand down her side as he leaned over her propped up on one elbow and stared at her with those eyes of his that had the power to intoxicate her. "You are so beautiful. Your skin is so soft, like silk." He dipped his head and flicked his tongue over her collarbone, watched as she shivered.

"You taste like you smell, honey and berries. I love your taste." Another stroke of his tongue along her neck as he moved down. He touched her arm and ran his fingers along her skin. "Your arms are so strong, so tender. Everything about you is strong. Yet you remain one of the softest people I know." He flicked his tongue along the same path his fingers had just traveled.

She squirmed. "No. Hold still. Or I will stop." Ciara moaned her frustration. "Look at your breasts. So full. Perfect for suckling." He did just that, and when his lips closed about her breast she arched her back and pressed herself into his mouth. When she tried to reach up and touch him he shook his head without leaving her breast. She got the message.

"So perfect. But you have two and I can't ignore the other one." He lavished attention on her other breast until both her nipples were taut and stiff. His breath made her shiver as it hit the spots where he had suckled and left her wet. "Further down we come to your stomach." He delved into her belly button with his tongue, eliciting a gasp, but she held firm. "You have a wonderfully flat stomach. Lovely hips." He nipped at her sides, making her whimpers grow in volume.

Lucien slid down and settled himself between her legs and brushed light touches there. "Legs. Your legs are in amazing condition. All this mountain climbing has made them so strong." He moved his tongue down the inside of her leg all the way to her foot. "Your ankles are small, your feet are delicate." Taking her toe into his mouth, he sucked on it as he had her breasts. The reaction was the same—her body quivered with need.

He ran his tongue up the inside of her other leg after loving her other foot and ankle in the same fashion.

He moved back up and gave her stomach more love bites. As her mewls grew louder, he spread her thighs farther apart. "And then there is my favorite part. Your core. You smell like a mixture of spices." He slid his fingers through the hair and along the slit but never did he enter her. When he ran one along her opening, she tried to move herself onto it. "No, no, no. I told you not to move. I shall have to stop."

"No, don't stop. I won't move again." Her voice was breathless as she gripped the blankets with a hold that should have wrung the colors out of them.

"One more chance, no moving. Understand?"

"Yes." Her voice was almost nonexistent.

"Very well then. Where was I? Oh yes, I was enjoying your smell." He wedged his body between her thighs and draped her legs over his shoulders. Ciara could feel his warm breath at the juncture of her thighs but he wouldn't touch her. She begged with her whimpers. He spread her lips and dipped one finger inside her. Lucien pushed a finger into her wetness. She tightened around him to try to keep him inside as he removed his finger.

"Look at me." The timbre of his voice made her shiver with anticipation. "Look at me." She slowly sat up and braced herself on arms that were none too steady. "Scoot back to the headboard." He stayed where he was between her legs as she moved back with her arms since her legs were still draped over his shoulders.

When she was back against the headboard with a pillow behind her he smiled at her and drove two fingers deep within her, never once taking his eyes off hers. Ciara's body shuddered with pleasure as her eyes fluttered closed. He started to withdraw his fingers. "No. Look at me. Don't close your eyes. Watch me, princess."

The hypnotic pull of his velvety voice gave her no choice as she dragged her eyes open to find herself riveted by eyes that appeared almost black with passion that was barely kept under restraint. He smiled as he saw her meet his eyes.

"Your reward." He slid his fingers back into her, making her eyes almost—she caught herself in time—roll back in her head. His thick fingers were covered with the juices flowing out of her body. Lucien maintained a steady but forceful rhythm. He held her gaze as she came on his fingers.

"You are a thing of beauty when you come." Her cries had turned to full-out moans. She tried to keep her sounds contained but he flicked his thumb on her hard clit, and as he realized she was trying to stay quiet, he shook his head. "I wish to hear you. Don't keep it to yourself. I want to hear what you are feeling."

"Please," she cried.

"Please what? More of this? Tell me. Tell me what you wish, my princess." His fingers stretched her as she approached the edge of the chasm again.

"Please. More... I want... Let me... I am going to..." Her voice was agitated as she tried to concentrate on what she was asking for.

"What do you want? What are you going to do? Come? Yes you are. No, don't look away. Keep looking at me. Keep your eyes open. Watch me as I make you come. That's my girl. My beauty. Watch as my fingers slide in and out of your wetness. I feel you tightening around me. You're almost there, aren't you?" His inhalations had increased along with hers. Indigo eyes locked with amber as his fingers moved like pistons in and out of her heated core. "Now! I want it now. Come for me."

At his words, her head dropped back against the headboard and her thighs clamped around him as she came in waves. She managed to keep eye contact with him. "Good girl." He withdrew his fingers and sucked them clean.

That sight alone was almost enough to make her come again. He lowered his head and placed his mouth over her. He drank every bit of her essence that was present. When she whimpered again, he rose and settled himself on his knees, leaving her legs on either side of his waist. His member jutted out from the nest of black hair. It pulsated and it drew her gaze. Velvet over steel.

Lucien grabbed her legs and dragged her to him. He moved over her and teased her with the tip of his dick. "What do you want?" His voice was rough with need.

"You."

He pushed the tip inside her and she sighed. He stopped and she complained. "What do you want?" he asked again as he inched in a little deeper.

"You," she cried.

Lucien began to withdraw. "What do you want?"

"You, damn it. I want you," she screamed in frustration.

He lowered himself so his mouth was by her ear, teasing her more as he gritted out his question, as he tried to maintain his hold on his control.

"My name. Say my name. Tell me you want me." His tone was pleading.

"I want you. Please. I need you to fill me. I need to feel you deep inside of me. I need you. I want you. I want you. Lucien."

That was all it took. He slammed home in one stroke and came. His body shook with aftermath as he buried his face in her neck, inhaling her scent, imprinting this moment in his brain.

Ciara wrapped her arms around him and placed kisses along his shoulder. "That was by far the best Christmas present I have ever received."

Lucien laughed.

They got back up and spent the rest of the day doing other things until it was time to sleep again.

As they lay in bed, Lucien asked, "How did you do the statue? When did you?"

"It was the one on the shelf up there. I really just had to add the saying. I hope you like it."

"I love it. Thank you."

"Mmm. You're welcome." She was asleep in moments.

Chapter Fifteen

When Ciara awoke in the morning a week after Christmas had passed, she was alone. She rose and dressed in haste, only to find that the cabin was empty. She heard Lucien before she saw him. Ciara looked through the curtains. She laughed as he was tripped by Faolan and pounced on by Kosse.

She swung on her cloak and went out to join them. A grin split his face when he saw her coming through the door. "Good morning, princess."

"Morning, Wolf. What are you doing?" The familiar thrum ran through her body as he called her 'princess.'

"We are shoveling." His imperious tone didn't do much to impress when Kosse sat on his chest and hampered his attempts to rise.

"I see, and what are you shoveling exactly?"

"Watch it, woman. You are outnumbered. There are three of us men versus one of you."

Ciara quirked a brow. "Those two will do anything I say."

He huffed with false indignation. "I know, I know you have them bewitched." He shoved Kosse off and rose. Lucien stopped in front of her. Skin flush with cold, he added, "You have me bewitched as well." He gave her a light kiss on the lips and, with a jaunty whistle, struck out for the shovel and got back to work.

Ciara had a smile on her face until a breeze turned her attention from the dark-haired man shoveling snow. Faolan came to stand beside her. She spoke in a language, one she knew Lucien wouldn't understand, to the wolf in case he overheard. "I know. I feel it too. A warm spell comes. We will take him down today and be back within the week."

She turned toward the hut where she did her tanning. She checked her rations of grain. There was enough for her to take the trip down and back. Her heart heavy in her chest, she observed Lucien as he entered the building behind her.

"What's wrong? You seem sad." He reached out to brush some grain off her cheek.

"Nothing is wrong. There is a warm spell coming. I will be able to take you back to town. You will be there in a few days. We leave today." She strode past him into the sunlight.

He grabbed her arm and spun her toward him. "What are you talking about? I thought you said all winter."

"Maybe I did. I was wrong. This good weather will hold. I can get you to town in three days. It is unusual for January but it does happen. I will pack some things. You should gather your things. Not that you have much." She entered the cabin, which left him to follow. He did.

"I'm confused. Why are we leaving today?"

"You need to go. You were supposed to be headed for England now. This warm weather is a surprise to me as well, but we will put it to good use."

"Now? You want to leave now? Will you stay in one place and talk to me?"

Ciara had gone to the bedroom. No, she didn't want him to leave. He *had* to leave. As she turned to him, she questioned, "What do you want to know? My guess is that since there is a warm spell the winter will come back in full force and stay longer. This is the perfect time for me to get you down the mountain." She stripped off her clothes and stretched for her thick buckskins.

Lucien grabbed her before she could reach the clothes.

"Wolf, please. Your hands are cold and we have to go."

"If you are sending me away, I want you once more. Please."

Her hands as they ripped away his clothes were his answer. They fell back on the bed in a tangle of blankets. They coupled with ferocity and yet tenderness. She almost wept as he came deep within her.

They separated and acted like strangers as they dressed. Ciara took a bag and put his papers in there along with the statue. She flicked a glance at him as she gamely tried for a smile.

"The first son of Nyama and Epona will be yours. You have my word."

"Good. Um, you have my address in England so you know where to send the horse."

"Aye. I put the statue and your stable plans in the bag."

She packed food and put out the fire in the fireplace. Ciara faced him by the door. "Is there anything else you think you will need?"

"No. I think that will do. I still have my things in Paradise Cove. What about payment for the horse?"

"Leave it with Marie and I will get it from her later. I would also appreciate it if you would give her this quilt for me."

"Yes, sure. I can do that."

She nodded. "Right, well, we should go. It will be a long trip." She took the rolled-up furs and gave him the pouch with his things in it.

They stepped out on the porch and Ciara let loose a whistle that pierced across the snow-covered mountain. Moments later, Epona, followed by his stallion, trotted into the copse. They mounted in silence and headed off, accompanied by Kosse and Faolan.

After their two nights in the woods, part of her wished that he'd never shown up in her life while another part never wanted to let him go.

When they started off the final morning, Ciara was nervous. She wove in and out of trees and backtracked. When she stopped she was at the end of a glade, but they were still hidden. It was late afternoon. She dismounted and Lucien did the same.

"This is where I leave you. Paradise Cove is across this clearing. You should be there by dark." Her eyes welled up with tears as she looked at him.

Lucien reached for her and she went without hesitation into his arms. "Come with me."

"Safe journey, Wolf. Good luck with your stable. I hope you find what you are looking for."

Lucien looked down at her and tried for a smile. "Thank you. For everything."

"My pleasure." She glanced at the sky. "You should get going. Take care of him. And yourself."

"You too."

"Aye, I will." She made a motion and Faolan came up. "Say goodbye, Faolan." The wolf took his hand in its mouth. Jaws that could kill with ease caressed him like silk. He was released after a brief spot of pressure. It was the wolf's way of saying goodbye.

Lucien patted the wolf on the head. "Take care of her, boy. Take care of her." He turned and pulled Kosse's ears with affection. He rose to look back at Ciara.

He strode over to her and swept her up in his arms. He almost crushed her. Lucien lowered her as he kissed her forehead then pressed his mouth to hers. He devoured her, she devoured him. After a long, heated exchange, they both stepped back.

Ciara licked her lips and touched her fingers to his bearded jaw. "Goodbye, Wolf."

He stepped close again and spoke so hushed she almost missed it. "Why don't you call me Lucien? You did once. No one but you ever has."

She raised her eyes to his as she memorized the face. "Go. It grows late. Stay to the middle of the field." Her jaw trembled in an effort not to cry. She reached out and pulled him in for one last kiss.

"Goodbye, princess." His eyes kissed her just as much as his lips did. Then he spun and swung up on Colonial Star and rode off without looking back.

"Goodbye, Lucien," came the whispered response that she knew would not be heard. She swung up on Epona's back, motioned for her to leave as well. She headed off as Faolan and Kosse followed in her silent wake.

Chapter Sixteen

England

"What the hell do you mean you are starting your own racing stable? What happened to you over in those bloody colonies? I had hoped that you would come back a man, but I guess I was wrong." Spittle flew from the mouth of the man in the chair. Lucien stood at attention in front of his father as he was yelled at.

"Just what I said. I am leaving Stokley and going home to Heartstone. I will build my stables there. I am also taking Devonna with me." His pronouncements made his stepmother gasp with shock.

"Why would you wish to go there? The ladies are in London. If you leave, then you will not find a bride." Her high-pitched, whiney voice grated on his nerves.

"That's it? That is all you have to say? Don't go so I can find a bride. What about your daughter?"

"She stays," yelled his stepmother.

"Take the stupid bitch. All she does is stare out of the window. It is embarrassing. Take her with my blessing." The venom in his father's voice was a punch to the gut. His stepmother backed down under the glare of her husband.

"We will be gone within the hour."

He walked out of the room as he swore under his breath. It had been like this ever since he had returned from America. His father had more nice words for the horse than for his own son. He had *at least* been pleased with the horse.

Lucien climbed the stairs to his sister's room and knocked on the door. He opened it a little and stuck his head in. "Devonna? Are you in here?" He heard movement by the window and entered the room.

His sister sat in silence by the window dressed in a drab black gown. Her hair was lifeless and dull. He sat on a cushion by her and tried not to show how her cringing away from him hurt.

"Devonna. I am going to take you with me to Heartstone. It's in the country. I think that you will like it there. Wide open spaces, woods, lakes. What do you think? Would you like to go with me?"

Although her face remained impassive and still, Lucien told himself that he caught a flicker of hope in those eyes. Something had happened to his sister. She used to be so full of life and laughter.

He reached out to pat her on the arm and she visibly flinched away from him. Careful to keep his face straight, he pulled his hand back and smiled at her.

"We leave in an hour. I will have your things packed."

He exited and, as the door shut, the caring brother was gone, leaving in his place a marquess that whipped out orders as fast as his mouth would work.

They were headed to Heartstone in just under an hour. He was shocked at how little clothing his sister had. They rode together in the carriage for a six-hour ride. He would have preferred to be on horseback but he thought he should spend some time with his sister.

"Are you excited, Devonna? I think it will be a grand adventure. Do you remember the adventures we took as children?"

He watched her face for any sign of recognition and found none. If anything, she withdrew farther into herself.

"I am going to start a stable for racers. Would you like to have a horse of your own? Or maybe a dog, or cat?" When she didn't answer, he just plodded on with the one-sided conversation. "Well, let me know. Would you like to hear of my time in America?"

That time he knew he caught a glimmer of excitement. "Well, you know," he said even though she didn't, "I had to go get a racer from America for Father. The town I had to go to was called Paradise Cove. Very small, very quaint. The people there were all different and yet they treated each one the same. I met an old woman, which is the one I got the horse from, and she reminded me of a grandmother that we used to hear about in stories. Always smiling and ready with hugs.

"Well, I took the horse, the one I brought back—his name is Colonial Star—out for a ride. I was not as good a rider as I had thought for he got away from me and took me high into the mountains. Then a bear came and attacked us."

Devonna tried to pretend she wasn't interested but he caught the look on her face. Lucien suppressed a smile as he continued.

"When I woke up I was in a cabin. The whole thing was not much bigger than a receiving room at Stokley. I was alone and the first thing I saw was a woman. She had saved me. Her name is Ciara. She had found me and carried me back to her cabin." At his sister's look of disbelief he did smile, and nodded. "It's true. She lived there all alone and we were stuck there together because the snows came and we couldn't leave."

There was a panicked look in his sister's eyes at the mention of him being alone with a woman. A clue perhaps why she was so withdrawn. "Well, I shouldn't say alone. She had a wolf for a pet. And while I was there, she also got a mountain lion kitten. She also had horses. She wore pants and did things like a man."

She may have done things like a man, but there were some things that she did which were *all* woman. He brought his focus back on his sister and continued with his story. He noticed that she listened with wide eyes.

"She taught me all about the woods, how to trap animals—which was really messy—and how to survive a winter in the mountains."

That wasn't all she had taught him, but his sister didn't need to know that.

"I think you would like Ciara, Devonna. She is a very kind person. She loves life and smiles and laughs a lot." He saw tears well up in his sister's eyes. "She is supposed to send me a horse for my stable." He broke off as tears began to stream down his sister's face.

He reached into his pocket, pulled out his handkerchief and handed it to her. She flinched back. That was getting old.

"Devonna. You have to know that I am not going to hurt you. I would never hurt you."

Devonna wedged herself back into a corner of the carriage and watched him with scared eyes. When they stopped to rest the horses, he got out and rode on his gray gelding to leave her alone in the carriage. Damn, he wished he knew what was wrong.

They arrived at Heartstone in the early evening. As he rode up the drive, his heart swelled. This was where he *would* make a name for himself. The servants were all lined up to wait for him. They waited for a chance to see the famed Black Marquess.

He dismounted at the steps and issued orders to his man of affairs. He helped his sister down out of the carriage after steeling himself for her wince. He took her to her rooms, which were on the opposite wing of the home from his.

As he opened the door to her suite of rooms, he peered at her. Her eyes skimmed over the room, going instead to the big window that had extra thick cushions placed in front of it. The room was done in a pale lilac with dark blue accents. There was a large bed and lots of space for her things, which he realized she didn't have many of. *Why not?*

"I will come for you at dinner." Her eyes flew wide with fright and she stumbled backward. "Devonna? What's wrong?"

He reached out to her and she put her shaking hand in his. Lucien could see that she was mortified and scared beyond belief but she didn't disobey his hand reaching for hers.

"Maybe you would wish to take a walk or get some sleep. I will see you in a bit."

Lucien left the room and realized that he was shaking. From anger. He kept his counsel until he found his man of affairs getting ready to leave. *Why is my sister so petrified of me?* Although they couldn't be classified as close, he had never done anything to hurt her.

"Foley. A word."

"Yes, my lord?" Foley was a thin man. Very competent and loyal.

"What the hell happened in that house when I was gone?"

"My lord? To what are you referring?"

"The treatment of my sister. What the hell did they do to her there?"

"I am not sure. I know that when you were gone your brother was there a lot. Your family did not see fit to include me in many of the discussions."

"Find out."

"Yes, my lord." He took his leave and rode away from Heartstone.

* * * *

America

"Are you going to let him know?" Marie's question invaded her thoughts.

"No," Ciara said with a very determined look at the woman who was questioning her.

"He has a right to know. We both know that."

"Maybe someday. Not now."

"Child. You should tell him." Her tone was unusually sharp for Marie, the woman she viewed as a surrogate mother.

Ciara looked at the old woman and smiled. A smile full of serenity and calmness, one that belied the rolling of her insides at the mention of 'the man.'

"This child is mine. I am not ready to tell him."

Him. Lucien. The man who still invaded her dreams. The father of her unborn child.

"Tell him." Angelique spoke, which surprised them both.

Ciara shook her head at Angelique. Marie clucked in disapproval and rose. "The quilt he sent from you was beautiful. Thank you."

"You know I like making things for you. It was my pleasure." Ciara's mind drifted to the time she had spent with Lucien. He had never been far from her mind.

"He had nothing but good things to say about you and now I know why." Marie gestured to her protruding belly.

"Marie. Shame on you." Ciara felt the heat of her blush rush across her face. "I brought you some honey. The first batch I had."

"You should not be riding around in those mountains. Not when you're about to give birth." The older woman respected her desire to change the subject.

"I am fine. Besides, I never go anywhere without Faolan and Kosse. They would die before they let anything happen to me."

"How is that old wolf? And that little devil cat?"

"They are both fine. You know you could go open the door and let them in."

"And have animal fur in the house? Never."

"Don't ever change, Marie. I couldn't stand it. I have to get going."

Ciara rose, kissed both women on the cheeks and walked outside with them. She whistled and Nyama came from the thicket where he waited. He stood as she awkwardly mounted him. Her belly had already begun to get in the way.

"Come before the birth. You shouldn't be alone then."

Marie reached out and handed her a money pouch with a seal embroidered on the side that caused Ciara's heart to skip a beat.

As she traced the pattern on the money pouch, Ciara acknowledged them with a wave of her hand then she headed home, her mind focused on past memories. As soon as she entered the woods a glossy black wolf and a lustrous, albeit gangly mountain lion placed themselves on either side of the stallion.

* * * *

As the time of her impending birth grew closer, she fluctuated back and forth about going down to Marie's. One day the decision was made for her. Marie and Angelique showed up at her cabin. How they knew where it was, she would never know. How the old ladies made the journey alone, she would also never know.

They couldn't have timed it better. Within the week she gave birth. She gave birth to a boy. She named him Brenden Kumi McKay. He was a beautiful boy. His skin had a golden tint to it, but he was still lighter than his mother. He had a head of thick black hair and his eyes were blue. Well, they were the shade identical to his father's. A deep midnight blue that could penetrate your soul.

Kosse and Faolan loved him and he became a member of the group. They took care of him when she had work to do. Later that same winter, she found that Epona had been successful with her breeding to Nyama and so she expected a foal late fall the next year.

The years passed, and as Brenden grew, her heart ached each time she looked at him. He was a very bright child who grew up able to speak all the languages she did. One autumn five years after the birth of her son, Bryn, she found that Epona was carrying again. Her other foals had all been fillies. Still she waited for the first colt. The next fall came, and when Epona gave birth, she bore a colt. Black like his father with a white lightning-bolt pattern on his left haunch. She had no more excuses. It was time to go. She trembled at the thought.

The colt was weaned at six months and she gathered the eldest daughter of Epona, whom she had named Artemis, her sister Angel, Brenden's gelding Toka, along with the colt. She, her son, the four horses, a black wolf and a mountain lion, no longer gangly, headed to catch the first ship to England to deliver on a promise that had been made seven years earlier.

The traveling group attracted much attention, in particular the horses, but the presence of the large black wolf seemed to deter any people that would think to take them even though his muzzle was grizzled, a testament to his age. If the wolf alone wasn't enough then the mountain lion, a lush deep red tipped with copper brown, which was no awkward little cub but a sleek animal whose every movement spoke of raw power, got the message across.

Chapter Seventeen

England

Lucien accepted the congratulations that came his way as another one of his horses won. He glanced at his sister who had been opening up over the past seven years. It had been a difficult road both with his sister and with starting the stables.

His father had thrown in every sort of obstacle possible. Lucien had succeeded, however, despite the problems he had faced. He had become successful at something that was his very own. Proud, he gathered his sister and headed back to Heartstone.

Lucien entered his study and poured himself a brandy while he sat at his desk. At one corner sat a carving of a wolf with a message at the bottom. *Ciara.* He thought about her often. More than often. Daily. Nightly. It seemed that his heart tattooed out her name. He realized that he had known love.

His two friends, Rafe and Phillip, joined him in the study and helped themselves to some brandy. "Some race today, Luc. Your stables are doing well." Rafe Carson, Viscount Harrington, spoke as he took a long drink of the smooth brandy. "I bet your old man hates it."

Lucien smiled, one of pure male satisfaction. "Probably."

Phillip Vallence, Earl of Edais, spoke next. "I say, Luc, you are a different man since you returned from that heathen country."

"America, Phillip?" *Bloody hell, man, it was seven years ago. Seven long years.*

"That's the place. What happened to you over there?"

"I went and got a horse for my father."

Rafe snorted his disbelief. He spied the carving and walked over to pick it up. "Where did you get this? I don't remember seeing it before." He whistled low as he read the inscription. "Wolf?"

"Put it down, Rafe." Lucien's tone brooked no argument.

"Who is Wolf? Is that you? Where did you get this? Better yet, when did you get this?" His friend kept pushing.

"Leave it alone, Rafe."

Phillip spoke up. "I say, I bet it's some colonial whore who secured a place in his heart." He laughed as if he had told a hilarious joke.

The sound of glass breaking snapped both Phillip and Rafe to attention. Lucien spoke low but there was no way to miss the daggered tone of his voice. The glass he had been drinking from lay in shards and his hand bled. His eyes were like ice shards. "She is not a whore and if you speak of her in such a way again, I will kill you."

"Sorry. I didn't know she meant..."

"You don't know anything. You are drunk, Edais. Go home. Take Rafe with you." Lucien waved a dismissive hand and shut his eyes against the onslaught of pain every thought of Ciara brought. It had been seven years and he still dreamed of her every night.

Seven years and no sign of the horse she had promised. She could be married now, with children. At the thought of another man with her—he groaned as he put his head on his desk. He couldn't get her out of his mind no matter what he did. The women he pursued now looked nothing like her. Who was he kidding? No one in England looked like her. She was amazing. She was gone.

He was thirty-three and needed to get an heir. Lucien was still one of the most sought-after men for the mothers in the 'marriage mart.' He kept to Heartstone. He didn't want a blushing debutante, and he wanted someone with curves who made him weak in the knees. Someone who smelled fresh. Someone who would stand up to him and make his life interesting. Someone like Ciara. No, there was no woman in the world like her.

He wanted Ciara.

His sister, Devonna, had begun to come out of her shell. They'd had a rocky start but she was doing well. If she saw her brother or father she would fall silent and withdraw. Not like they ever came out to Heartstone. Foley had found nothing to report on the happenings while she was at Stokley.

His stables had taken a lot of time and a lot of hard work, but he was proud of them. He looked up as Rafe came back into the room. He glared at his friend.

"What do you want, Rafe? I thought you were leaving?"

Lucien had wrapped his hand to stop the blood and summoned someone to clean up the mess he had made.

"I sent Phillip back home. I came to apologize. I didn't know that you had met someone over there. I never would have said anything about the statue if I had known."

Lucien shook his head. "That's all right. No one knows. I am going down to the stables. Want to come?"

Rafe nodded and turned toward the door. It opened and in walked Devonna garbed in a deep purple that brought out her violet-blue eyes. Lucien began to speak to Rafe when he noticed the two of them. They were staring at each other like they were each other's lifeline and they needed to look at each other to survive. Lucien was as good as invisible.

Humm humm. Lucien cleared his throat and hid a grin as his sister and best friend blushed to their roots. Devonna managed an awkward curtsy and mumbled, "My lord, Lord Harrington."

Lucien took pity on them. "Was there something you needed, Devonna?"

"Um. No. No. I was only going to ask you if I could go for a ride. Sorry, I didn't know you had company."

"Nonsense. Rafe and I were just on our way to the stables. Why don't you join us? We could all go for a ride." He glanced at Rafe and raised one brow in a dare. "Rafe, what do you think? Care to join us?"

"I would love to." His eyes flared as he nodded to Lucien. They all headed for the stable. Lucien watched in amusement as the two with him pretended not to notice each other, when in fact they couldn't take their eyes off each other. It was the most animated he had ever seen his sister. It encouraged him for she was twenty-five now.

When they arrived at the stable, a liveried servant from the house ran up to him. "My lord," he panted. "His Grace is coming. Up the drive."

Lucien slanted a glance at his sister, noticing how her color faded. "Thank you, Thomas. Ready some rooms."

Devonna was pale and had backed up into a stall, completely ignorant of the fact that there was a horse in it.

Lucien took a deep breath before he headed for the house. Partway out of the barn, he swung back and asked Rafe, "Will you escort my sister on her ride? Take a groom with you so it is proper. Return in about one to two hours."

The urgency in his tone was not lost on his friend who nodded his agreement right away.

Lucien cracked his neck on his way up to the house as he prepared himself for this confrontation. He waited on the steps when the carriages pulled in. His father descended and looked at him.

"Your Grace. To what do I owe the honor of your presence?"

"Don't get smart, boy. We came because we found someone to marry your sister. Even though she is on the shelf and dumb."

Lucien's eyes narrowed in warning. "Watch how you speak of my sister."

"She is my child and I will speak to her or of her any way I wish. Bring her to me. I have no wish to remain in this place longer than necessary."

Lucien smirked. "Good, I have no wish for you to remain. She is not here. She is out riding."

"Go get her, boy." The voice rose. "I have promised her hand to Viscount Dansworthy. They will be wed within the month."

Viscount Dansworthy was a letch. The small progress Devonna had made would be lost under him.

"No. She won't marry him."

"You dare tell me who she will and will not marry?"

"No, I do." Rafe entered the conversation. "I am sorry, Your Grace, I have compromised your daughter and I was discussing the details with her brother since it was here that it happened. I will do the honorable thing and marry her."

Devonna stood behind Rafe and at his announcement Lucien could have sworn that she smiled.

Teeth gritted in an attempt to control himself, Lucien turned to his father and said, "Perhaps we could go inside and finish discussing the details."

The look he sent to Rafe promised that his time was not long in coming for that stunt. The duke stomped inside, followed by his wife, his son Lucien, daughter Devonna and soon-to-be-son-in-law Rafe.

Lucien's younger brother—stepbrother—stayed outside to smoke and see what trouble he could get into. Richard Nidels, stepbrother to the Marquess of Heartstone, was an angry man.

Not a handsome man, he was whip thin with a very large nose, and eyes that were a light watery blue. His teeth were crooked and he was not built to wear clothes so they looked nice on him.

The butler entered after a brief, sharp knock on the door.

"My lord. There is someone here to see you."

"Weeks. We are busy here. Tell them to leave their card and wait or come back later."

"I tried, my lord. They insist that they have an appointment with you. They don't have a card."

Lucien's brother rose and said, "I'll deal with it." He walked past the butler who didn't even flinch, just gazed at his employer.

Lucien wondered if maybe it was his current mistress, Christie. But the normally unflappable Weeks seemed very nervous. Hell, he'd not even see his brother return to the room.

"Stupid butler. Do your job, we are busy here," the duke put in.

"Enough," Lucien roared, furious. "This is my house. These are my servants. Do *not* speak to them in that tone. Everything will be dealt with in due time. I will go with Weeks, deal with this person, come back and we will finish this. Get some food, for His Grace will be staying longer than expected. Everyone understand?"

"Bloody hell!" The scream came from the hall as his stepbrother Richard bolted back into the study, pale and shaking like he had seen a ghost. "There are creatures out there."

Lucian groaned. His stepbrother was an idiot.

Weeks spoke up. "My lord. That is what I wished to advise you of. This person has animals with them."

"What is so odd about that, Weeks? Most people have animals. Did you ask them for a name?"

His butler looked affronted. He sniffed. "Of course. I can't tell you, though, for aside from asking for you, they said nothing except that I was to give this to you." Weeks crossed the room and handed him a money pouch on a silver platter. It was his. He knew that from the seal. "I was told there was a note inside, my lord."

A headache loomed. He rubbed his temples as he asked, "What did they look like, Weeks?" He opened the bag and took out the note.

"Couldn't tell you, milord."

"What kind of butler are you? All you have to do is look at them and then…"

"Stop," Lucien snapped. "Not another word out of you, Father. Emma, close your mouth because I am not in the mood to hear it from you either. Continue, Weeks." He opened the note and the words that jumped off the paper at him made him shaky.

A promise once made
has been fulfilled.

It was unsigned. It didn't have to be signed, for he knew who it was from.

"They are wearing a hooded cloak and I can't see what they look like."

Lucien's knees gave out and he sat with a thump in his chair. "Weeks, what type of animals?"

It couldn't be. After all this time, after seven years could she really be here? Or was he just imagining what he had dreamed of so often, what he longed for?

"Horses, what looks like a wolf and a…" Lucien jumped up and sprinted through the doorway.

Lucien stumbled through the open door to his manorial home and looked down the steps. The sight he saw almost made him weep.

Chapter Eighteen

There were three horses, two grown and one small, a black with a white jagged mark on his haunch that Lucien saw when the horse turned sideways. There was a figure garbed in a black cloak, hooded so that it obscured the face of the person beneath the folds of cloth.

At one side of the silent figure was a glossy black wolf, with a dark green collar, and on the other side a fully mature mountain lion with a silken coat of ruddy brown and sporting a deep blue collar. Both animals were ominous-looking, and as Lucien gazed upon them, he had never seen a more welcome sight.

He heard his family appear behind him. They all muttered to themselves about the strange group presenting themselves at the door.

His father spoke loudest. "I would see those horses. Who is that? What kind of person goes around with those kind of animals?"

Lucien walked down the steps, ignoring his family and the noises they made. Her pull on him was too strong to disregard—like a bee to a flower—and he stopped a short distance away from the figure that was well-protected by the animals. He could have heard a pin drop—for the first time, his entire family was silent as they watched the scene unfold before them.

"Hello, Wolf." The husky voice tinged with velvet floated from beneath the hood, enveloping his wounded soul like the coolness of a summer breeze on a sweltering day.

"Ciara." He spoke the word almost reverently, as if she might disappear and he would wake to find it was all another dream.

"As promised, the first son of Nyama and Epona." The hood bobbed in the direction of the colt between the mares.

"Take off your hood. Let me see you." His order was quiet but everyone heard. Everyone watched as the command was obeyed.

Ciara stood tall and pushed back her hood.

When her hood fell, Lucien drank in the sight of her. She was just as beautiful as he remembered in his dreams. With all the regality of a queen, she stood for his perusal and that of all others present. Her eyes stayed wary and he saw that the animals had not relaxed their guard either.

"Faolan? Kosse?" Lucien got down on one knee. He had to focus on something else or he would grab her. Both animals looked at Ciara and, at her minuscule hand gesture, she released them. The animals swarmed him, Faolan wagged his tail and Kosse purred. His stepmother screamed and fainted—for once not a fake swoon because she hit her head hard—while his brother paled even more and retreated behind the nosy servants.

Ciara spoke a single word and both the animals were back on either side of her.

"Who are you?" the duke yelled as he came down the stairs. "Where did you get these horses?"

Ciara never even blinked. Her eyes followed him and only when he got close to the horses did she speak, her voice impassive as if he were not worth her time.

"Those are not your horses. Keep away from them."

"Wench, I am a duke. I can do whatever I damn well please."

Lucian saw the flash in her eyes and stepped forward to intervene when she flicked her hand and Faolan placed himself in front of the duke and between him and the horses.

"*He* does not ask. You will get no more warnings. Step away from the horses." She turned back to Lucien, her voice soft once again. "The bay mare next to the colt is a gift for your sister. Her name is Angel. Epona's second daughter."

Devonna walked down the stairs and past her brother, who was trying not to run up and grab this woman, and stopped in front of her.

In a soft voice she asked, "Are you Ciara?"

"Aye. I am. You must be Devonna." A slight nod of her head was all the deference she acquitted her regardless of her station.

She blushed. "I am. Thank you for the horse. Can I see her?"

Lucien was shocked to see his sister speak so open with a stranger like that, as was the rest of the staff.

"Of course." She gave a low whistle and Angel broke away from the group and trotted up to Ciara. Picking up the rope, she placed it in Devonna's hand. "She is very gentle. I hope you find happiness with her."

Another whistle brought a mare and the colt to her. That left the duke facing a large wolf. She untied the colt and placed the rope in Lucien's hands.

"My promise has been fulfilled."

"Where are you going?"

"I am staying… That is none of your business. I have to go. It was wonderful to see you again, Wolf. I hope you have found your happiness."

"Wait." He couldn't let her leave, not now after all this time. "Would you like to see my stables? I mean, after all, you helped with the planning."

"Just let her go. She is obviously not of your class." A high, nasal voice reached everyone.

"Emma. Shut up." Lucien faced them both. "In fact, if the two of you, and you as well, Richard, can't be nice to her then you will be removed from the property. That is it. If you stay, you will be polite." He turned back to Ciara. "Well?"

"Fine. Can I water my horses?"

"Sure, your horse?" He bit back the urge to grin like a schoolboy. She was within his reach again. He didn't intend to let her go *this* time.

"No, horses." She made a sound like a bird and out of the trees came another horse with a small person on its back. It was a very nice gelding, chestnut in color. It was the passenger who caught Lucien's attention, though.

A boy, lanky with youth, rode tall on the horse. He was golden-skinned but not as dark as the woman he was with. His hair was thick and wavy, an inky black. As he stopped beside her, he swung down with agility, despite the height of the horse, which bespoke his familiarity with horses. He stood beside Ciara.

"Are we here to rest for a bit, Mama?"

Mama? A sword pierced his heart. She did have children, which would explain the cool reaction she gave him. Here he had been dreaming of a woman who had gone and had a child.

"You have a son? Congratulations." His voice was sharp and tense. Even he heard the pain. The knife settled between his ribs as he saw his dreams leave his reach. "How old is he?"

"Yes. This is my son, Brenden Kumi McKay. Bryn say hello to Wo… His lord, the Marquess of Heartstone."

"Good day. Thank you for allowing us to rest our horses."

The boy was polite even though his address to the marquess was not correct. His voice was like a gentle rain, falling anywhere without fear. And why should he fear? He was well-protected.

"Not a problem." Each word killed him a little more. The boy even sounded like her, with an accent on certain words. He looked at Ciara and saw her gaze on her son, full of love.

"Bryn, go play with Kosse and Faolan. I don't think his horses are used to them." She turned her amber gaze back to Lucien. "Is there a place they can play?"

"By the lake."

"You heard him, Bryn. What do you say?" A small victory as Lucien noticed that she didn't ask if he would be safe.

"Thank you." The child who went by Bryn looked up at him and smiled. Lucien stared in shock, his heart coming to a halt as he gazed into a mirror image of his own eyes. Thick dark lashes framed them, giving him a very exotic and innocent look. His eyes were going to be a very big attraction for the ladies when he was older. His eyes did not leave the boy until he was headed to the lake.

"How old did you say he was?"

It couldn't be. It's impossible, isn't it?

"I didn't. A little over six years." Her amber eyes were guileless as she looked at him.

"He's mine." He swore. He grabbed her arm and pulled her up flush against his chest. He heard the gasps of shock from his father, stepmother and the rest of the vultures listening in on them. "Deny it! Damn you, deny it."

His entire body quivered with rage. Rage that he had been denied his son.

Faolan looked back, and as he saw Lucien reach for her, he turned. Ciara sent a word to him. The large black wolf continued with Kosse and Bryn.

"I can't. He is yours." Ciara still spoke with the calm assurance that he had always admired about her. Now it just added fuel to the fire.

Meeting his gaze head-on, she asked, "I thought you were going to show me your stables. Has that changed?" She was unflappable—her calm settled over her like a suit of armor nothing could get through.

Eyes hardened. "No, it hasn't. This conversation isn't over."

He knew she didn't lie about him being the father—it wasn't in her to do so. But she *had* kept it from him for seven years. She hadn't even sent him a missive. Looking over his shoulder, he saw Weeks still watched.

"Weeks, see that the green room is made up for her. She and *her son* will be staying the night."

He swung off toward the barn, never once letting go of her arm. He entered the stables and stopped a stable boy and gave him the reins to Artemis. "Take care of her horse. It needs water and some grain. The other ones need some as well."

He stalked to the back of the stable where it was low light and found an open stall and pushed her through then followed. He snapped the door shut behind him and glared at her.

"Explain yourself."

The edge in that tone could have cut steel. This was the tone that made him good at being a marquess, it demanded an answer—her answer. He was beyond angry. He shook with untold anger as he tried not to put his hands on her. Truth was he wasn't sure he wouldn't do her harm.

"I don't owe you any explanations."

"You don't owe me any— You can't believe that? That's my son, damn you! I had a right to know he even existed. You had no right, none, to keep that from me." Lucien's voice rose and he shouted with no regard to who might overhear.

"Perhaps not. Maybe I handled that bad—"

"Maybe? There is no maybe about it, you—"

"But surely you gave some thought to what happened between us. You never once pulled out of me. Or did you forget that when you got back here to your 'golden-haired' beauties with their 'skin the color of cream'? Don't take this out on me." Ciara's bitterness cracked through her normally calm demeanor.

"I never held any idea of trying to get money from you or anything for him. I love my son. I came to fulfill my promise and to let you know of his existence. I will not let him come to harm in your society."

She meant to leave him. Fresh rage swept through him. "I could keep him with me. He is my son. I have the right to keep him with me."

Ciara's eyes flashed with danger as she advanced on Lucien. He had found the chink in her armor. Her entire body trembled with fury. "Don't you *dare* threaten me with taking my son from me. He is mine."

Lucien found himself retreating a step under the wrath of her vehemence. As he realized that there was also fear in her gaze, he understood what he had done. He held up his hands in a surrendering gesture. Bloody hell, this woman—his woman—was magnificent.

Ciara stopped when he put up his hands. Her breaths came short and fast. It wasn't only from the yelling match either. She was aroused.

Lucien saw her eyes darken, with desire this time. His eyes flared and he grabbed her into his arms and kissed her. Kissed her with all of his worry and love for the past seven years. He crushed her to him as he imbibed deeply her smell.

"Umm. Humm." The sound of a throat being cleared brought them back to earth. Lucien snapped his gaze to the door and saw Rafe there with a smug grin on his face. "As the rest of your family is on their way, perhaps you would like to put some light between your bodies."

They stepped out of the stall just as his family came down the aisle. All speaking—no, demanding—at once so it was hard for him to tell which person was yelling at him.

"Who is she? What is this about your son?"

"Where did she come from?" Richard asked.

"What is she to you? What is her family line?"

"Where did she get those horses? I want some like them." That from his father.

Ciara stood erect between the two men and faced the storm that was his family. Lucien placed his hand on the small of her back and stared at them until they quieted. "I will answer your questions, inside. One at a time." Once again he had become the unflappable marquess, no task too great for him to handle.

The family glared at her but stepped to one side of the aisle to allow them to pass. When they got back outside, Ciara stopped. Lucien looked down at her and tried to nudge her forward but she wouldn't move.

"What?" he asked in a low tone.

"I will go to check on Bryn."

"Will you leave?" She stared out toward the lake where her son, their son, played and didn't answer. "I would have your word you won't leave."

"Very well. I will not leave until I speak to you again."

"No. You will stay the night. Your word or I drag you with me." Lucien knew that his family was shocked by his behavior. He didn't care. He wanted her word of honor.

"One night we will stay." She pinned a look on him and added, "As long as he is safe."

He sketched a bow at her and smiled.

"Until later then."

He strode off to the house while his father continued to berate him. Lucien didn't even take offense when she had said that he might not be able to keep them safe. She was here. After seven long years she was here, with him. And he had a son.

"It is just a woman. Who cares if she leaves? Her word is useless to you."

Chapter Nineteen

Devonna began to follow her family but, at the sight of her stepbrother, she stopped. She turned to Ciara, who watched Lucien walk away with a longing gaze, and Devonna asked, "Could I go with you? To the lake?"

Ciara snapped her attention off the male who had sucked up all too much of her common sense to face his sister. "Of course."

Richard glared at his sister as she stepped closer to the guest. "Coming to the house, sis? I would be glad to escort you."

Devonna sucked in a breath and tried hard not to cringe. Ciara's gaze flickered between them before she stepped forward to place herself between Devonna and her brother. Richard hesitated at the look, the silent challenge.

As they walked to the lake, Ciara snuck glances at the woman beside her. Although not in the start of her youth, she was still beautiful. She had seen fear flash in those eyes when her brother looked at her.

"How did you meet my brother? He said you saved his life?" Devonna's voice was raspy from lack of use.

Ciara smiled. "Yes. He had been attacked by a bear. I found him in the woods and took him back to my cabin to heal him. He caught the fever and for two weeks it was uncertain whether he would pull through. Good thing he was a healthy man. He will have scars but, other than that, I think he pulled through fine." She picked up her son and held him close, inhaling his clean scent until he struggled to be let down.

"Weren't you scared with him alone in the cabin?" Her question hid a silent inquiry, that instinctively Ciara knew she was too ashamed to ask.

Ciara sat down on the ground by the lake. She kissed her son and sent him back off to play with Faolan and Kosse. Then she answered Devonna's question.

"At first it was difficult. I had an advantage, though, since I had Faolan—he is the wolf. One night after he was walking again, he came to my room." At Devonna's shocked gasp, she hurried on to finish. "I was having a nightmare and he sought only to wake me from it. When he touched me, I knocked him to the floor and was in the process of sliding my knife into his throat when I realized who he was and what he had been doing." She did not look at Devonna but stared after her son.

"That night he asked me to tell him why I had reacted how I did. I couldn't tell him for it hurt too much. Sometimes, though, it helps to tell someone who has experienced the same thing. If you wish to talk about it, Devonna, I am here to listen."

Devonna swung toward Ciara but she was looking at her son. "How did you know?" Her voice filled with shame.

Ciara put the full intensity of her eyes on Devonna. "Don't ever feel like you have anything to be ashamed of. I know because I was raped myself a long time ago."

Devonna crumbled. Sobs racked her body as she laid her head in Ciara's lap. The story came out among the sobs.

"It started when I was sixteen. He would come on different nights that he stayed at the house, claiming that I had been screaming in my sleep and how he was worried for my safety. I was forced to do things to him, touching and kissing on him. He said that my father would never believe me so not to tell." Her body shook.

"Then he started to give me to his friends and they bragged about me to others. I know the only reason they want to marry me off is because I am on the shelf and they don't want me in the house. Since I have been here with Lucien, he hasn't been able to touch me. He would never dream of touching me with Lucien around."

Ciara put two and two together by her reaction to her brother and her comments and figured out whom she spoke of. Her brother Richard had committed the ultimate sin.

"Rafe told them today that he compromised me. He sought to protect me. I have always thought he was a wonderful man and now I know it. But I can't let him marry me. I am spoiled, used, worthless to him."

Ciara stroked the head in her lap, her calm words hiding the fact that she was furious. Where had Lucien been during this time?

"You are not used or worthless. That was taken from you, not given. You are still pure, and when you find a man who loves you and you love, it will be like your first time. It will be wonderful."

Devonna turned her violet eyes up at her. "Like you and Saint? Your boy there, Bryn, he is my brother's son, isn't he? He has his eyes. Males get those vivid blue eyes."

"Yes."

"Do you love my brother?"

* * * *

Lucien looked at his parents as they sat on opposite sides of the room from each other. It seemed the only thing they did together was glare at him. They were doing it now.

"Who is she? What is she to you? What were her parents? Her skin is too dark," his stepmother asked.

"She is the one who saved my life in America. From the bear. She has the father to the horse that you got from over there."

His father jumped in next. "Did you bed her? Is that why she is here? To try to pass off that boy as your own. Don't let her. All she wants is money. How can you be sure it is your son after all this time? We will not have one of her skin in our family. It won't happen."

Lucien slammed his hands on the desk as he spoke firmly. "This is none of your business. She is none of your business. She is my guest and will be treated with the respect due. I will not have you disrespecting her or her son in this home. Now, what are your wishes about Devonna and Rafe?"

His father spit he was so angry. "I will not be paying a dowry for that slut. She isn't worth it." His stepmother seemed to agree although with a small hesitation.

"Fine. I will give a dowry. If that is all, I would like to go and speak to my guest." He headed for the door. "If you kill each other, try not to make a mess of my house."

Lucien found Rafe sitting in the library, holding a glass of brandy but not drinking. He just stared at the amber liquid.

"Why? Why did you do it, Rafe? You know that she is not all there upstairs. I won't have you hurting her more than she has been hurt."

There was menace beneath his words to his friend. He wanted to be furious with Rafe, but Lucien's mind was on the whiskey-eyed woman by the lake.

Rafe looked at his friend and took a deep breath before he made his declaration. "I love her. I have always loved her." His voice spoke volumes to Lucien.

Lucien smiled as he walked to his friend.

"I guess I should have known that from the look you were giving her. Congratulations then, my friend. Welcome to the family. Care to walk with me? I am going to find some females."

Rafe stood and asked Lucien, "Have you told her how you feel?"

"Who?"

"I am not blind nor am I stupid, Luc. I saw how you looked at her. In all of our trips to visit professional women, I have seen the looks you give. Ones to seduce, ones to scare people, but never like the one you gave her. It was tender, for lack of a better word. If I didn't know you better, I would also say I saw tears, but I don't wish to anger you."

Rafe walked out on his friend's stunned expression. They strolled in companionable silence to the lake. What they saw when they got there surprised them both. It took a moment for the men to pick their jaws up off the ground and regain their composure.

Devonna was screeching and laughing as she chased Bryn around. Faolan and Kosse chased her. The scene was observed by a woman who had shed her cloak and stood protectively over her charges. Ever the guardian. Lucien heard Rafe's sharp intake of breath at the sight of her.

Jealousy swarmed him. She still wore her buckskins. If anything, having a child had filled her out more. She was still firm, but he knew what lay beneath that hard exterior. Passion. Endless, inexhaustible passion.

Bryn turned and ran toward his mother and launched himself at her. She caught him and spun him around. A tight hug for him before she set him down and sent him once again on his way.

Ciara felt Lucien's presence and didn't turn to face him, just waited until they got close enough to speak. "Hello again, Wolf."

"Why do you call him Wolf? I'm Rafe by the way."

The pale-haired man with the green eyes spoke. He was almost as tall as Lucien, but lacked his broadness. Lucien was big and broad while Rafe seemed to be lean and dangerous.

She pivoted and her lips turned up as she looked at the man that Devonna was to marry.

"It is nice to meet you, Rafe. I am Ciara."

There was kindness in his eyes. It would be a good match.

"You can call her Miss McKay," Lucien snapped.

With a negative shake of her head, she corrected, "Call me Ciara. I don't know how to answer to anything else."

"Yes you do. I have seen you."

Ciara arched a brow at his comment as she continued her conversation with Rafe.

"This is why I call him Wolf. He is ornery and pushy, always thinking that he should get his way." She waved a hand in the direction of Faolan who was in the process of tripping Devonna. "You see? Pushy." She looked at Lucien. "What do you want? What was so important for you to be rude to your friend?"

Lucien stood in silence for a moment. "I want to show you your room. Come with me."

Ciara turned toward Devonna and Bryn. She motioned with her hand and all four of them came up. Devonna curtsied to her brother and to Viscount Harrington, her skin flushed and her expression full of life for once. They all walked up to the house.

She entered the house and Ciara's breath caught in her throat. It was huge. Her entire cabin could fit in the entrance. Everything was large and clean. There were servants by doors who opened them before people got there.

"I put you in the green room. Come, I will show it to you." Lucien interrupted her study of the house.

"Mrs. Ashley, I would like you to meet my guests, Miss McKay and her son, Bryn."

"Pleasure to meet you, miss. And you, little sir. Perhaps the young lad is hungry? We've some sweets in the kitchen."

Bryn looked up at his mom. With a smile she nodded.

"Bryn?"

"Yes, Mama?" He turned and looked at her before he ran back to her and jumped into her arms.

Placing a kiss on his head, she sent him back to Mrs. Ashley. "Bryn, remember your manners. Say 'please' and 'thank you.'"

"Yes, Mama."

"Speak English, Bryn."

"Yes, Mama. I love you."

"I love you too, Bryn. Have fun."

Chapter Twenty

Lucien opened the door with a push then stepped back to let her enter. The spacious room had been done in forest greens with amber edging. On one wall were paintings of mountains. The windows were large and open, which allowed the cool country air to come in. Large cushions lay scattered on the benches under the windows and on the floor by the fireplace.

"It's beautiful. Thank you. We will be very happy here tonight."

Lucien didn't tell her about the adjoining rooms. His rooms. He stepped into the room behind her and shut the door. Given that he stood at her back, he let his gaze flow over her body. Her top fit looser than he remembered over her usual buckskins. He draped her cloak over a chair and watched as Faolan and Kosse settled under the windows.

Ciara stepped toward him and grabbed his waistcoat, yanking him near. Not expecting the attack, Lucien stumbled forward. Before he knew what had hit him, she had latched on to his lips with her own. She moved her hands up and tugged on his hair as she tried to pull him in closer.

With a growl, he wrapped his arms around her and kissed her back. He jerked at her top. Ciara shook her head as she whimpered her need into his mouth.

"Now."

As he braced her body with one hand, he freed himself from his breeches and lowered hers seconds later. Lucien turned and put her back against the wall by the door. She had slipped one leg out of her buckskins and without hesitation wrapped her legs around his waist.

He felt her moisture and his member swelled as it bobbed up and down. She yanked his hair as she pulled his mouth back to hers as he plunged into her with one fierce thrust.

She bit his lip, drawing blood as she tried to keep quiet. He pounded into her, pressing her harder and harder into the wall, Not caring one iota that the windows and curtains were wide open in the room, exposing them to the outside world. When they came it was within moments of each other. It was like an explosion had gone off. Both were breathing hard as their gazes met.

Panting with exhaustion, Ciara smiled at him as she unlocked her legs from around his waist and slid to the floor.

"I didn't expect that to happen." Ciara straightened up and swallowed.

Lucien looked at himself, covered in their combined juices, and shook his head. He had treated her no better than some dockside doxy. He'd had her up against the wall like that. He smiled as he touched his lip and saw the blood. Maybe she didn't care. Perhaps she had wanted it as much as he did. That quick liaison had left him more breathless than a night with one of the mistresses he'd had over the years.

He found a cloth and cleaned himself off then refastened his pants before he tugged her down on a green and amber chaise. Lucien snuggled her in the crook of his arm. He just sat in silence as they brought their breathing under control.

"Why didn't you tell me about Brenden?"

With one hand he stroked her arm. There were wide bands under the sleeves of her shirt by her wrists and he wondered what they were.

"Marie said I should. We come from two different worlds. I guess I was scared."

"I know what I said, but I would never take your son away from you. Tell me about him. What was he like as a baby? Why did you name him Brenden? Thank you for naming him Brenden." His son carried his name and for that he was forever grateful.

"Bryn was a very happy baby. He still is. I am sorry that I kept the knowledge from you but I am not sorry that I didn't bring him here to you. Your family is so full of hate. I wanted him to grow up with the love that I had. As for his name, I don't know. It just fit. I have liked it since I heard it in your name."

"You don't think that I would have loved him?"

"I wasn't thinking of you at all. I know that is selfish of me. I remembered the hate in your eyes when you spoke of your family. I did what I thought was best for my son—"

"Our son."

"Our son, and I would do it again in an instant."

"Where are you staying?" He changed the subject, not wanting to think of her leaving him again, especially since he now knew about his son.

"I am staying in the country with some people."

"Who?" This was all country.

"Friends. Leave it at that. You have no claim on me, so don't pretend to be jealous of something that you have no right to." Faolan rose from under the window and gazed at the door with a stance that made her rise right away.

"What do you mean by that?" He had every right to place his claim on her. "Where are you going?"

Ciara swung on her cloak and opened the door, following her animals down the stairs without giving him a response. He felt the change in her—she became cold and withdrawn in a second.

Lucien followed her, not sure what had happened to elicit this abrupt change in her demeanor. Weeks saw her approach and opened the door. By the time she hit the bottom of the steps she was in a full run. The animals matched her strides. Toward a small shed by the stables her powerful legs carried her. Lucien ran after her.

Faolan stopped in front of the door. His growls sent chills up Lucien's spine as he neared Ciara. Kosse's low growl echoed the wolf's with frightening menace.

Lucien watched as Faolan and Kosse crouched in position to attack. He heard cries coming from inside the shed accompanied by adult voices. His father came up behind him followed by Rafe and Devonna.

Ciara flipped her cloak back so her arms were free. Before anyone could move she had kicked the door to the shed. It splintered under the force of her single blow and fell to the ground.

Four coachmen of the duke's had Bryn trapped in the shed. They were beating him with whips, calling him names like 'gypsy boy' and much worse. Ciara moved with blinding speed, Lucien saw, as she flicked her arms and sent the daggers that had been concealed in her sleeves flying toward the men who were hurting their son. Faolan and Kosse hadn't even waited for the door to hit the ground before they attacked.

Each animal took a man and her daggers found their marks in the other two. A rage unlike any that Lucien had known, flowed through his veins. They had attacked *his* son. He stepped forward to intervene as well but, just like at the cabin, she didn't need his help.

Ciara yelled a command and Bryn was instantly surrounded by the animals. He didn't even cringe away from the blood on their mouths, just delved his hands into their thick pelts. He stood tall and silent as tears fell from his lapis eyes.

An unholy light burned within the amber eyes of his mother that turned them almost yellow. She flew across the room and picked up the one who had been doing the actual whipping of her son when she entered and threw him to the other side of the small shed.

"Mama?"

Ciara spun, opening her arms to him as she sank to her knees on the floor. Bryn launched himself in her arms and shook with what Lucien assumed to be fear and pain.

Lucien got the four rounded up. He turned on his father. "These are your men. This is on your head. They will die. That was *my son* they were whipping." A wind picked up, bringing with it a chill that coincided with his tone.

His old man didn't speak.

Ciara rose and strode out of the building, her son once again safe and protected in her arms, flanked by her loyal guardians. The iciness in her gaze could have frozen hell. Her gaze flicked to Devonna who without a word stepped forward and took a very reluctant Bryn from her.

A motion of her hands sent Faolan and Kosse with them. She continued on her path toward the men. She had punched one in the face before Lucien got behind her. It took both him and Rafe to bring her under control.

His father spoke. "You slept with that. No woman should be that strong. Why would you want to claim her, son? She is no better than a slave." A mistake he would surely never repeat for now he was the object of her anger.

"You! You bastard," she seethed. "Of course a woman should be weak, that way they can't defend themselves against you. I hold you responsible for this attack against my son. My son. He has done nothing to you." She raged against the holds of Lucien and Rafe, but their combined strength defeated hers, though only just. "Unlike you, I love my child, you heartless bastard of a man."

Her voice lowered so it was borderline noticeable. "I swear by all that's holy if you come near my son again I will kill you. That goes for your servants as well. Heed my warning for it is my vow." She turned her head and spoke a sharp word to Faolan. He sprang away and disappeared into the shadows of the forest.

The duke's face grew mottled. His eyes grew dark with anger as he raised himself up to his full height and glared at her. Sebastian pinned her with the look that quelled many people who would dare question a duke.

"You little bitch. Do you know who I am? I can have you imprisoned. You are threatening a member of the peerage. You are nothing, do you understand me? Do you think I am scared of you?" He jabbed the air with one finger toward her to punctuate his statement.

Ciara hissed at him as her eyes spit venom. "You are so brave when they have a hold of me. Say those words to my face when two men aren't holding me back. I would *love* to show you just how scared of me you really are. Tell your son to release me. I am not nothing, I am a mother and you…you threatened *my* son. I would chase you through the deepest, darkest pits of hell for that alone.

"You don't have the first idea of what it is to be a parent. And you have *no* idea what I am capable of. I am not scared of you. You, I would bet, are petrified of me. I may be a woman, but I will not cower before you." She struggled again. "Damn you. Let me go." Lucien and Rafe loosened their grips. As soon as they did, she made for the duke with her hands curled into claws. Lucien caught her at the last moment. She was inches away from the duke.

Lucien watched in amazement as his father paled at her words and stumbled back from her actions. It was the first time he had ever seen fear flash across his father's face. Lucien met Rafe's gaze over Ciara's head and saw the shock and admiration that he held for the woman he'd helped to restrain.

"Let me go. Let me go! I want my son."

He released her once more, still ready should she go after his father again.

She went over to Devonna and took her son out of her arms and held him. Ciara walked away from them with

Kosse and sat down on a bench and rocked him back and forth as she hummed to him.

Lucien turned his gaze to his father. "Leave. Now." Now that the danger was past, his anger surfaced again.

The duke had the grace to look ashamed. "I will see that they are punished. Let me stay for a week. Please, son. We should talk about this. I will make it better, I will take care of it."

"Son? I am not your son. You have never been anything but a tyrant to Devonna and me. Stay if you wish, but stay out of my sight." He turned and walked over to where Ciara sat with her child. *Their* child. He had not been able to protect his own child from his grandfather's anger and hatred.

"I'm sorry, Ciara. The men will be punished. Is he all right? Is he hurt?" Lucien sat down on the bench next to her.

"I can't stay here. We are leaving as soon as Faolan gets back."

"You said you would stay the night."

"That was before my son was attacked. I told you I would do whatever necessary to protect him. It is obvious that he isn't safe here. Your father's hatred is too much when it includes my son." Bryn's eyes were closed as he was snuggled up to his mother.

"Our son, Ciara. Don't forget that."

"Keep your mouth shut. He doesn't know," she snapped at him.

A new pain washed over Lucien. His son didn't know about him. She hadn't told him. He was losing her for a second time but this time there was also something more to lose. A son.

Bryn stirred in her arms and mumbled something that he couldn't understand. She answered him in the same language. He cuddled up closer to her in a manner that broke Lucien's heart.

Chapter Twenty-One

A shadow fell over them and she looked up to see Mrs. Ashley standing there, wringing her hands. The woman didn't glance at her but focused on the man beside her.

"My lord. My son is about the same age as Bryn and I would be happy to give some clothes for him."

"Yes please. Thank you, Mrs. Ashley."

She curtsied and headed off to send a footman to her house for them.

"Mama, I'm sleepy." Bryn spoke into her chest.

Ciara gazed at Lucien. "Can he have a room to sleep in until Faolan returns?" She'd recognized the anger in his own eyes during the attack on her boy.

"Of course. We will put him in the room for you." Lucien rose and reached out to take him. When Ciara pulled him tighter against her chest, he blinked back the unexpected sting of tears. "I just want to carry him for you, Ciara." Her name came out a plea. "I only wish to hold him."

I wish to hold my son was the unspoken statement.

"Bryn." When her son looked up, she smiled as she brushed a hair out of his face. "This man is going to carry you to a room for a nap. He won't hurt you. Kosse will be beside you and I will be right there as well."

"Okay, Mama." Bryn turned in her arms and reached out to the man whom he didn't know was his father, without fear. Lucien smiled at him.

As they walked, she noticed Bryn had laid his head on Lucien's shoulder and had fallen asleep.

Ciara pulled back the blankets and motioned for Lucien to lay him down. As she undressed her son, she looked over at Lucien who watched every movement she made.

"Would you like to do this?"

Lucien flashed a grateful look in her direction then stepped forward and finished undressing him. He made sure to cover him up with the blankets. Kosse jumped up on the bed and placed himself between Bryn and the door. Lucien stroked his son's soft cheek before he stepped back.

"It kinda gets you right in the chest, doesn't it." Ciara made it a statement.

He nodded. "I don't understand why…"

"Why your own father was the way he was? I don't know either." Ciara sat on the chaise, patted the spot next to her and waited for him to sit down. She leaned on him to soak up his quiet strength. "I am guessing maybe he was just scared. But isn't how you were raised the way most of your class does it?"

"Yes. Ciara. I'm sorry I couldn't protect him today." The self-loathing in his tone ripped her apart. She had no doubt that this man protected people, she knew it.

"What's done is done. If they had busted the skin, I would have killed them all. He will be shaken up but, overall, he will be fine. I trust that you will take care of it from here."

"Then why are you leaving? Stay."

"I don't belong here. No matter how mean your father is, he was right about one thing. I *don't* belong here. I have some business to complete and then we will be going home."

He pulled her onto his lap and slid back until he was in the corner of the chaise with her cuddled up to him. "Where are you staying? You are welcome to stay here."

"No. Don't make this any harder than it is." A low growl from Kosse came just before a muted knock.

"Enter." It was Mrs. Ashley. She set the clothes on a chair and smiled as she saw them, looking quite cozy.

They must have dozed off as well, for they both started when another knock came. It was Devonna. It was time for dinner and Faolan had returned.

"Stay for the evening meal, at least?"

"Sorry, Wolf. We have to go."

Lucien sent his sister to have someone ready their mounts. Ciara roused Bryn and dressed him in the borrowed clothes. When he went into the side room to use the chamber pot, Lucien grabbed Ciara around the waist and pulled her up against him.

"Don't do this. Stay."

His mouth was inches from hers when she heard her son come back into the room. He pressed a quick kiss on his mouth before she stepped back and took her son's hand and left the room.

Lucien followed her down the stairs when he heard a commotion outside. Weeks opened the door to admit his stepbrother. He was followed by Christie Smyth, his current mistress. A small and petite woman, she had golden hair and a peaches-and-cream complexion. She was also a vindictive woman.

"Saint," she cooed as she floated across the floor to wait for him by the stairs. "How wonderful to see you. I miss you so when we are apart. Your brother was kind enough to invite me out." She leaned against him as she offered him a view of her bosom that appeared to be in danger of falling out of her dress.

She gasped and clung to him when she saw Faolan and Kosse as they walked across the floor. "What are they?"

"Come, Christie, they won't hurt you. You stay here. I have to see my guests out."

With a gaze that was all too personal and knowing, she simpered as she fluttered her eyelashes at him. "Take your time with that person, I can wait. I will have you all night." Then she stepped back like she would get dirty by being too close to Ciara or her animals.

By the time he had pried himself away from Christie, Ciara and Bryn were already at the bottom of the steps by their horses. As he stepped outside, he noticed a horse flying up the drive. Lather flew from the animal and as the horse slammed to a halt a man jumped off.

Bryn ran at the man who picked him up and hugged him with a familiarity that had Lucien narrowing his eyes. A footman claimed his horse and walked him around. The man's gaze lit upon Ciara and he set Bryn down, saying something that the boy understood, because he climbed up on his horse and waited for them both.

The man was tall. As tall as Lucien. He was leaner but no doubt just as strong, maybe stronger. He moved with a natural grace that reminded Lucien of a wild animal. Reminded him of Ciara's easy movements. He had sandy-brown hair and gray eyes. Handsome. Very much so, even with the scar on his face. Lucien's eyes narrowed to slits as he watched their interaction.

"Are ye all right, lass?" The stranger's question was asked with a rich brogue.

"Aye. We are."

He opened his arms and she walked into them with no hesitation, her own arms curling around his waist to return the embrace. Lucien saw red as the man's arms closed around her. "Who are you?" he snapped as he approached the couple.

"That is not really any of your business, lad. Who are you to let harm come to this woman and her son?" The man was tense and more than ready to battle.

"Conar. Let it go. Let us take our leave." Her voice rang with exhaustion.

"As you wish, lass." The man named Conar released her and lifted her onto her horse in a way that spoke of familiarity as Lucien trembled with jealousy.

"Who are you?" he bit out. "She isn't going anywhere with you." The tone of one used to being obeyed.

"Aye. She is. She is staying with me. That is all there is to it. The name, if you need it, is McKay."

"Ciara, get down from that horse. You aren't going with him."

"Goodbye, Wolf. Enjoy your horse." She spoke to the man beside her in a language they both understood, while he sprang onto his horse and they trotted off down the road. The only one who looked back was Bryn, who waved. At whom, Lucien couldn't be sure.

Lucien shut himself in his study and began to drink. He stared at the wolf carving that sat on his desk. As he ran his fingers over it, he swore to himself. He heard the door open and, without looking up, snapped at the intruder. "Get out."

"Saint?"

It was his sister. He couldn't snap at her.

"What, Devonna?"

"I was wondering if we could have the wedding here and I could invite Ciara and Bryn. I would like her to stand up with me."

"Whatever you want. If she agrees that is fine." He waved her away.

Chapter Twenty-Two

Do you love my brother? The question ran as a litany in her head as Ciara rode with her cousin toward the home they were staying at, her Aunt Fiona's. She had gone to Ireland to search out her kinsmen. To her immense surprise, they had welcomed her with open arms, Bryn also. They had been saddened by the news of her father's death.

Her grandfather, Rory McKay, Laird of Clan McKay, had asked her to stay for a while. She compromised with them to stay in the Randolph house while she concluded her business in England. Her Aunt Fiona had married an English viscount and they resided—much to her surprise—not far from Heartstone. Her grandfather and some of the clan had come on the journey and she found herself surrounded by family that loved her.

Did she? Did she love him? Probably. Regardless of her being so different from him, she did love him. Her newfound family smiled at her unconventional ways and applauded her success with raising Bryn on her own.

Bryn loved the attention. Being a great-grandson was a big thing for him. He was happy with his cousins, but he loved most to sit on his great-grandfather's lap and listen to stories of when his grandpa was a tyke.

Going back to America would be hard on him. As Bryn rode ahead, Conar looked at her. Her cousin was forever flirting with her and she could only laugh. "What happened for you to send Faolan to us, lass?"

"Some of the duke's men were whipping Bryn. We couldn't stay there. Nae, Conar. Head home. I took care of it. It's over."

"You've a family, lass, that loves ya. If they attack you, they attack us." Conar trembled with anger but turned his horse back around at her request.

"No. I don't want any more trouble. Please. Can we just go home?"

"Aye. As you wish it. We have the party tomorrow night. Are you excited?"

"To be paraded around like an object? No. I will go because Auntie Fi has gone through so much to set it up. I would rather be in the open away from these people. They make my head hurt to tell the truth."

"I agree. But you promised to attend and dance a waltz with me. I intend to hold you to that."

"I haven't forgotten."

"I don't intend to let ye forget it."

"Conar. I would have your word that you will keep calm about this. Please. If it gets out, there is no telling what will happen. To either side."

"Are ye content with the punishment of the ones who did it?"

"As content as I can be." In her mind there was nothing that would ever make it okay.

"Ye love him." A statement. "The marquess, he is the father o' Bryn, right?"

"Aye. He is and I do."

"Why dinna he marry ye, lass, when he found out about the bairn?"

They dismounted at the house. As they walked in, Conar steered her into the study, where her aunt and uncle-by-marriage sat, unbeknownst to her. Bryn headed for bed with Kosse and Faolan.

"Well, lass? Why dinna he?"

"He didn't know, Conar. Today was the first day he saw his son. I never told him."

Conar sat hard on a chair as his breath escaped him. Fi and her husband, Trenton, sat in silence as they listened to the story. "How, lass? How could ye do that to the man? A man has a right to know his children." His tone admonished and that made her feel worse.

"I know what I did was wrong, but…" She rose and paced the room. "Damn it, Conar. When he told me about his family I saw nothing but hate in his face. After he had left and come back here and I found out I was carrying his baby, all I could think about was the hate he said he grew up around. I couldn't let that happen to Bryn. He deserved to have love. Like I did.

"I know that I'm not rich like he is, but I gave my son something that he wouldn't have gotten here. Love. If he had been raised here, he would have known his father in passing only. If that wouldn't have bad enough for him to endure, to be labeled the bastard child of the marquess would have been. He is my son. Mine!" Tears streamed unchecked down her face.

"Damn him. Why do I have to love him?" Ciara crumpled to the floor and sobbed. Trenton motioned for Conar to come with him while Fi saw to Ciara.

* * * *

"My lord, you have a visitor." Weeks walked forward with the calling card on the silver platter.

Lucien picked up the card. It read Viscount Trenton. "Show him in, Weeks." He knew of the viscount. An older gentleman who lived on property that bordered his own. Rather a quiet man. He wondered what this could be about.

Christie was somewhere with his stepbrother and his parents had left after dinner to head back to London. He was grateful for that at least.

The door opened and the viscount was shown in. "My lord."

"Saint, please. What can I do for you, Trenton?"

"I come to you on a serious matter."

"Speak. Would you care for a drink?"

"Brandy please." Trenton sat in a chair that faced the desk.

Lucien made them both a drink and sat down across from the viscount. He noticed the direction of his gaze and merely waited for a comment.

"Nice carving."

"I think so."

"If I may ask, where did you get it?"

"A gift. Did you come all this way at night to ask me about a statue you didn't know I had?" Lucien raised a brow and waited for him to continue.

The viscount appeared nonplussed. "I have come for two reasons. The first to extend a welcome to the party my wife is throwing tomorrow night."

"I am not sure if I will be available."

"It is a party to introduce my niece to the families in the area."

Great, a matchmaking party. Just what I don't need. He needed to find out who that man, McKay, was that Ciara rode off with. "As I said, I am not sure of my schedule. I may be able to put in an appearance."

"That would be wonderful. It begins at ten o'clock. The second item is of a more delicate nature. My niece fancies herself in love with you. Although she tries to deny it, my wife and I know this for a fact."

"Sir." The imperious tone of one talking down to a member of lesser status coming out. "I am sorry that your niece fancies that. I don't believe I know your niece and with this new information I shouldn't make an appearance at your party for fear of encouraging her further."

"Forgive me for being blunt, but is there someone that you fancy?"

"You, sir, are out of line. You are right—it is none of your business. However, I will answer your question. Yes. My attentions are otherwise occupied and will not be squandered on some country miss."

Trenton rose. He set the glass on the desk then showed himself to the door. With his back to the marquess, he allowed himself a grin. At the door he turned and spoke, "I do apologize if I have offended, my lord. It's just that my niece claims you know her in a—shall we say—biblical sense."

Lucien rose from the chair, fury evident in every line of his body. "Are you saying that your niece claims I slept with her? Sir, unless you have proof of this you should leave before I lose my good nature. I have not slept with any country miss. Your niece, sir, is a liar. Good night, Viscount Trenton."

Trenton opened the door and slid through the opening. As he turned to pull the door shut, he stopped and glanced at the marquess. The man looked angry enough to spit nails. "With all due respect, sir, my niece doesn't lie. And before you say anything else, I do have proof. A child."

"A child? I don't have children." *Except one. And he doesn't know about me.*

A sad look came over Trenton's face. "That is a shame, my lord. I shall tell my niece she must be wrong. Perhaps she will come to apologize as well. I thought you knew her. Her name is Ciara McKay."

Lucien sat frozen as he heard the words. His niece. Ciara McKay. Oh god, what had he done? Trenton had said that his niece was in love with him. Ciara loved him. She *loved* him.

And he'd told her uncle he didn't have children. Amidst a groan, he yelled for Weeks. When the butler arrived, he asked, "Did we get an invitation to the Trenton party?"

"Of course, my lord. You chose to decline."

"Damn. Can we secure another one?"

"Excuse me, my lord, I believe that your sister received one as well and accepted." Lucien waved his hand and Weeks nodded. "I will get her, my lord."

When his sister entered his study, his mission was almost planned. "You sent for me?"

"Devonna. Come sit down. Did you get an invite to the Trenton party?"

"Yes. The party is tomorrow night."

"I wish to accompany you." At her raised brows, he just shrugged. "I have to get out sometime."

"Um-hum. As you say. Is that all?"

"What? Oh, yes."

Lucien stayed at his desk, staring at the wolf. Picking it up, he looked at the words engraved although he had them memorized.

Wolf,
Aim to the heavens for your dreams,
No matter the obstacle, you will triumph.

He set down the statue. Oh yes. His plan was made. He spoke aloud to the room as he walked to the door and smiled. "Okay, Ciara. You said yourself, no matter the obstacle I will triumph. You are my dreams, you and Bryn, and I will get rid of all obstacles. Your days of being single are numbered, princess. I am coming for you."

Lucien stepped into the hall and ordered his horse. If he rode hard, he could catch up to his parents. "While you're at it, get my carriage and take Ms. Smyth back to her home."

Rafe shot him a strange look as he headed for the door.

"Care for some company?"

"I ride to overcome some obstacles. If you care to join me, feel free."

Rafe sent word for his mount. "I feel I have to go with you, for this mood you are in is a strange one. Care to explain it to me?"

"On the way." The men swung up onto their horses and set their heels to them. They rode fast and hard. After about two hours of hard riding they came up on the carriage that carried the duke and duchess.

"Stop the carriage."

"We are being robbed," a servant screamed.

"I am the duke's son. I wish to speak to him."

The carriage stopped. Lucien rode over to the window and waited for the duke to pull back the covering. "I am here to let you know that I have every intention of marrying Ciara. Her…our son will be my heir. If you can accept that you will be welcome back at

Heartstone anytime. If not, I never want to see you again.

"You see, I learned something when I was with her in America. She taught me that having someone's love is the most important thing. All the riches in the world are useless without someone to share them with. Bottom line, I love her. If I can convince her to marry me, I will do so that very day. I will not give her another chance to turn me down." His stepmother gasped and sputtered but the duke silenced her with a wave of the hand.

"She opened my eyes to love. True love, something that before I met her I had no idea what it was. You never showed us love growing up. I had hatred in my heart when I spoke of you, which is part of the reason she did not let me know of my son. Now all I feel is pity. I pity the both of you, for you are bitter and hateful to those around you. You wear your title like a shield and don't allow anyone to know you have feelings. I don't understand because you sought a mistress so you must have wanted something.

"I dream of the love that her parents had. I find myself wanting her to glance at me and smile a smile that only I know what it means. I think that the title of the Black Marquess is gone forever. I really don't care what you do with this information. Devonna will be getting married at my estate. You could try to make it up to her, to show up, show your support. I am not sure what happened to her. I have been searching for seven years and I still don't know.

"If you wish to be a part of your grandchild's life, you will do so on my terms. But if you hurt him again, I will not be held responsible for my actions. Goodbye."

He wheeled his horse around and he and Rafe headed back toward his house.

Chapter Twenty-Three

They hadn't ridden very far when Rafe stopped. Lucien followed suit. He knew that his friend would not be able to resist the questions. "Are you serious about all that you said back there?"

Rafe was closer to him than any brother. So he had no qualms about letting Rafe see this side of him.

"I meant every word. I live for her smile. A smile that is open, complete and just for me. You read the inscription on the wolf—she made that for me. Those are her words. She believes it. Rafe, she carried me to her cabin when I was wounded."

They started walking the horses.

"Carried you? You mean with a horse and carriage?"

"No. I mean, carried. She lives alone up in the mountains. You were there when she was trying for the duke. She is strong. Full of life. Unlike anyone I have ever met. She encouraged me to find my life and pursue it. I learned what it was like to enjoy my life. To live. For the first time I had someone who treated me like a person, not a title or a potential husband for a daughter.

A person. An ordinary, everyday person. I ran trap lines, shoveled snow. It was amazing. I found myself out there." He shoved a hand over his face.

"She said that I had been fevered for two weeks. I still have the scars from the bear. The nearest town to her was days away. She didn't care. She was happy. They call her the 'heart of the mountain.' It is where she gets her life, her spirit."

Rafe rode in silence before he commented. "If this was before you left to go over there I would have said you were crazy. Even a month ago, but since I have seen her and you with her, I believe you. I also envy you. All this talk of marrying for a duty is not right. You know that I am in love with your sister. I have told you as much. But I want her to love me back. Seeing her laugh with Bryn and playing, it has been so long since I have seen that in her. You said that Ciara helped you find who you were. Do you think she could help Devonna? I would do anything to give her that kind of joy."

"I don't know. For the past seven years I have tried to find out what happened to my sister. She would cringe away from me when I would reach for her. I asked servants—no one saw any marks on her. Whatever happened to her could be what is holding her back from joining the world."

Rafe laughed. "Listen to us. We are worse than women. Talking about love and feelings."

"Yes, I am in love. It is a wonderful feeling."

"I agree. So what are you planning on doing to get Ciara back? Are you going to buy her something? Give her your stables?"

"She helped me design those. I don't think she would want them. I can't buy her anything. I don't know what she could want. I asked her to come back with me and she told me that she had everything she needed right there."

"What about a statue like she gave you? Where did she get that made?"

"She made it herself. Her dad taught her."

"I don't envy the work you have ahead of you. I am going to leave you here and go to my home. I have to get ready for the party tomorrow at the Trenton house. Will you attend? Or are you going to be busy planning on how to get Ciara?"

"I will be there. Ciara is Trenton's niece. That was one of the reasons he was at the house tonight. I will see you at the party. Goodnight, Rafe."

"Goodnight, Luc. Until tomorrow." As Rafe rode toward his home, Lucien sat and just looked at the sky. He had to get her back. He would find a way.

* * * *

The party was in full swing. Young men jostled each other to be near her. She was standing by a table when the butler made the announcement. "The Marquess of Heartstone, Lady Devonna St. Martin, and the Viscount Harrington." Ciara's heart skipped a beat. He was here.

"Good evening, Ciara… I mean Miss McKay."

For the first time that night, a smile that wasn't forced crossed Ciara's face. "Good evening, Devonna. Or am I supposed to call you Lady St. Martin?"

"Devonna, please. I like to believe we are friends."

"Devonna then. But you must continue to call me Ciara."

"Agreed. Can I have a private word with you?"

Ciara followed Devonna to a row of chairs that were empty for the moment. They sat side by side as Ciara waited for Lucien's sister to speak.

"As you probably heard, I am getting married to Viscount Harrington."

"Yes. To Rafe, isn't it? He seems a wonderful guy. Congratulations."

"Yes, well thank you. I was wondering if you would attend?"

A look of amazement crossed her features, followed by a smile. "I would be honored. When is the wedding?"

"Saint says that we will have it next week, since the whole thing was rushed. Thank you. Thank you so much." Devonna squeezed her hand and left her alone.

Ciara rose and was once more surrounded by young bucks again. Lucien watched her from across the room.

Ciara stood next to Conar by an open window as she watched Lucien move toward her. He moved like Kosse, like a predator. He was dressed in black, as was Conar, with a white cravat at his throat. His hair was tousled and he looked delectable. The gazes he sent her made her legs feel like pudding.

Before he got there, a servant came up and whispered in her ear. She turned, all else forgotten, and hurried out of the room.

Lucien saw as she gazed at him then left, following the servant. As soon as he saw Conar head in that way, he found himself hugging the shadows as he snuck up the darkened staircase to find where she went in such a rush. Was she running from him?

He heard her voice as it came from a room. He peered in the open crack and saw her seated on the edge of a bed as she held her son in her arms, not worried about the condition of her dress at all. "Mama's here. It's all right, Bryn. I'm here. Shhh. You're fine now."

A noise in the hall made him realize the danger of his situation. He shrank back into the shadows where he would not be seen, but could still overhear Ciara.

"I was scared, Mama."

"I know, baby. Everyone has bad dreams."

"I am sorry I took you from your party."

"Nothing, nothing is more important to me than you. You are my son."

"You look beautiful, Mama."

She sighed, "Thank you, Bryn. You should lie back down. Would you like me to tell you a story?"

"Yes."

"All right, what story would you like?" Lucien could imagine her hand as it stroked his hair as she smiled down into his face.

"Mama?"

"Yes?"

"Will I be beautiful like you when I grow up?"

She laughed a light husky laugh. "No. Men become handsome. And you will be the most handsome of them all."

"Like my father?"

Lucien held his breath as he waited for her answer.

"Yes, Bryn. Like your father."

"Do I look like him now?"

"More and more every day." Pain laced her voice with that admission. "What story do you want to hear?"

"Tell me how you met my father."

"Is that the story you want?"

Yes. Yes.

"Yes. That is the one I want."

A sigh reached his ears. "Very well. It happened by home."

"Home in the mountains?"

"Aye, home. Home in the mountains. I was out with Kosse."

"Mama. You were out with Faolan. You didn't have Kosse yet. You forgot."

"That's right. Faolan. Are you sure you don't want to tell the story? I am old and I may not remember it all."

"You're playing, Mama. You're not old. You're the beautifulest woman in the world."

"Oh, Bryn. You are so sweet to say so." Lucien heard loud smacking kisses.

"Mama. The story."

"Right, sorry. I forgot you are getting too old for kisses."

"Not all the time, Mama."

"Okay. So, I was out with Faolan. I heard a bear and I told myself 'that is strange, bears are usually sleeping by now.' Faolan had indicated that there was trouble so I checked the signs and saw that a horse had ridden between a mama bear and her cub. That was why she sounded so angry."

Lucien hadn't known about the cub.

"So when I found them, she was tossing him around like a doll and I had to have Faolan's help to get her away from him, so I could help him."

"Like yesterday, Mama? At that man's house? When you got so angry? That man and his friend had to hold you. Kinda like that?"

Tears pricked her eyes as she gazed at her son. "Yes, baby. Like that. I am so sorry you saw me like that."

"I was scared, Mama, but I think when you kicked in the door, they were scareder."

Ciara smiled as she looked at her son, staring at her with eyes that were like his daddy's. How resilient kids were. "Probably right. Do you want me to finish the story?"

"Sorry."

"After the bear had been chased away by Faolan, I had to get the man back to the cabin, for he was in pretty bad shape. I had to carry him. So I picked him up like I was carrying a deer."

"Over your shoulders?"

"Aye. Over my shoulders. Then I walked back to the cabin with him."

"It was snowing also."

"Right. It was snowing also. He had a fever for two weeks and…"

"You're really strong, aren't you, Mama? Did you pick him up like you did the men you threw around the building?"

"No." For the first time, her tone was sharp. "Bryn, listen to me. What I did was wrong. I was angry."

"You were stronger than them. You threw them like they were a piece of cloth."

"Enough of that kind of talk, Bryn. What they did was wrong. What I did was wrong. Just because you are stronger than someone does not mean you should use your strength on them. When I carried your father back, it was different, I was helping him. In that case, using your strength is important.

"When you are grown, you will be strong, like your father. But you must use your strength only to help those in need. Those weaker than you. Never use your strength in anger, like I did. It is to be used to help, not hurt. Understand?"

"Yes, Mama. Mama, did you like my father?"

"Yes, Bryn. Very much."

"Why did he leave? Did he hate you?" Six-year-old anger in his tone rang clear to Lucien.

"No. He didn't hate me. He had to go back home. He didn't belong there."

"He had to come back here?"

"Aye. He lives in England."

"Do you think he would like me? Would I like him? Can I meet him?"

"I know he would like you. And I am sure you would like him."

"I like Conar, Mama."

"Me too. You need to get to sleep. I have to go back downstairs or Auntie Fi will come looking for me."

"Is Conar my father?"

Lucien stiffened as he waited for her answer.

"No. He isn't your father. Enough questions for one night. Get some sleep."

"How do I look like my father?"

Ciara shook her head as she tucked her son in. "You have his hair, dark and thick."

"You have dark hair too."

"You have his eyes. The same blue like the deep part of the lake. Now, go to sleep."

"Can Conar be my daddy? I like him a lot."

Lucien's nails bit into his hands. There was no way he would let her marry that man.

"No. Conar can't be your daddy. No more questions."

"Who is my father? I want to meet him."

"Enough, Bryn. Goodnight." Her tone brooked no room for argument and the boy obviously knew that for he fell silent. Lucien shrank back as he saw the door open wider and she slipped through to head down the hall.

"Goodnight, Mama," he heard Bryn whisper. "I love you. Night, Faolan, night, Kosse."

Lucien was shocked. Even though his son didn't know who he was, he knew about him. Rising, he glanced in the door and saw Faolan and Kosse asleep on either side of his son.

"Goodnight, son." He slipped away from the door with only the wolf and cougar as witnesses.

Lucien strolled outside. He needed time to think. He approached the gardens and walked in them. There were courting couples scattered around. Lucien headed for a place he thought would be secluded. He heard Ciara's voice. And Conar's.

"Is he okay?" Conar asked.

"Aye. He just had another nightmare. Then he wanted a story."

"Ye are a wonderful mother, lass."

"I have good material to work with. He is a wonderful son. Conar, he wants to know who his father is." She ran her hands over her face in desperation.

"Aye. He is coming into that age. He has a right to know. Are you going to tell him?"

"I don't know. He has already met his father."

"That's not fair, lass, he didn't know it at the time. I may not like the man, but he has a right to have his son know who he is."

"It's just that…"

"What's going on out here?" A tall, gray-haired man came onto the scene.

"Grandpa. What are you doing here?"

"I was looking for me grandchild. Have you seen her?" His brogue was thicker than Conar's.

"I thought you weren't feeling well. I'm glad you are up and about."

"That tea you gave me did the trick, lass. Give your grandpa a hug. I have years to catch up on." As Ciara walked into his arms, he asked Conar, "What are you two doing out here?"

"We were discussing the fact that she needs to tell her son who his father is."

"Aye. Conar has the right of it, lass."

"It's not fair. He is my son. Why can't I be the one to decide?" Anger sparked her tone.

"Lass, let me tell you a story about an auld man that sent his son away. The man in question was the Laird of the Clan McKay, one of the largest, fiercest clans on the isle of Erie. He sent his only son to get some slaves from the passing trader ships. His son came back with about six. One, a woman, was standing tall in her chains. Her eyes burned with pride and resistance at being a slave. Not even the journey she had endured could dampen her spirit. She was like an Amazon princess.

"I firmly believe that if she had spoken our tongue that day my skin would have been flailed off my body with her wicked words. The son, the sole heir of the chieftain, took the slave for himself. As days passed they learned each other's language. The chieftain told his son that if he felt that strong for the slave to tup her and get it o'er with.' He was to be laird and a slave was beneath him.

"His son, as fiery as the hair on his head, freed the slave and handfasted with her. The laird went into a rage. He verbally attacked his son, in front of the woman he had joined with. She stood up to the man and gave him twice what he had inflicted on his son. That night his son and his beautiful princess left for America. I never saw my son again.

"Never had I seen anyone so brave before. Before now. You have your mother's spirit in ye, lass. You don't back down, no matter what. Don't keep the man from his son. I regret what I did every single day. I will spend the rest of my days doing so and trying to make it up to you. You shouldna have been alone.

"I thought that your mother wasn't worthy of my son. She claimed to be a princess and she was. I have since traveled to where the slavers said they got her. You are a princess, you are also my grandchild. I love you, lass. Something I never got to tell my son or his wife. Don't deny his father the same chance. Please.

"You don't have to go back to America. We are your family now. You and your son will be always welcomed on Erie. Think about it."

Sniffing back tears, she kissed her grandpa on the cheek.

"Thank you, Grandpa. For everything. I remember Papa used to tell me stories about you. He missed you, you know. Mama would yell at him and tell him to just go home. He never did, his pride wouldn't allow it. I just don't know what to do. Tonight Bryn asked me if Conar could be his daddy."

Conar laughed and grabbed Ciara around the waist, planting a kiss on her mouth. "Great. When do we marry?"

"Get off me, Conar. Even if I wanted to marry you, which I don't, I couldn't. We're family."

"But I could make you happy. Who cares what people would say," he teased.

"Get off with you." She shoved against his chest as she grinned at the absurdity of his words. "I will think about what you both said as far as him knowing his father. It is just not fair. What if he wants to stay with his father? I could lose him forever. Then I would be alone. I don't know. I will think on it. But right now we had better get back to the party before Auntie Fi sends the rest of the clan to find us." Her voice wobbled as she tried to control her emotions.

Ciara and her grandpa walked off arm in arm.

Chapter Twenty-Four

Conar stood still as he watched them walk off. "I know you're back there, English. I know you heard. Know this, if you allow her to be hurt again, you will answer to me." Conar walked away without another word.

Lucien was surprised that Conar had known he was there and not said a word. The man was honorable. Someday he would have to thank him. She wasn't letting their son know for fear of losing her son. Not because she hated him.

By the time Lucien made it back to the party, the band had begun to strike up another waltz. As he approached Ciara, he heard some pimply faced boy ask her for the dance. Before she could respond, he swooped in, "I believe that she has promised this dance to me. Gentleman."

He swung her onto the floor, almost groaning aloud at the feel of having her in his arms again. "Smile, love, or people will think that you don't wish to dance with me."

"I don't."

He arched a brow and looked down at her. "Why not? I have been told that I am a passable dancer. By the way, you look ravenous tonight. You are the most beautiful one here. With the possible exception of my sister, but familial loyalty decrees I say that."

He grinned at her, once again a marquess overly confident in himself. A grin that faltered when he saw the look in her eyes.

"It seems we have come full circle. You are using your title to get what you wish, for you know that I never promised you this dance. And since you know that I am upset, you are spouting compliments to try to soothe me. Unfortunately for you, in the same way you spout them, they flow off me, like water off a duck's back. Save your pretty words for someone else. Like maybe Christie or whichever other woman is your current mistress."

"Jealous, princess?"

"Like I tell you over and over, one can't be jealous of what one doesn't have. I just resent being grouped with the collection of brainless women who find your compliments endearing, when I am nothing like them."

"No, you are most definitely not. You are..."

"I know. Different. I am nothing more to these people and you than a freak show. I am different and they want to see how the 'wild American' will act. Don't insult me by adding to it. Just, can we finish the dance in silence?"

The detachment in her voice struck a nerve with him. He hadn't looked at it from her point of view. She was correct, and while no one would insult her openly because it was her aunt and uncle who hosted the party, there were titters behind fluttering fans. Men joked about how it would be to 'make it' with the dark-skinned savage.

The dance ended. Before she could pull away, he whispered for her ears alone. "I never thought that of you. For what it's worth, princess, I think you are the most beautiful woman here."

He thought to appease her. It had the opposite effect.

Eyes flashing fire, she glowered at him. "I know. I am beautiful, for a savage, a heathen. Anything someone would wish to sleep with just to say that they had. I know. For all your pretty words I am still only good enough to be a mistress. Never a wife. Goodnight."

She spun around and pleaded a headache to her aunt then sought her room.

Ciara left Lucien with a swirl of jade silk and the teasing scent of honey and berries. Her scent. He watched her disappear up the stairs. He didn't know how to proceed. She was unlike any other. Compliments didn't work. Trinkets *wouldn't* work.

"She's full of fire, isn't she?" Rafe stood at his elbow as he posed the question. "So what's your plan? Are you going to kidnap her, take her to Gretna Green and marry her?"

Lucien laughed at his friend. "No way. I wouldn't get within three feet of her."

"What's the problem? Her animals know you. Just go grab her."

"The last time I went into her room to wake her from a nightmare, her knife was sliding in my throat before she was fully awake. No thanks. I don't plan on doing that anytime soon."

"Are you sure you wish to be saddled with such a woman? Perhaps she is a little much for you to handle."

"Silence. There is no woman alive that is too much for me to handle. In all honesty, Rafe, I am not sure what to do here. I don't know how to get time alone with her. I have to consider Bryn as well."

"You are asking the wrong man, I know nothing. Now if you will excuse me, I am going to take my fiancée away from all those slobbering fools." Rafe walked off toward Devonna.

"You know her animals are with her son tonight. Her room is the third on the left, English." The words came to him from behind a pillar. Lucien moved off with just a nod of his head. Now was his chance to speak to her.

Lucien went to her room and approached on silent feet. The breeze blew her fragrance to him and he stiffened like a hound on the scent.

Lucien stood in the middle of the darkened room and watched her framed by the moonlight. Her dress was tossed without care on the floor and she sat cross-legged in her buckskins. Her hair was braided and hung down her back.

Even from this distance he could read her like a book. She wanted to be out there. Not trapped in this world that he lived in. It was killing her spirit. "Ciara." The name spoken like a lover's caress was soft and gentle.

"Good evening, Wolf. Why have you come here?" She didn't start at his voice, so he knew she had known he was there.

"I came to speak to you. Will you give me a chance to explain?"

"Come sit down and speak your piece." Tiredness was evident in her entire body.

Lucien sat down beside her and looked at her. Her skin shone in the moonlight. "How do you like England? It is pretty, is it not? I was surprised to find out that Trenton was your uncle. Why didn't you tell me?"

"It wasn't any of your business." Leave it to his princess to ignore the niceties and hit the heart of the matter.

"If I had known that this was where you were staying, I wouldn't have said anything. I—"

"You have no right. I didn't tell you because where I stay is not your business." Her voice came hard and fast. "The only reason you wondered is because you thought I was with some male."

"Well, yes. I have a right to—"

"No. You don't. Whether I chose to stay with a male is not your concern. I ceased being your concern the moment you crossed that field back in America. Before that even. Why are you trying to lay claim to me? I am not yours." Ciara sighed. "I have never been yours."

"Damn it. Yes you are. You always have been, since I woke up in your cabin. Nobody else can have you." *I won't let anyone else have you.*

"Why? Why not? I am nothing but a novelty to you. Not good enough to marry, but good enough to sleep with. Why can't I allow the same for someone else? Did you even think of me over the past seven years?"

"Every day and don't say that about yourself. You are not a whore. Do you understand me?"

"Oh. I get it. I am just *your* whore. I see. So I am to be set up for use at your disposal but not for anyone else's?" The bitterness she spewed only fueled his own determination.

"You are not my whore. Not any whore. Do you understand?" His words fell like chips of ice.

"I forgot. I am the mother of your bastard. Listen to me. I don't understand what you are doing. I don't understand why you feel like you have the right to be jealous of someone like Conar."

"Damn it. Because you belong to me." He grabbed her and applied a bruising kiss to her lips as he hauled her up against his body that was rigid. With anger. Maybe fear. "I won't share you with anyone. You are mine. You always have been." There was fortitude in the force of those words.

Wrenching free, she stared at him, tears pouring down her face. "You won't share me? Tell me then, since I am yours, does that mean during all this time that I belonged to you that you belonged to me as well?"

"Yes." He gritted out. "You have always been with me."

"That was not my question. Tell me, did you think of me when you were sleeping with your mistress? I am assuming that you had more than one, a man with your reputation. You didn't belong to me and I don't belong to you. Don't you see?"

"I'm a man."

"I'm a mother. Do you understand that? Regardless of what you think, it is not flattering to tell a woman that you thought about her every time you were sleeping with another."

"Yes. You are a mother, of *my* son." This wasn't working. Maybe he should be honest with himself and her.

Ciara fell back against the window, as she just had no strength left to support her own body. "I hated you, you know. For leaving me. For leaving me pregnant. Alone." She spoke in hushed tones, almost as if speaking to herself.

"I didn't know." His voice pleaded with her for understanding.

"I know. I was losing my independence and you had left to find your dreams. Then Bryn was born and my world changed. He is my everything. If he likes it here, I will lose him. You have the power to take him from me. You can give him things I can't even dream of. And I will be left alone again."

Oh, sweetheart, what have I done to you? "No. You gave him life, and you fill his life with love. You are his mother and I can't take that away from you. I don't want to take that away from you. He loves you so much. His smile, when he sees, you could rival the sun for brightness. I have no wish to take him from you. Ciara, don't you understand that?

"I'll admit that I haven't been a monk since my return, but I compared everyone I was with to you. They all fell short. I know that is not what you want to hear, but it is the truth." He ran his hands through his hair. This wasn't going well. "Ciara, there is something unique about you. You are so special. It breaks my heart to think that I hurt you. I never wanted to do so.

"What you said to me tonight, on the dance floor, is so untrue. Maybe at one time but not now, definitely not now. I don't see you as a conquest to be lorded over my friends. I don't have the words for the exact way you make me feel, but when I do, I will be sure to tell you."

Lucien slid his body between hers and the window, so she leaned on him, and he wrapped her in his warm embrace as he spoke softly into her ear.

"I want you to stay with me. I want you to marry me. I want to marry you. I want to have what your parents had. I know that you don't believe me, and I will spend every day trying to make you do so. Don't go back to America without giving me a chance. Please. I will find a way to prove myself to you. I will.

"I love you. I love you, Ciara Malika McKay. One day you will believe me and that will be the happiest day of my life. Then I will marry you and we will grow old together and watch our son grow up with his siblings. Together. You and me. You will never have to be alone again."

He rose and wiped her tears away with his thumbs. Lucien drew her up into his embrace, buried his nose in her hair and just held her. When he felt her relax, he leaned back and kissed her on the mouth, with the utmost tenderness. He kissed her again and again until he felt his body stir in response. To the bed he carried her. After he took off her clothes, he tucked her in.

Lucien pulled back and placed one last kiss on her lips. "I know my limit. I have to go. I will see you soon. Goodnight, princess. I love you." Lucien left the room as quiet as he had arrived, leaving an emotionally exhausted Ciara alone in the bed. Confused. Wondering. Wishing. Hoping.

* * * *

Ciara rose late the next day. She dressed slowly as though the night had added fifty years onto her life. She made her way downstairs and looked for her son. He was outside playing. With Lucien.

"Morning, princess." Lucien's deep voice reached her as she stepped out into the late morning light.

"Morning, Mama. I was going to wake you, but he said I should let you sleep." There was no need for her son to identify who 'he' was. "I was going to go with him to name the baby horse we brought him, but he said we had to ask you first. Can I go with him, Mama? Please? I'll be good. Promise."

"Give me a minute, Bryn. Come give me a kiss first. Then I need to speak to him alone."

Bryn ran up the stairs and threw his arms around his mother. He kissed her soundly on the cheeks, hugged her and let her go to run back down the stairs. "Well, can we? Mama? Please?"

"I need to speak to him alone first, Bryn. Go play with Faolan and Kosse for a bit."

"I promise to take care of him, Ciara." Lucien's voice intruded, unwelcome, into the conversation.

"See, Mama. It's all right. He said."

"Brenden Kumi. Enough. I said go. I will not repeat myself." Ciara glared at her son, knowing he knew better than to add anything else.

As he walked away, he looked back at Lucien and added in a whisper his mom was not supposed to hear, "Mama's mad. Better be nice to her."

"I will." He sent the response with a wink to the boy who grinned and scampered off.

Before he could fully turn his attention back to the woman on the stairs, she ripped into him. "Damn you! I will not have you undermining my authority with my son."

"Our son."

"*My* son. You will not put him in the middle of this. Don't expect him to fight your battles for you. I won't have it."

"Okay, okay. It was poorly done. I just want to spend some time with him. Let him come with me."

A footman brought out a message for Ciara on a tray. She read it in silence. Not so much as a flicker giving away what it said. She placed it back on the tray then spoke quietly to the servant and he disappeared into the house.

"What was that?"

"Nothing for you to concern yourself with." She bit her lip as she watched her son. "Very well. You win. We tell him now, that you are his father and that he can spend the day with you, on one condition. Faolan goes with."

"Why the sudden change?"

"What now? You don't want him to know?"

"No. I do, I just don't understand why you have decided to agree now?"

"I never disagreed. I just wasn't sure of the right time to tell him." Ciara wouldn't meet his gaze as she walked over toward her son, leaving him to follow.

"Bryn. Come sit. There is something that we need to tell you."

He ran over and plopped down beside his mom. He looked up at her with such love and trust it damn near brought tears to her eyes. "What, Mama? Can I go with him? To see the horses?"

"Aye. You can. But first there is something I have to tell you. I should have told you a long time ago." Lucien sat beside her and rubbed the lower part of her back in quiet support. "It is about your father." Bryn sat still then and looked between his mom and the man next to her.

Eyes that were wiser than they had any right to be took in the picture. "It's you." Not a question. Just a plain statement. "You are my father. You have my eyes."

"Yes." Lucien's voice cracked as he answered.

Bryn looked at his mom. "Did he not want me, Mama? Is that why you didn't tell me?"

Ciara reached down for Lucien's hand and squeezed it as she answered her son in the same language. "No. That is not why. He didn't know about you until the other day at his house. He wants you so much and loves you. If you are to be angry, be mad at me, not him. Give him a chance, Bryn. He really wants to be a father to you. He would love for you to go with him still today, but it is up to you."

"I like him too, Mama. I think I will like having him as a father. Besides, Conar told me that sometimes surprises are the best things that can happen to you. We can be a family now."

"One thing at a time. Right now, we should speak English because it is rude to speak with him not being able to understand us. Are you all right?"

"Yes, Mama. I am strong." Bryn glanced at Lucien before he asked his mom, "What should I call him?"

"I think that is something the two of you should work out. Now, no more unless it is in English."

Bryn turned to Lucien and looked him in the eye. "What am I supposed to call you? Mama said I should ask you."

Lucien swallowed. "What would you like to call me? My name is Lucien but some people call me Saint."

A thoughtful look crossed Bryn's face. "Well, Mama says that you do want me and that the reason I didn't know about you was because of her. She says you love me. Is that true?"

"Yes. I love you very much."

He rose and scrambled to sit in Lucien's lap. "Papa." His decision firm. "I will call you Papa. That way I have both a mama and a papa." He gave Lucien a hug.

Bryn pulled back from him and touched his face. "Your face is wet. Are you hurt? You are crying. Mama can fix just anything. You should have her look at it." He jumped into his mom's lap and kissed her. "I will go with him still. Are you coming, Mama?"

"No. There is something that I have to do. You go with Faolan. Have fun and make sure you listen to him."

"Yes, Mama." He jumped up and ran off, yelling behind him, "Come on, Papa, Faolan, let's go."

Lucien rose and pulled Ciara up into his arms. He pressed a kiss to her neck as he whispered into her ear, his words trembling with emotion both shed and unshed. "Thank you. Thank you for giving me a son, my son."

She pulled back and wiped the tears from his eyes. "Go on. Have fun. Keep him safe."

"Are you sure you won't come with us?"

"You two need some time together." She smiled as she watched her son beckon to the man he had just learned was his father.

"I love you, Ciara." Lucien placed a caressing kiss on her lips, making her sigh and lean into him on instinct. His chuckle made her realize where they were. As she pulled back, he smiled at her. "You may not be ready to tell me how you feel, but your body is and does."

Ciara backed up to put some much-needed distance between them. "Be good, Bryn, and have fun."

"Bye, Mama. Love you."

"I love you too, baby."

"What about me? Don't you have something to say to me?" Lucien purred in her ear.

"Take care of him."

"That's it?"

"That's it."

Ciara didn't even get one complete step in before she was spun around. Her eyes wide with shock, she looked into Lucien's hard gaze. With a jerk he had her up against him and kissed her once more. No caressing kiss, this one spoke of possession.

He had made his claim and she had just realized it was on her. The kiss was fast, hard, deep and commanding. He had issued his command, *remember me, and remember this for you belong to me.* Just as fast as it began, it was over, leaving her shaky and wanting more.

"Have a nice day, princess." He walked off toward their son.

Ciara watched as they left for his estate on horseback before she got ready for her appointment. She had sent Faolan with her son and had kept Kosse with her. She would need the support.

She rode her horse hard. It was a little over four hours on horseback to her destination and she wanted the confrontation over with. Kosse kept pace with her in the shadows of the trees. Artemis held her own as she rode up to the ducal house.

She swung down and took a deep breath before she handed the reins over to a footman who waited and walked up the steps with Kosse flanking her. As she knocked on the door, a dour-faced butler answered her summons.

"Where is he?" Ciara asked the pinched-face man.

"His Grace is waiting for you in the library." Disdain was evident in the man. "That creature will have to wait outside." He acted as if he had managed to disrupt her plans.

"He comes with."

She brushed past him and entered the house. Museum would be more apt a word. It was sterile in its cleanness and there was no feeling of warmth present. There were many priceless items, but nothing to make it feel like a home. Ciara suppressed a cold chill as she looked around.

"He was most insistent that no creatures come with."

"Then he will have to be upset. Where is he? You tell me or I will find him myself." She moved through the foyer as she guessed where the library would be.

"Wait," the imperious tone of the butler came. "Follow me." He led the way past gaping servants to a door that was solid oak. There were intricate carvings in the wood.

For a moment she forget where she was and gazed at the door as her fingers skimmed over the markings. It was a mythological scene depicting Zeus as he enslaved the Titans. It was beautiful.

The butler knocked and, when bidden, stood back and let her enter. Then he shut the door behind him leaving her alone in the room with the duke.

"What do you want?"

"You were told that you were to leave the animals outside."

"I would not be dumb enough to face you without someone I trusted at my back."

"Humph. Come in and sit down. We have business to discuss." A liver-spotted hand waved her forward.

Ciara went and sat in a straight-backed chair while Kosse stayed between her and the door. "What did you send for me for?"

"Did you tell my son?"

"I don't need your son to protect me. No, I said nothing to him."

"Have you no manners? You did not even curtsy when you came in, never mind your dress. Pants are for men."

"Why bother with niceties? I did not ride for four hours to discuss what honors you believe I should bestow upon you. You called me. I came. Be happy with that much. What do you want? You are wasting both our time." Ciara kept her tone hard.

"How much?" the duke rasped. "How much will it take?" When she raised her eyebrows, he cackled with glee. "I knew it. Money always works for your kind. That is what you were after from the beginning."

"Enough," Ciara broke in. "What are you talking about? How much what? What is it you are trying to buy?"

"Why, your leaving, girl. I am willing to pay you to go away and not try to marry my son. How much? I will have the money for you before the end of the day. How much will it cost for you and that brat of yours to disappear?"

"Don't call my son a brat. I won't take your money. I never wanted your money. I never wanted your son's money. I don't need it. Is that what all this was about? You wasted my day. Goodbye." Ciara rose and headed for the door.

"Get back here. I am not finished with you." His tone caused her to narrow her eyes in response. She turned inch by inch and approached the desk, moving with all the grace of the wildcat that kept pace with her.

"What? Why do you keep me here?" Ciara placed her hands on the edge of the desk and in silence dared the duke not to back away from her gaze.

"I could have you thrown onto a ship never to be seen or heard from again," he spat.

Her voice dropped to a purr as she leaned in closer to his face. "Aye. And I could have Kosse kill you here and now. Your threats don't scare me. You are a lot of talk. You hide behind your title and use it to intimidate people. That doesn't work for me."

"Why did you come here?" This sudden change in conversation almost caught her off guard. Almost.

"To fulfill a promise I made to your son."

"And the kid." She noticed he didn't say brat. "Was he an attempt to get money?"

"No. If that was the case, I would have said something when he was born."

"My son claims to wish to marry you. Regardless of how I feel about this, I can't and will not have the family name hurt. Soon this will be just another one of his scandals that will blow over. The wedding will take place here. We will show our support."

That did catch her off guard. "I have not said I would marry your son."

The duke continued as if she had not spoken. "After the novelty of you wears off, he will be back with his mistress and forget all about you. Perhaps leave you in the country or send you away somewhere. Then we could just forget about you." The duke leveled a stare at her that shot fire. "He changed, you know. When he came back from your bloody country of upstarts. What did you do to him?"

"Do you even know what your son went through?" Ciara backed off and stood arms crossed as she looked at this old man in front of her.

"He said that he was injured for a bit. Unimportant. I was concerned with the horse he was bringing."

Ciara shook her head in disbelief. No wonder Lucien was the way he was. "He almost died. Do you realize that? Died. Dead. As in, no more son. Can you comprehend that?"

The duke's mouth shut with a snap. "What are you talking about? He said he got knocked off a horse. Stupid boy never could ride like he should be able to." The duke narrowed his eyes at her.

"Aye, he did get knocked off his horse. Because a bear attacked them. When I found him he was being tossed around like a rag doll. He was near death for two weeks." Indignation rose along with her voice. "You should be ashamed. You are the worst kind of man. Your son almost died. Your own daughter has been tormented in her own home and you allow it. You can't see past your own face."

She slapped her hands down on the desk, calling the complete attention of the duke as she lowered her face even to his withered one. "You are a bastard of a man and if I never see you again it will be too soon. Stay away from me. Stay away from my son. This conversation is over."

Ciara made it to the door when she heard a single word from behind her. "Wait." She turned back to the duke who looked paler than usual. "Wait. What did you mean? About my daughter?"

"I didn't speak in tongues. You figure it out. Whatever dislike you have for me, well, I don't understand it, but I don't care. Your daughter still loves you even though you have neglected her for her entire life and for some reason your son would love for you to be proud of him. Although why I couldn't tell you.

"I don't know what you have against me. You don't even know me. The only connection we have is through your son and the horse he brought you. My meeting him was an accident, for I am sure that he would never have wished to have been attacked by the bear. I healed him, for that is what I do. Nothing more. I am sorry that you lead such a bitter life. I saw that in your son when he first woke up. You're right, he did change. He learned what it was like to enjoy life. Good day." Ciara left before the duke could form a response.

Striding down the hall, she walked to the entrance of the house, trying to imagine what it was like to grow up in a place sans love. Her life had been full of it and she couldn't even begin to picture what they went through. A shocked gasp caught her attention.

The duchess was coming down the large staircase. "What are you doing here?" the duchess demanded. "Why are you in my home?"

"I'm not. I'm leaving." She did. Jogging down the steps, she vaulted into her saddle and turned Artemis down the drive and set her off with a touch of her heels. Soon the house and its eerie feel were far behind.

She rode up to her aunt's house but instead of handing the reins over to the footman, she asked, "Has my son returned yet?"

"No, miss. He is still with the marquess, I mean his father." The man blushed.

"Thank you." It was time for him to eat his dinner. She waved goodbye to the footman and, as he raised his hand in return, she grinned.

When she first came, they had looked at her like she was too crazy to pay attention to them. She overcame their reservations with her normal ease and cheer.

Weeks opened the door. "Hello, Weeks. Is my son here?"

"Good afternoon, miss. He is out with his father. I believe they were going to the stables to name the horses."

"Thank you, Weeks." Turning, she was brought up short by a soft voice.

"Wait. Miss… Ciara. Do you have a moment?" It was Devonna. She was wearing a light green day dress that enhanced her beauty and yet still she looked sad.

Smiling at the woman, she nodded. "Of course, I was just heading to the stables. Would you care to join me?" Devonna came outside with her and stared at her. Ciara watched as she worked her bottom lip with her teeth. "Maybe a walk to the lake? I could go for stretching my legs after such a long ride."

"Yes. I would like that." She gestured for her to walk and fell in beside her. Devonna was quiet as they walked and Ciara waited for her to start.

A large black streak came running up and she bent to say hello to Faolan. She knew that Bryn must know she was here. "Was there something you wished to tell me?" Devonna looked close to tears. Ciara rose and opened her arms and Devonna fell into them as her cries came out of her in a torrent.

Ciara just held her and let her cry. Devonna's legs began to shake so Ciara led her over to beneath a tree and continued to hold her as she would hold her own child if he was crying like this. Rocking her back and forth, she let her cry it all out, knowing she would speak when she was ready.

Chapter Twenty-Five

Lucien had seen Faolan run off and knew that she was there. Bryn knew it as well. He sent Bryn in for some food and promised to bring his mom to him. "You go in and get some food while I look for your mother."

"I want to tell her what we did today, Papa."

That word still made him choke up with tears.

"Fine. You tell her, but first we have to eat. Run inside and tell Cook to get you something."

"Okay. See you inside, Papa."

"I'll be along soon." He ruffled his son's hair. His son. And swallowed back tears when he got a hug.

"Love you, Papa." Then he was gone, off running with the spirit of a child.

Lucien looked toward the lake and saw Faolan so he headed that direction. What he saw when he arrived was more than he'd ever expected. His sister was sitting in Ciara's lap like a little child. Her head was tucked up under Ciara's chin and she was shaking.

Ciara rubbed her back as she began to sing a quiet song. It was not in English but Devonna seemed to understand the feeling of the song. Her sobs slowed until she was almost silent. Ciara didn't stop, simply continued as if she were doing something ordinary, as if it was normal for her to hold a grown woman in her lap as she cried.

Faolan rose and she followed his gaze to look into the blue eyes of Lucien. One eyebrow rose in silent question. Without stopping her song or the rocking, she gave a slight shake of her head. Lucien nodded as he stepped back

After Lucien had disappeared from sight, Devonna raised her head. Her face was streaked with tears, red and blotchy. She scooted off Ciara's lap and hung her head in shame. "I am s-so s-sorry," she stammered. "I don't know what came over me."

"Everyone needs a shoulder to cry on from time to time." There was no censure in her tone, only quiet understanding.

"Why aren't you asking me what's wrong? Or telling me to stop crying because a lady never shows her emotions?"

"If you wish to talk about it, you will. And I am the last person that can be telling you what a 'lady' would do. I'm wearing pants."

Ciara turned to Devonna and took one of her hands in her own. She looked her right in the eye and spoke softly. "I am here if you do wish to talk about it. But I will never force you to do so."

"I feel so bad about deceiving Rafe. I mean Lord Harrington."

"Why? What are you deceiving him about? Are you not going to marry him?" Ciara furrowed her brow.

"No. No. Nothing like that. I am so excited about marrying him. I have always had a crush on him." A girlish smile crossed her face. "No, about him marrying someone who isn't a virgin." She blushed at the word virgin.

"Look at you. You blush just saying the word. How can he think you are anything but one?"

"But I lost proof."

"No. It was taken from you. Devonna, do you trust me?"

"Yes. I'll admit I don't know you very well but I think I trust you." She nodded. "I am sure I trust you."

"Tell your brother." The look of horror that crossed her face made Ciara reach out and take hold of her arm to keep her from bolting away. "Listen to me." She adopted a tone that she used with Bryn when he was being stubborn. It worked like it did with her son. Devonna stayed even though she was nervous.

"Your brother loves you. I have seen the look of pain on his face when you pull away from him. He would never hold that against you. And I don't believe Rafe would either. He took you away from them seven years ago. In that time, has he ever done anything that would make you think that he would be like Richard?"

"How did you know who?" Her breath came in short gasps.

"I figured it out. Answer me. Has he?" Her tone sharp.

"No. He hasn't."

"Then why are you punishing him? All he sees is a sister who can't stand him. And yet, he still stands by you. He stood up to your father when he wanted you to marry that other man. You trusted him for that, why not with this? He won't turn his back on you.

"Think about it. In the seven years that you have been here, have you ever felt threatened by him? Has he ever made you uncomfortable? I would bet not. I know that what Richard did was horrible and inexcusable, but that was Richard, not Lucien. Don't punish the brother that loves you for something the other one did." She rose.

"I am going to the house to see my son. Think about what I said. I think that you should also tell Rafe. If you wish to tell them, I would be there with you should you desire it. Both your brother and fiancé are good men, don't forget that. Don't let Richard win by ruling your life with fear." She left her then and headed toward her son.

"Mama." He jumped at her and hugged her. "I missed you today. Where did you go? What did you do? I had fun. I got to name the baby we brought for Papa. Guess what I named him? Guess, Mama!"

She set him down and ruffled his hair. "Give me a minute, Bryn. You are asking too many questions at once. One at a time. I missed you too. Now, what did you name the colt?"

"What fun is that? Guess, Mama." Hands on hips, he looked affronted that she would dare to take his fun away.

"All right. A guess. Let's see."

Ciara chewed on her bottom lip as she pretended to think hard on this question, while Bryn danced from foot to foot with impatience as he chanted, "You'll never guess."

Aware that Lucien stood in the doorway to the kitchen and watched the interaction with mother and son, she continued to think hard. "Humm. I think…

No, I'm going to say" – she leaned down to his ear and said in a stage whisper – "Storm."

Astonishment crossed his face, Lucien's as well. Bryn stamped his foot and demanded as his lower lip stuck out, "How did you know that? Who told you?"

"No one told me, no one had to." She smiled as she placed a kiss on his scrunched-up face. "I'm your mother. I know all." She winked at him and rose. "How was he today?" The question was directed to the man in the doorway who took up more space than he had a right to.

Lucien entered the room, making it feel even smaller. "He was a very well-behaved boy. My son did wonderful." He watched as Bryn darted off to play with Kosse with a wave to them both. "How did you know what he would name the colt?"

She gifted him with a rare full-blown smile. "Like I said, I am his mother and I know."

He crossed over to her, immune to, or perhaps it was uncaring of, the kitchen staff that watched them with amazement and drew her into his arms.

"Tell me then, 'mother who knows all', what am I going to do?"

His voice was throaty and sent shivers flying all through her. His passion-filled stare ran over her body with hunger.

Ciara's own body flared in response as her tone deepened with desire. "Kiss me." A plead? A wish? Who knew?

"As my princess commands."

Growling low in his throat, he did just that. Melting into his embrace, Ciara forgot where she was, who she was. Forgot everything except the feel of his lips on hers, his body pressed intimately against hers.

A low whistle brought them both back to the present. Lucien raised his head to look at the kitchen staff that was trying not to smile, and failing. Ciara tried to pull away, but his arms locked around her like chains, holding her prisoner. A willing prisoner.

"Let me go, Wolf." She spoke in a soft tone.

"Never." The word so quiet she wasn't sure she had heard correct. He opened his arms so she could step back. His gaze belied his motion. They agreed with the single word he spoke. They heard childish laughter and saw Bryn and Devonna standing in the doorway watching them.

Devonna raised an eyebrow in perfect imitation of her brother. Which caused Bryn to laugh even harder.

"You two look like you got caught doing something bad." His voice was full of joy.

"Bryn."

The warning came from his mother. He ran off, trying not to laugh, knowing that his mother wasn't really angry with him at all.

"Saint?"

"Yes, Devonna?"

"Can you arrange for a meeting with Lord Harrington two days from now? I wish to speak to the both of you."

"About what?"

"Please. In two days. Can you do that?"

"Yes. I will send a note today."

"Ciara, will you be there as well, please?"

"Aye."

As his sister left, Lucien turned to Ciara and asked, "What did you do today?"

He settled his hand on the small of her back as they walked out of the kitchens and to a sitting room.

"Nothing important. Just answered a letter."

"From whom?" He felt a wave of jealousy hit him.

"Don't worry about it. I have to get back. It will be time for Bryn to find his bed soon. Thank you for keeping him today."

"There is no need to thank me for watching my own son, Ciara."

He settled her on a small couch then sat beside her. Draping his arm over the back and also her shoulders, he accepted the silence just enjoying being with her.

After a bit he asked, "How *did* you know what he named the colt?"

Leaning her head against his shoulder, she chuckled. "The night the colt was born, a wild storm raged through the mountains. When Bryn saw him the next day for the first time, he asked me if the storm had left him the baby to play with. I knew from that day on he would always think of the colt as Storm."

"Was he disappointed that he didn't get the colt?"

"No. He had Toka, and since he was allowed to play with all of them, it never occurred to him to want the colt. He loves horses and is very good with them."

"I know. I was amazed the first time I saw him on that horse. He handles him like a pro."

"He wants to race them. Maybe if you helped him then I wouldn't feel so nervous about it. Or talked him out of it. From what I remember, the races can get very nasty at times. When it's just the two of us, I don't worry 'cause we are just racing for fun. Not money."

"You let him race? Are you crazy, woman? He is too young to be racing."

"He has been on horseback since before he was born. Toka would never hurt him, nor would any of the other horses I've put him on. Don't you think that I would be the first one to tell him no if I thought he would be in danger? Look, life in the mountains is dangerous. He needed to know how to ride. Besides, a growing boy likes adventure."

"All right. You're right. You wouldn't put him danger. I could take him to a race with me tomorrow. I have two horses racing. You could come as well." *A family outing.*

"No. I need to get away from people for a while. If you are sure you wish to have him with and he agrees, then I see no problem with it."

"We can ask him." Pulling her back when she rose, he tucked her in along his side again. "When he comes in. I don't want to share you right now. Just let me hold you."

She relaxed against him and he watched as the sun started to set.

"Mama. Mama." The childish yell reached her long before the child did.

"Brenden Kumi. What have I told you about yelling inside?"

"Not to do it. Sorry, Mama." He looked only a little put out as he climbed up onto her lap. "I'm hungry. When do we eat?"

Lucien shook with silent laughter. Always hungry. What a kid. "Dinner will be served in three hours."

"That long? I'm hungry now."

"Bryn, that is when the adults eat. You will be sleeping." Ciara's words were soft.

"Mama, why can't I eat with you? I miss eating with you."

"I miss eating with you too, baby. Normally I would have eaten with you, but you were here, remember? I will have dinner with you tonight, but we should go now."

"Why don't you eat here? That way Bryn can spend the night and we can leave in the morning?"

The words were out of Lucien's mouth before he knew he'd spoken them. He blanched at the look on her face.

"Where are we going in the morning, Mama?" The promise of an adventure overrode the immediate need for sustenance.

"Your father wanted to take you with him to a horse race. He has two horses entered. What do you think? Would you like to go?"

If bouncing was any indication that he did, he was ready now. She stilled him with a touch as he repeated, "Yes. Yes. Yes." Over and over.

"Don't tell me. Tell your papa."

She had a hard time getting out the word *papa,* Lucien noticed.

Bryn jumped over onto his lap and hugged him hard. "Can I go with you, Papa? I will be good and all that other icky stuff Mama makes me promise to do."

"Yes, you can come with me. Are you going to sleep here tonight?" he asked his son, evading Ciara's gaze as he tried to stifle a grin at his son's words.

"That will be fine. Mama and I can share a room." He looked to his mother for confirmation.

"No, baby. I won't be staying. It would just be you. I have to go back to Aunt Fi's."

Lucien noticed his son withdrawing from him and leaning back toward his mother.

Bryn glanced at her with a scared look. "I don't want to stay here if you are not going to be here, Mama."

This was it. Right now, she had a chance to sever all ties with Lucien, make him continue to depend on her. He held his breath, waiting. When she began speaking in a language he didn't know, his gut plummeted to the ground.

Her son digested whatever she had said and looked at him. Lucien struggled to remain impassive.

"Mama. You said we were only supposed to speak English around Papa, 'cause he couldn't understand, 'member? You said it was rude."

"You are right, Bryn. I apologize." She rose from the couch. "Come give me a hug. I have to go." Bryn hopped off and ran over to her and wrapped his arms around her neck as she knelt on the floor. "You'll be fine. Have fun."

Lucien rose as well. "What about dinner? You said you would have dinner with him. We can have something within a few minutes." He implored with his gaze.

"Will you stay for dinner, Mama? I am not quite as brave as I thought." Her son spoke in a hushed tone, but Lucien heard.

"I will stay for dinner. Then you need to go to bed."

"Will you show him how to tuck me in? He might not do it right." Bryn spoke as if that were a cardinal sin.

"Your papa is a very smart man. I'm sure he will learn the proper way to tuck in little boys."

"With your help, Mama, maybe he will learn. It's just that you've done it much longer and I know you do it the proper way."

Bryn tucked his hand into Lucien's and led him to the door, chatting about the 'proper' way to tuck a boy in.

* * * *

Two hours later Lucien told their son a story, after tucking him in, the proper way, while Ciara stood in the doorway.

"Mama?"

"Yes, baby?" She approached and stood next to Lucien who still sat on the bed.

"I love you, Mama."

"I love you too, baby. Goodnight. Have fun tomorrow. Mind your father and…"

"Mama. I will." His lower lip trembled. He spoke with rapid fire to his mother in a language Lucien couldn't understand, as a tear leaked out of the corner of his eye.

Ciara leaned over and wiped the tear away. Rising, she placed her whiskey gaze on Lucien as she answered in English, "Aye, Bryn. I trust him. I trust him with my life." Then she leaned over to give her son one more kiss and she was gone.

Lucien said goodnight to his son and as he left the room he comprehended what Bryn had asked his mother. Did she trust him? She'd said yes, which banished the last bit of fear her son had about staying with him.

He strode down the stairs, hoping to catch her. She was swinging up into her saddle when he did.

"Ciara. Wait."

"What is it, Wolf? I have to go." Her voice was tight, controlled.

"Thank you for that. You could have taken him from me forever. Instead, you gave him the strength to stay with me."

"He is your son as well." She wheeled Artemis around and rode off without a backward glance.

Chapter Twenty-Six

The next day Ciara kept busy. She rode all over the property with Faolan and Kosse. She had never felt so alone. This was the first time she had been separated from her son.

A warning growl from her animals alerted her to a rider coming up. It was Richard. He stopped his horse beside her. It was covered with scars from whippings. Even now it was lathered and blowing hard.

"A word?" His tone didn't escape her.

"What do you want?" There was no civility in her question, for she didn't see the need. She didn't like him and she didn't trust him.

"I was just wondering why you were allowing your son to be the subject of ridicule?" At her blank look he continued, "I was at the races, where I saw my brother conversing with not one, not two, but three of his old mistresses. He introduced your son, excuse me, his son too, as 'just a boy' he was bringing to the races for a day. He even made some assignations."

He looked as if she should be upset by his claim.

"Why should you care what he does to my son? Isn't it true that if he claims him, you have even less chance of inheriting the dukedom? So why would I believe you, for all I know you just want him out of the way so you can get your nasty hands on the title?"

Ciara didn't let him see how those words that he had spoken hurt her. She would deal with Wolf later.

"Your son is still a bastard, since you aren't married. Not to mention he is just a kid, and children are prone to accidents." Richard's attitude raised her protective instincts in an instant.

"I know he is a child, which is why he is well watched. I will know of any harm that would befall him. I will allow nothing, nor anyone, to hurt my son."

"Are you threatening me?" He seemed almost incredulous.

"No more than you are threatening my son." Her words spoken laid down the stakes. At his raised eyebrows, she nodded. "Good. I see we understand each other." She rode off, thinking that the sooner she left this country, the better.

When she got back to her aunt's house, there was a note from Lucien waiting for her. It read—

Bryn did well, we had a wonderful time. My horses won (in case you wondered).

He decided that he would stay the night again. I said it would be all right.

If you wish to come over, I have room in my bed for you.

Maybe you could tuck me in properly.

We miss you. Some of us are lonely for your company.

On the chance that you will decline to join me in bed,

The meeting my sister requested is scheduled for ten o'clock.

I will see you then, if not before.

Love,

Your Wolf

Ciara crumpled up the note and threw it into the fire. He was teasing her. He wanted her to rush over there to see her son. She wouldn't do it. She trusted him. Her son would be safe.

To keep her mind occupied, she spent the night carving a statue. Her uncle had given her some wood and she was making him a statue. Her grandfather and cousin were spending the evening with her so she was not lacking in company. It just wasn't the company she wanted to be with. If they noticed her agitation, they made no mention of it.

"We will be leaving at the end of the week." Her grandfather spoke, breaking the silence.

"So soon?"

"We need to get home with the winter coming on. You know you and Bryn are always welcome on the Isle. Come for a visit. Please, the rest of the clan would love to meet you and my great-grandson." Pride shone in his eyes. "He is a wonderful boy and my boy did a wonderful job of raising you. I am proud of you, Ciara McKay. Don't ever forget that. And don't e'er forget that we are family."

Ciara nodded as she rose to give him a hug. On impulse she gave one to Conar as well, who whooped and grabbed her for a long kiss on the mouth. "Get off me, oaf."

"Here now, lass. I thought you were coming with me." The rest of her cousins that were present just laughed. She looked around. There were twelve men present plus her grandfather.

All of them tall and brawny. A good-looking lot. All cousins, all family. All clan. They all began hollering for a kiss and soon she was being handed from one to the next as they claimed their kisses. By the time she was back on solid ground, her aunt and uncle were in the room and they were laughing along with everyone else.

She gave her grandpa a carving of a mountain lion that her father had started and she'd helped with. There were tears in the old man's eyes as he accepted the gift. She went to bed with a happy heart. It had been a good night.

* * * *

She rode into Heartstone a little before ten. Bryn was waiting on the steps and came running before she had dismounted. He looked so happy.

"Morning, Mama. I am going to take Toka for a ride. Can I bring Faolan and Kosse with me?"

"Of course, baby. Have fun and be mindful of the men riding with you."

"Bye, Mama. Papa says that you are having a meeting. Are you going to marry him so we can all live together?"

Bryn ran off before she could even think to answer his question. "Yes, Ciara. Are you going to marry his papa so you can be one family?" Lucien asked from the top of the steps, the serious gleam belying the smile on his face.

Yes. I would love to marry you and live with you forever. Her heart spoke one thing. Her mouth said nothing of the sort.

"Good morning, Wolf. Stop putting ideas in his head." She brushed past him on the stairs and didn't get more than two steps away before she was pulled back.

"Uh-uh, princess. I need a good-morning kiss."

He tugged on her shirt, reeling her in a slow, but constant motion. He lightly touched her lips with his before begging entrance to her mouth with his tongue. When she opened, he sucked on her lower lip until she shuddered in his arms. He made a broad sweep of her mouth then pulled back, leaving her wanting. Again.

Grabbing her by the arm, he propelled her into the house.

"They are in the library waiting. Do you know what this is about?"

Lucien was nowhere near as calm as he was portraying. He was as hard as the stone his home was made of. All he had to do was inhale her honey and berry scent and he was as randy as a goat.

Damn her pride. He knew she wanted him—every response he got said as much. She wouldn't, or couldn't, let go of needing to go back to America. He was about ready to abduct her and take her to Scotland.

They entered the library to find Devonna fiddling with her hands and Rafe looking as confused as Lucien felt. They waited in silence as the servants brought the tea and Devonna served all present.

After a time, Lucien looked at his sister and said, "Well? Devonna, what is it you have to tell us?"

Devonna had moved and was sitting alone in a chair closest to the door. Rafe sat on a settee facing her. Lucien occupied a tall-backed chair by Rafe and Ciara had claimed the couch with her back to the large windows in the room.

"Devonna. Come sit by me."

Ciara issued the order and to his surprise Devonna didn't hesitate but came right over and sat next to her. The woman who owned his heart then turned her gaze to the men. "You two need to hear her out before you say anything and before you judge." That was also a command. Lucien recognized this Ciara, the protector. He and Rafe nodded their agreement.

With a little additional prodding from Ciara, Devonna began, her voice so low he had to sit up to hear.

"First, I want to start off by saying that I understand that you may wish to cry off from the wedding after you hear this."

Christ, she's pregnant.

"I have to thank you, Saint, for taking me with you seven years ago when you left Stokley. I know I didn't make it easy for you, with flinching from you every time you came near me. I am sorry for that and wish I could take it all back." Her voice shook with each word she spoke.

"I just feel that it is not fair, especially to Lord Harrington, to marry me under such pretenses. I don't know how to say this, but…" Her voice faltered.

Lucien looked to Ciara for an explanation but she pinned him with a glare. Obviously, she had meant what she said about hearing her out.

"Go ahead, Devonna. Tell them."

She offered her hand and Devonna latched on to it. Lucien noticed Ciara's wince.

"I'm not a virgin." She never raised her voice but they all heard.

"What!" Lucien roared.

Devonna cringed as tears began to fall. He spun on Rafe who had the same look on his face, so Lucien knew his friend hadn't done it.

"Who did it? Damn it, Devonna, who? Quit cringing. Tell me who did this."

He stood, flexing his hands, longing to hurt someone. Since his direction was focused on Devonna, she shrank back even farther. The marquess had returned in full form.

"Enough. Sit down. Let her finish," Ciara interjected and Lucien ignored her words but not her intrusion.

"Keep out of this. It is not your business."

He was so mad. How could Devonna have done this?

"How could you have done this? Were they right when they called you a slut?"

"Enough, Luc. I will still marry her. It doesn't matter to me. There is no need to put her through this," Rafe said.

"Of course you will. You would never go back on your word. But, Devonna, how could you? With who? Damn you, tell me!"

Lucien watched his sister flinch back and try to hide behind Ciara.

"Luc, enough. Leave her alone."

Rafe had risen as well, facing off with Lucien.

"I will get to the bottom of this, Rafe. Stay out of this."

"That is my future wife you are yelling at. I have every right to be in it."

"She behaved like a whore. She gave herself to someone knowing that she should go to marriage a virgin," Lucien grated out, with an accusing finger jabbing at his sister.

"Enough! Sit down both of you and keep your mouths shut."

Ciara had risen and was in full fury. Lucien looked at her as. She narrowed her eyes, pointing at the chairs they'd vacated, and snapped, "Sit!"

He did and in his periphery noticed that Rafe had as well. She pinned them each with a glare that froze him to their seats. "Both of you promised to hear her out. So listen."

Lucien shook his head. "Emma was right. She called her a slut. She just—"

"Shut up, St. Martin. Listen to your sister." Ciara's tone and words made him take notice. She never called him St. Martin.

Devonna amended her last statement. "Ciara says I still am a virgin since…since it was not given away freely. I am sorry that I had to put you through this." She sank to the couch and covered her face with her trembling hands. "I can't do this, Ciara. Will you tell them?"

Ciara rounded on him and Rafe. "Don't the two of you realize what she is saying? She isn't a virgin anymore but it wasn't by choice." Pinning a glare on Lucien, she snarled, "Your sister was raped. Since she was sixteen until you took her away. That was why she cringed from you. For if *one* brother would do it, why not the other? It's not like her father helped her."

"I'll kill him," Rafe growled.

"Not before I will." Lucien echoed his friend's growl. It all made sense. *I have been so blind. How could I not have known?*

He looked at Ciara. "Have you always known?" His tone was tortured.

"I figured it out."

"How?" He begged to be told how he could have missed this.

Ciara swallowed. "Like recognizes like. I knew the signs."

Her meaning sank in. His heart broke anew. "That is why your parents? Oh god, princess, I am so sorry." He reached for her, but she waved him off.

"Tend to your own. I will leave you all alone for a while."

Ciara offered a tiny smile to Devonna before she left. Lucien enfolded his sister in the first hug he'd received since she came to live with him.

They would deal with Richard after.

* * * *

Ciara called for her horse and rode out to find her son. She caught up to them deep in the woods. He was trying to get the footman to race. She sent them on their way and spoke to her son.

"We need to go to Auntie Fi's. We can race on the way there."

"Why, Mama?"

"Your great-grandfather and all the cousins are leaving. We need to say goodbye."

"Will we see them again?" He fell in beside her as they rode through the woods.

"Aye. We could go visit them in Ireland. Would you like that?"

"Could Papa come?"

Ciara looked around for Faolan and Kosse as she got control of her emotions. "We'll see." They were slinking through the shadows of the trees, present but hidden.

"Mama? Can I ask a question?"

"Of course, baby? What is it?"

"Well, I know that Auntie Dev is getting married to Uncle Rafe. They say that if people are to be a family, the parents should be married. When I was at the races with Papa, he had lots of women coming up to him asking when he would marry them. They sent me evil looks. Why aren't you and Papa married? Auntie Fi loves Uncle Trent and Auntie Dev says she loves Uncle Rafe. Do you not love Papa? Is that why we aren't a family?"

Bryn had stopped the horse and was looking at his mother with a sadness that tore her heart out of her chest.

"It's not that simple, Bryn. Your papa and I have some things to work out between us."

"I want to be a family. Like you always talked about. Is it me?"

"No. Never think that. England is different than back home. Your papa is a very wealthy man and over here there are certain rules about who he should marry. I will talk to him, all right? I think it is time the two of us had a chat."

"Okay, Mama. You look sad. I didn't mean to make you sad. Please don't be sad."

"I'm not sad. Just thinking. Have you thought of what you would like to give Auntie Dev as a gift for her wedding?"

"No. I don't have anything. Maybe you could carve something from the both of us." He sounded so hopeful all she could do was laugh.

"Maybe I could. We'll see. Let's race to the other side of the clearing. Stay on the road, though."

"I'm gonna win."

"Ready. Set. Go." Both horses took off like a shot. Toka was running all out. Ciara knew that she could win, but she let her son have his victory. They were laughing as they rode up to the Trenton house.

* * * *

Lucien rode hard to Stokley. It was time for some answers. He had convinced Rafe to stay with his sister while he confronted their father.

"I promise not to confront Richard without you."

"I will hold you to your word, Luc."

Lucien was entering the house before his horse had been led away. "Father!" he bellowed.

"My lord, the duke is in his study," the butler said. "He is not to be disturbed."

"Good. See we aren't disturbed." He brushed past him, knowing full well that wasn't what the butler had meant, and headed off to confront his father. At the door he stopped for about two seconds before he ripped it open.

"Damn it, didn't I say I wasn't to be disturbed?" There was a lot of shuffling in the chair that was turned from the door.

"I heard something to that effect."

The duke spun his chair around in surprise. "What are you doing here? Did that bitch whine to you about me sending for her a few days ago, or was it the fact that I offered her money?"

So that was where Ciara had gone. "Neither. She has not spoken of it to me. Thanks for telling me. This is about Devonna. Tell me you didn't know."

"Know what? Is this going to take long? I'm busy."

"Did you know?" His voice was dangerous and low.

"Know what? And watch your tone with me." He raised his walking stick and shook it at Lucien.

Snatching the cane, Lucien broke it over his knee and threw the pieces back at the duke. "The fact that your daughter was being raped by your stepson. Did you know?"

If his father had paled when his walking stick was tossed back to him in two pieces, it was nothing compared to the paling his face did at Lucien's blunt announcement.

"What…what did you say?"

"You heard what I said. Answer my question. Did you know?" Lucien was shaking he was so angry.

"No. I had no idea. Are you sure about this?"

"I have no reason to lie. Even you must have noticed that she pulls away from males."

"How do you know it was Richard?"

"She told me. Where is he?"

"I don't know. He left yesterday saying he had something to take care of." The duke slumped in his chair, at the moment looking all the older for his years. "Is she all right?"

"I don't believe you have the right to ask that. You have despised her since she was born."

"I was mourning the loss of my wife."

"And ignoring your child. She has endured the hate-filled stares and your comments about her with a quiet pride. You have ignored her for her whole life, and now you wish to play the hero. Forget it. If and when you see Richard, you tell him *I* am looking for him." There was no mistaking his meaning.

"Why are you looking for my son?" Emma asked from the door.

Lucien spun around.

"For what he did to Devonna." The expression that flashed across her face was not one of curiosity, but one of fear. "You knew. You knew what he was doing to her. How could you?"

"He said that she came on to him. It was not my place to say or do anything." She spoke with the authority of one used to being a duchess. "Boys will always take what is freely given."

"You bitch. Were you a man, I would call you out for this and kill you." He spun on his father. "You are to blame for this. You." He strode to the door, his penetrating gaze making his stepmother jump out of his way. With a final glance over his shoulder, he frowned. "I will find him. He will pay for harming my sister."

* * * *

Lucien rode hard to the Trenton house. "Where is Ciara?" he asked the butler as soon as the door opened.

"I believe she is up in her room. Shall I let her know you wish to see her?"

"I'll go tell her myself." He started to brush past the butler when he saw Trenton come into the foyer.

"Good day, my lord. Was there a reason for your visit?"

"I need to see Ciara. Now."

"This is my home. If you will follow Potter to the sitting room, I will let her know you are here."

Lucien struggled with his desire to just march up there and kick in her door. "Very well." He followed Potter down the hall to an amber sitting room.

"I will have refreshments here soon, my lord." Potter bowed and left the room. He waited for about five minutes when the door opened and two servants brought in trays with food on them. Still no Ciara.

Pacing the room, he munched on a sandwich. About to go get her himself, he turned and saw her entering the room. The vision walking toward him made his knees weak and he sat down on a chaise. She was dressed in a dress that was like the one she had worn at the cabin. Her feet, bare, were peeking out from beneath the flowing hem. It was green with colorful designs on it.

The fringes were dangling off a belt that accentuated her narrow waist. Her hair was in tight braids and threaded through with ribbons and beads. She looked comfortable. She looked beautiful.

"Good afternoon, Wolf. What brings you here?" She offered him a small smile as she approached.

This was the woman he knew. The woman he had fallen in love with. The one who made nothing seem impossible to accomplish.

He needed to hold her. He needed to be held. He didn't know how to ask, so he just sat there and looked at her.

Ciara walked up to him, slid between his thighs and wrapped her arms around him. She pressed his head to her breast and let her strength flow into him. Neither of them spoke.

Lucien drank deep of her warmth and her scent. She had known. She always knew.

"Emma knew. My stepmother knew what he was doing."

"It wasn't your fault. You did what you could. You are there for her now." She began to pull back so she could look at him, but his arms tightened and he kept his face buried against her.

"I failed my sister. I failed my mother." She massaged his shoulders and when he relaxed, she pushed him back. He gazed up at her.

The door opened and Auntie Fi entered in a swirl of yellow silk and flowers.

"Ciara. Take him up to your room and let the poor dear get some rest. I am having tea soon and it wouldn't do for them to see the marquess like this. Then you two need to have a talk." She walked over and patted Lucien on the cheek. "Dear boy. You look so tired. Treat my niece right." Then she was gone, leaving behind petals and the feeling of being run over by a carriage.

Lucien looked up at Ciara, uncertain if a trap had been set. "Did I hear that right? Did she just tell you to take me to your room?"

"Aye. We'd better go. Come on." Ciara led the way out of the door and up the stairs.

Entering her room behind her, Lucien shut the door.

"Where are Faolan and Kosse? Where is Bryn?"

"They are with him in his room. He is sleeping. He was up late last night saying goodbye to his cousins." She directed him to the chaise beneath her window. "Here, sit."

He sat and watched her from lowered lids as she moved around her room. She sent for some hot water and lemon for herself and some brandy for him. She had an inborn grace that made him just sit back and wonder.

She brought him the brandy when the servant had set down the tray and left. She curled up next to him, drawing her legs underneath her as she sipped her drink. "Do you want to talk about it?"

"No. Not right now. Why didn't you tell me my father summoned you?"

"Because it wasn't important."

"Did he really try to pay you to leave?"

"Aye. He was pretty sure he knew why I had come to England. We reached an agreement of sorts. He will stay out of my way and I will let him live."

He couldn't help himself. He burst out laughing. "I can just imagine you confronting him. I would have loved to have seen it. Does no one frighten you?" He hugged her hard as he shook with amusement.

Ciara continued facing the fire burning in her room. "You do. You frighten me."

The solemnness in her tone banished the laughter from him.

"Why?"

"Because you make me feel things, things I can't control. I don't want to control them when I am with you. And because you have the power to take my son from me."

"I would never do that." His hand tipped her face so they had eye contact. "I hope you believe that."

"I do. It is just hard for me to share him. He's all I have." She looked away.

"Don't look away from me."

He set down his glass and took her cup from her. Lifting her, he set her on his lap. He placed her legs on either side of his hips, which made her dress ride up midthigh, exposing her smooth legs to his gaze. Clenching his teeth, he tried to ignore the fact that his body was responding to her and focused on his words.

"I am willing to give you everything I have. I promise not to take every bit of your freedom away from you. I want to be what you have." His voice dropped to a whisper as he drew her mouth within inches of his own. "Marry me. I love you. Will you do me the honor of becoming my wife, a marchioness and future duchess of Stokley?"

Chapter Twenty-Seven

"Yes. I will marry you."

Lucien had gone cold when she fell silent for so long. When her answer came it was like having a fog lifted off from around his eyes. The world looked brighter. He kissed her lips. "I love you."

Ciara kissed him back, not ready to admit that to him. She rose and pulled him with her to the bed. "Time for a nap. You still look exhausted." Drawing back the covers, she helped him out of his boots and shirt.

Sliding into bed in only his trousers, he was enfolded by her honey and berry scent. The fatigue took over. As he closed his eyes, he felt her slide in next to him. She cuddled up to him like she had done in the cabin. One hand over his heart and her head on his shoulder.

* * * *

Lucien woke to the bed bouncing. He smiled, recalling that Ciara had agreed to marry him.

They were going to get married as soon as he got the special license, for he wasn't going to give her a chance to change her mind. As he thought of his wife-to-be, he realized the warmth that had been next to him was gone, but the bed was still bouncing.

His eyes opened into mere slits as he heard childish laughter. His son was sitting on the end of the bed between Faolan and Kosse, staring at him. Every now and then he would bounce and shake the bed.

Bryn was obviously trying to stay quiet but was losing his patience with that. Lucien opened his eyes and blinked as he saw the smile cross his son's face.

"Finally. You woke up. Mama said I couldn't make any noise to wake you. I didn't. But I bounced some. That should be okay 'cause she didn't say I couldn't bounce, only that I had to be quiet. Are you awake now?"

Sitting, he looked at his child and nodded. "I'm awake. What can I do for you?"

"Why aren't you wearing a shirt? Why are you in Mama's bed naked?" The child's eyes narrowed.

"I'm not naked." *Is this the sort of conversation one should have with a child? Even if it's my own child?* "Where is your mother?"

"She is with Aunt Fi. They are planning a wedding. Or, rather, Fi is. Mama looks like she has a headache. Are you marrying Mama? Does that mean we will be a family now? I asked her and she said she would talk to you about it." Bryn bounded into his lap and continued to chatter.

I spoke to Mama about it. She was marrying him for her son. Not because she loved him, or wanted to. It was for her son. The joy that had been with him when he woke disappeared like a puff of smoke. Was he going to have a marriage like his father, after all?

"Bryn, leave your father alone. Go find something to give Faolan and Kosse to eat. I have to speak to your father for a minute."

"Okay, Mama." He reached up and kissed Lucien on the cheek before running to his mother and kissing her as well. Full of happiness, he left with Faolan and Kosse who stopped by Ciara to get pats as well.

Lucien stared at her with mistrust. Sliding out of bed, he put on the shirt she held out to him. When she sat down on the bed, he remained standing.

"I am pretty sure that Bryn has spoken to you about what he talked to me about. I felt that you should know, while I did do this for him it wasn't all for him. I do want to marry you." She caught his gaze and held it with her own. "I would only hope that you realize I can't change overnight and some of your customs will take me a while to get used to. That is all I have to say, so I will let you finish dressing. I'll see you downstairs." She rose and slipped out of the room before he could formulate a sentence.

* * * *

Lucien ate dinner at the Trenton house. After he had drunk some after-dinner port with the viscount, he found Ciara sitting outside in the garden by herself on a bench. She was bathed by the moonlight and looked at peace.

She was sitting cross-legged on the bench, enjoying the cool night air and the scents that came with it. Listening to the bugs and night birds that croaked, chirped and sang made her breathe easier. She wore a loose-fitting dress, the one she had worn for dinner. It was a navy blue.

Lucien knew she didn't wear any of the corsets or stays that most women did under a dress. Knowing her, she was probably barefoot or wearing moccasin slippers. He pulled his cravat loose as he approached her.

"Ciara. What are you doing out here?"

Without opening her eyes, she answered him. "Faolan and Kosse are off hunting and I am enjoying the outdoors. What are you doing here? I thought you would be going home by now."

"Trying to get rid of me?" The question was lighthearted but the meaning behind it was not.

"No. You should probably know, however, that my aunt wants to go all out for this wedding. If she has her way, it won't be ready for a good six months or so. She wants everyone around to know."

"And you? What do you want?" He sat beside her on the bench and smiled as he saw one moccasin-clad foot peeking out from under her dress.

"I don't really care. I don't know most of the people she says she wants to invite anyway. I don't like the idea of being put on display." Her voice was heavy with a passiveness that was not like her—it was full of resignation.

"Are you having regrets about saying yes?"

"No. It's not that. Well, not in the way you are thinking. I am having to give up my freedom. That is hard for me to accept. Not marrying you." Her lids raised and he found himself ensnared by her whiskey eyes. "Never about marrying you."

"Would you like to have a quiet ceremony? I am afraid that you will have to go to breakfasts and such, as people will want to meet you. But I can have a special license by tomorrow if that would make it easier on you."

"Tomorrow? You can do that?"

"For you. Anything." He pulled her into his arms. "I want you to be happy. We will have to go into town for a while, but we can come back to Heartstone if you wish."

"And Faolan and Kosse?"

"They will come with, of course. You will have to ride sidesaddle and never faster than a trot, while in town." He finished in a rush at her look of horror.

"And my dress?"

"In the house you can wear anything. When going out, a dress befitting your station." He searched her face for the glint of defiance he knew his pronouncement would bring. It came, but disappeared quicker than he would have thought.

"I will have to take this one day at a time. Can't I just stay here?"

"And have people laugh at me that my wife stays with her family instead of me?" He raised his voice with censure. "No. Your place is with me."

Ciara sighed. "I meant at Heartstone. Instead of going to London, couldn't I just stay there?"

She gripped her dress with a grip that almost whitened her knuckles showing how distressed the conversation was making her.

"We will have to go to London, for a little while at least. You may like it there. Rafe and Devonna will come with us and we will be in Rafe's townhome." He kissed her on her temple. "I have to go get the license. We will wed tomorrow. I will bring Rafe and Devonna to stand as witnesses. All right?"

When she didn't answer, he turned her and tipped her face up to his. She was at war with herself. She nodded and slipped off his lap and walked to the edge of the garden.

Lucien followed. There was something wrong. She was not as happy as she should be. He gathered her in his arms and placed a very thorough kiss on her lips. Eyes darkened with desire and bodies responded. He set her down with reluctance and walked away with only a "Goodnight, princess."

****

Lucien rode to the Trenton house accompanied by Rafe and a very excited Devonna. Potter met them at the door and smiled as he opened the door to admit them.

"Where is my fiancée, Potter?"

"My niece is out riding." Aunt Fiona swept into the room, looking very bright in her orange dress.

"Well, we are early. Where is she riding at? I will go meet her." Lucien looked down at the woman who was to become his aunt by marriage. She was very vibrant and, if her brother, Ciara's father, had been anything like her, it was not any wonder that Ciara was so full of life.

"Perhaps she needs to be alone for a bit. We need to talk. Perhaps Lord Harrington would like to take Lady St. Martin to see the gardens, while we chat."

Rafe bowed to Fiona and led Devonna off to the gardens. Lucien followed her into a sitting room that was bright yellow. At her wave, he settled himself onto a settee and waited for her to begin.

Fiona sat across from him, clashing with the room. "Do you plan on allowing my niece to keep her freedom?" His brows rose in amazement. Scanning the room, he looked for the viscount. "Trenton's not here. This is between you and me. She is my only link to my brother and I will not have her hurt."

"I don't plan on hurting her. Some of her activities will have to cease, for she will become the wife of a marquess. I am allowing her to keep her animals and that should tell you something right there. When we come out to Heartstone, I will probably allow her to assist with the horses. She will not want for anything. I will provide for your niece."

"You will find her out riding past the lake. One of the grooms can give you directions." She didn't look back at him when she added, "Don't forget who she was when you met her. Ever." Then she left in a swish of silk.

Lucien let her words wash over him. He had to go find his wife-to-be. The minister would be here this afternoon. The special license was in his pocket. He had witnesses, had sent a note to his father letting him know what he was doing. All he needed was to see his son and his future wife.

He swung up into his saddle and got directions from the groom. When he rode up to the field he stopped as he saw Faolan and Kosse lying in the sun. Bryn was not with her. She was riding across the field. Her hair was loose and flowing out behind her.

Ciara was riding low and they were moving fast. Artemis was moving swift and powerful across the grass. Her hooves pounded the ground, sending up chunks of earth in their wake. As they approached the edge of the field, they moved as one into a smooth turn and headed back across.

Riding into the sun, Ciara sat up and reached her arms out to the warmth. Her head fell back and she moved with her horse, holding on with her legs. Lucien saw and realized that she was riding bareback. There was no saddle and no bridle on her horse. His breath caught in his throat.

A whistle reached his ears and, as he watched, Faolan and Kosse jumped up and ran after her. Without slowing, she turned Artemis toward a fallen tree. Urging her horse on to greater speed, she sent her flying over the tree, followed by both animals, and was soon out of sight.

Shaking with fury at her daring, he rode his horse down to look at the tree. It reached the chest of his horse. She could have killed herself. Wheeling his gelding around, he headed back to the stables. Ciara, however, wasn't there when he arrived.

Ciara rode off into the trees. She loved this, running fast and free. As she found herself on the road, she slowed Artemis to a walk and followed the winding path. Glancing at the sun, she realized she needed to get back to get ready for her wedding. Her wedding, that struck a nerve.

Turning Artemis around, she noticed that Faolan and Kosse had slipped back into the wood and Artemis was tossing her head. She heard it then, an approaching horse and rider. Moving Artemis over to one side, she continued walking on.

"Morning. What are you doing out here and who are you?" He pulled his horse up in front of hers so she would have to stop.

Cool eyes, the color of whiskey, ran an assessing gaze over him. He preened. He was very good-looking and knew it.

Ciara looked at the gentleman in front of her. He was built like Lucien but had sandy brown hair and gray eyes. His face was pointier and more hawklike. Lips were thinner. He was broad-shouldered and fit. He was a handsome man. Problem was, he knew it.

"I am riding. I am Ciara. You need to keep your horse moving. He is too hot to be made to stand still. Who are you?"

Arching a brow at her comment, he moved his horse alongside hers and walked with her. "I am Phillip Vallence, Earl of Edais. I am on my way to see the Marquess of Heartstone. He is getting married today."

He smiled like she should be heartbroken at the news. Or shocked to hear it. "Oh. How nice for you. Excuse me, I have to go." She turned to head Artemis off the road and onto a path when his voice stopped her.

"Do you know this chit he is supposed to marry? There are rumors all over London that she beat up the duke's men for no reason. They say that she is a heathen from the colonies and…" Dawning hit him. To his credit, he did blush.

"Looks like they say a lot in London. I believe you will find the marquess at Viscount Trenton's house, for that is where the wedding is supposed to be. Good day." She rode off into the trees without another word.

"Wait. Where are you going?" Phillip turned off the path and blanched as he saw the animals in his way. His horse rolled its eyes in fear and bolted off down the road, leaving him on his butt on the ground.

Ciara turned back when she heard the thump of him falling to the ground. This was not how she had wanted to spend her last free day. She saw her babies stalking the man. Calling them off, she looked down at the man on the ground.

"Are you all right?"

"Are they friends of yours?"

"Aye. They won't hurt you, unless you attempt to hurt me. Are you hurt?" She swung down from Artemis and walked over to him. Artemis began to eat the grass.

Phillip rose with caution, keeping an eye on the animals that were watching him. "I'm fine." He took a step and winced as his ankle flared with pain. "Ouch. That hurt."

Ciara was by him in a flash. "Sit. I need to look at that."

Phillip listened. She examined his ankle in a detached manner. As she slipped his boot back on, she said, "It's not broken, just sprained."

"How would you know?"

"I just do. I will help you to the Trenton house. There someone can summon a doctor if you prefer." She spoke with calm assurance.

"I can't walk on this, woman. It hurts. Send someone to help me. I will wait here."

"I can't leave you here. You will ride my horse with me."

"No way. Your horse has no saddle. For that matter, why is it still here? Why didn't it run away from those animals?"

Unamused by his hesitations, she struggled to contain her irritation. "They are friends. I will help you on her back and then I will ride in front of you." Her decision made, she rose and held out her hand to the man on the ground.

Shaking his head, he refused her hand. "I will stay here."

Another heavy sigh. "Look, the nice weather will not last. There is rain coming. You can do this the easy way or the hard way, but I am not leaving you here. Come on. Let's go." Ciara took the decision from him and lifted him.

Calling her horse to her, she looked between them both and made her decision. She spoke low to the horse and it got down on the ground. She gazed at the man standing next to her and gestured to the horse.

"You get on now. After she rises I will get on. I would help you up, but I think it best if I do not put my hands on you. Come on."

Phillip shook as she helped him on and Ciara wasn't sure if it was from pain or fear.

"Slide back. I will swing up in front of you and then you will have to scoot up so you can hold on to my waist." When he complied, she pulled herself up and brought her leg over the other side of the horse's neck. Waiting until she felt his arms go around her waist, she spoke and they were off.

"Are you really marrying Luc?"

"That's the rumor," Ciara answered.

"You don't speak much for a woman." He gripped her tighter as they went around a corner.

"I speak when it's important. Hang on, we are almost there." They broke from the covered road and saw the Trenton house in the distance.

Her passenger tried to hold himself upright as they rode in but he couldn't find it in himself to release her all the way. Lucien was waiting at the top of the steps with thunderclouds in his eyes. Rafe and Devonna were there as well.

Halting Artemis, she looked until she saw the footman she was searching for. "Go get a doctor. The earl has hurt his foot." The man ran off. She looked up at Lucien and Rafe. "Don't just stand there. Come help him off the horse. He can't stand on his own."

Lucien speared her with a glare. "You have some explaining to do. I saw you in the field." He grabbed his friend and pulled him down, asking, "What are you doing here? Why are you riding and holding on to her? Stay away from her."

Ciara turned Artemis toward the stable and rode off, ignoring the look of disbelief on Lucien's face. She would deal with him later. For now she had a horse to tend to. While she was in the stall brushing down Artemis, she felt rather than saw the door slide open.

When she looked up, she stared at a furious man. "Morning, Wolf." She kept on brushing.

"What in the hell do you think you were doing, riding around like that?" Lucien fisted his hands and stepped closer. "I saw that jump. For god's sake, woman, you weren't even using a saddle or a bridle. And then to come back riding with another man."

"Would you have had me leave him in the road, injured?"

"Yes. It would serve him right for falling off his horse. He should learn to ride better." His words were snarled.

"Funny, your father said the same about you. Should I have left you where you fell?"

"That wasn't the same thing."

"How do you know? His horse spooked. He fell, he was injured. There is a storm coming and, regardless of your feelings about it, I couldn't and wouldn't leave him there." She walked past him out of the stall. "Now I have to go and get ready. Excuse me."

* * * *

"Where are you going to celebrate the marriage?" Phillip asked Lucien.

"We are just going to Heartstone and after Devonna's wedding we will be going to London."

"We should be going." Lucien rose and pulled her to her feet amidst the sly looks of his friends. He had arranged for Bryn to stay here with Devonna for one night and they would return to Heartstone tomorrow, for Devonna's wedding was at the end of the week.

"Bye, Mama. Bye, Papa. I will see you tomorrow." He hugged his mom and whispered something in her ear.

"Yes, Bryn. They will stay with you. Take them with if you ride Toka. I love you, baby. See you tomorrow." One more hug and she turned to the rest of the family. "Thank you for everything." She kissed her uncle and said goodbye to the rest present.

Lucien handed her up in his carriage that had been sent and they set off for Heartstone. He couldn't believe it. He had just married Ciara. "Well, how do you feel, Lady Heartstone?"

"I think I am in shock. It seemed to happen so fast. What about you?" Ciara smiled at him.

"Happy. You are mine now. I will never let you go."

Chapter Twenty-Eight

"To the Marquess and Marchioness of Heartstone. Cheers." Everyone in the room echoed the shout and raised their glasses in a toast. Lucien took a drink, looked to his wife of two months and sent her a smile.

The townhouse was filled with members of the ton who were making an appearance at the wedding breakfast of the future duke of Stokley and his duchess. The Black Marquess had been tamed. Or had he? The paper wasn't so sure.

Ciara felt like screaming. She had been married to Lucien for two months and for six of those weeks they had been in London. He had changed. There were so many rules for her to follow.

At least Bryn was settling in well. He went with his father to the races and spent most of his time shadowing his footsteps. Lucien was gone until the wee hours of the morning, and if and when he made it home, he smelled of drink and women.

Through it all, Ciara smiled. She kept her own counsel and rarely ventured out to see Devonna and Rafe, who, also newly married, were in his townhome. The smile that she had on her face felt like it was etched in stone. When would it end?

Endless invitations came to the St. Martin house. Each one Lucien accepted on her behalf, as if she were an idiot and not capable of doing so herself. Her new husband seemed to avoid her unless there was a function to attend, during which he performed his obligatory duties then left her alone to fend for herself.

Most of her days passed in the large gardens in the back of the house with Faolan and Kosse. His friends would stop by to try to catch a glimpse of the elusive animals, but she always had them hidden away. This was what she had feared beyond all measure.

Ciara sent a smile back to her husband and nodded at him, her face schooled into a pleasant mask as she listened to the ramblings around her.

Ciara felt the duke's gaze on her. Enough was enough. Rising, she left the room, heedless of the other stares on her. Lucien was right behind her.

"Where are you going?"

"I don't feel well. I am going to lie down."

He placed his hand on her head. "Should I call a doctor?"

"No." Brushing off his hand, she walked away without looking back.

* * * *

A knock on her door surprised her. She opened it and found herself looking at Foley, her husband's man of affairs, and a bearded man that had a nasty look on his face. Arching a brow, she asked, "Can I help you?"

"I'm Dr. Roman. Your husband sent for me to check on you." He tried to push his way into the room.

Ciara slapped her arm across the opening. "I don't need a doctor."

"Your husband sent for me."

"Then go check on him. I don't need you." She shut the door in his face. Then she locked it. Sitting on her bed with Faolan and Kosse, she looked out of the window. The air was thick and blackened with coal smoke. There was a very pungent odor in the air that made her want to choke. *I want to go home. I want to ride in the clean air and swim.* Covering her face with her hands, she turned her back on the window and curled up against Kosse with Faolan at her feet.

* * * *

"I called the doctor to check on you. Why did you not let him?" Lucien asked.

"I don't need him." Ciara didn't even open her eyes. He had gained entrance to her rooms through a connecting door.

"You don't feel well. You need a doctor."

"No. That's not what I need." Her hand clutched as she tried to keep from breaking down.

"What then? There are things to do tonight, you know. We have places to go."

"Why don't you go? I feel like staying in tonight."

"Ciara, what's wrong?" The bed shifted as he sat next to her back.

"Just a change, I am not used to all this." All this dirt and congestion.

"I know. I forget that you are used to the country. I suppose it can be overwhelming. Maybe I will just go to White's with Phillip then if you are staying in." He patted her on the back. Like a child. "You rest. I will see you later. Maybe a walk in the park will do you some good." Rising, he left the room.

"Getting me out of this damn city will do me some good," she snapped at the closed door. "I hate it here."

She was a prisoner. Her son had a governess and otherwise spent time with his father. She, on the other hand, couldn't go outside without people following her and telling her what to do and where to go. For being a marchioness there certainly were a lot of people that got to order you around.

A walk. Maybe that was what she needed. If only she could take Faolan and Kosse. She changed into what Lucien considered a *proper walking dress*. She considered it uncomfortable. After telling Faolan and Kosse to stay, she opened the door and peeked out and came face to face with a pair of violet eyes.

Devonna. "Where are you going? I saw you leave. Are you feeling all right?"

"I am going to the park for a walk. Would you like to come?"

"Are you sure you should? Lucien said he sent for a doctor."

"I'm going out."

"I'm going with you. Let me just get our maids."

Ciara rolled her eyes. How she hated this, but she waited. Before long, the two women were off walking toward the park. They traveled in silence until they reached their destination.

"Is everything all right, Ciara?" Devonna glanced at their maids, not close enough to overhear but not far enough away to be improper. "You seem different. Are things all right between you and Saint?"

The women came to an open section where there were couples sitting on the ground and kids flying kites. Ciara sat down.

"I don't think I am fitting in here. I hate the city. My husband is gone all the time and sets up all these appointments for me to attend without asking me first." She ran a weary hand over her face. "I miss riding, I miss being able to go outside by myself. I miss my son." She turned her face up to the sun and shoved the bonnet off her head. The warmth on her face almost brought a smile to it. Almost.

Two women stopped by them, deep in their conversation. "Then what happened?"

"I'll tell you. Phillip said that he would bring a friend with him back to my house and that I should just go home and wait with Christie. Sure enough, he brought his friend the marquess with him. Imagine that. I spent the night with the Black Marquess, even though he is supposed to be married. Well, he is. I mean they are having his wedding breakfast this morning. She must not be very good for him to be with me at night. He is supposed to be back to my place again tonight." The women laughed and walked on.

Devonna made as though to jump up and confront them only to be stopped by Ciara. "Let it go." They waited until the women were gone then headed back to the house.

Devonna and Ciara walked back into Lucien's townhouse and saw him in the foyer with the Widow Levon pressed up against his arm, offering him a clear view down her dress front. The shock he had at seeing his wife come in from outside flashed across his face, but he didn't move.

"Saint." Devonna's voice was sharp with disdain. "Lady Levon." She brushed past with no further comment to find her husband.

Ciara looked at both of them. Her heart may have fell to her feet, but her expression didn't change or even offer the slightest bit of emotion. She nodded and walked past them both as she headed off after Devonna.

A bit later, she came back down and found the same widow pressed against him. Bitterness swam in her mouth but she swallowed it back.

"Ciara," he mumbled as he set Lady Levon away from him, "I need to talk to you."

"I am spending the day with the Harringtons. I will be accompanying them to the opera tonight, so you can go with your friends. Have a nice day." She walked past him and out through the door, her back ramrod straight.

"I will accompany you to the opera."

Spinning around, she flicked her eyes over him in a dismissive way. "Don't bother. It appears to me that you are busy." She walked down the steps without looking back and joined Rafe and Devonna in the carriage with her animals, which drove away the second she was inside.

* * * *

The opera was interesting. Ciara didn't pay much attention for she was thinking about her husband. She saw him sitting with the lovely widow in his box. His gaze was on her, however, and not the play, or the lady next to him. Keeping her own eyes fixed on the performance below, she didn't notice when he left. At least that was what she told herself.

As they left the opera house, Rafe helped the women into the carriage. "I will drop you off first and then escort Ciara home," he said to his wife. She nodded and soon it was just Rafe and Ciara in the carriage.

"Rafe, will you take me somewhere?"

"Where?"

"Lady Polly's. I assume that you know where it is."

"Why do you want to go there?"

"Will you take me there or not?"

"Yes. He is a good man, you know."

"Don't defend him to me. I don't want to hear it." She waved him quiet.

They pulled up across the street from the house and, as they watched, another carriage arrived. Out stumbled a very drunk Phillip followed by a scantily clad Christine. Lucien came next, just as drunk as Phillip, perhaps more so, and lifted Polly down. Their lips met as his hands roamed all over her body.

"I have seen enough. Take me home." Her voice was dead. Rafe knocked on the roof and the carriage rolled off, leaving the patrons to their business on the street.

As they stopped in front of the townhome, Rafe stretched out a hand to assist her. After he walked her to the door, she smiled at him and spoke. "Thank you for such a lovely night. I really enjoyed the opera."

Once in her room, Ciara stripped out of her clothes and dressed in her buckskins. She woke her son and readied him for the ride. She sent for a horse and the footman looked surprised but did as she ordered. Within the hour, she was riding back to Heartstone.

Only once she left London did she allow the tears to fall.

* * * *

Lucien came home the next afternoon. "Where is my wife?"

"She is gone." His words were hushed.

"Very well. When she returns, tell her, I wish to speak to her. Is my son with her?"

"Yes, my lord."

That was the routine for the next couple of months. Lucien immersed himself back into his old life and seemed to forget that he had a wife. He would ask about her rarely and didn't seem the least bit worried about his son either, for he was with his mother.

One day a message came from his father's house. The duke was in a bad way health-wise. Heading over right away, Lucien slowed as he entered the house and saw the same doctor his wife had turned away. The man was dirty, scruffy-looking for a doctor.

"How is my father?"

"He is very sick. He should be bled, but he is asking for you. You need to tell him to let me bleed him." The doctor glared at the son as he entered his father's room.

"Father. You sent for me?" Lucien was shocked. His father looked horrible. His skin was pasty and pale. There didn't look like he had any blood in him to be let.

"Where is she?"

"Who? Where is who?" Lucien stood by the bed wondering if his old man was delirious.

"Your wife. Ciara. I want her. You said that she could heal. This old sawbones wants to bleed me. Get her here." He collapsed back against the pillows, gasping for breath.

"My wife?"

"Yes, you idiot. Your wife."

"All right. I will have her come here." Rising, he went to the door and sent a footman with a note to his wife. Then he shut the door on the pacing doctor and went to sit by his father. His wife, he hadn't seen her for a while. He had been avoiding her, almost.

"Where is she?"

"I just sent for her. Why do you want her? I thought you didn't like her?"

"If she healed you after what you went through, she can help me. I am being poisoned. I don't trust the doctor."

"Poisoned? What makes you think that?" How long had it been since he had been with his wife? Too long. He missed her at night, well, the ones he was sober enough to remember.

"Pay attention, boy. Don't let that doctor near me, or my wife. Got it?" The words broke through and caused Lucien to stop and look at his father. He was not acting—he actually thought that he was being poisoned.

There was a knock on the door and he hollered for them to enter and it was to admit not his wife but the same footman with a missive for him. He opened it and just about roared in fury.

My lord, your wife is where she has been for the past two months, at Heartstone. I have sent a rider for her and hopefully she will return before the morning.

Foley

"Well, where is she?"

"Heartstone. She is at Heartstone."

Two months. How had he not noticed? Because he had been out with Phillip and the courtesans. God, he was such a fool. That was why the staff looked at him so strangely when he asked about his wife. He hadn't even gone into her room.

He had been so angry that she didn't want him at the opera, he hadn't spoken to her. Just drank, nothing else. Rafe and Devonna had not been around to see him either. Had Rafe been right?

He knew he had not been unfaithful in the manner of cheating, except for that first night when he kissed Lady Polly. Other than that, he gave off only the appearance of cheating, but his body wouldn't perform for another woman. His sole source of release had been by his own hand. And that he wouldn't admit to anyone, including his wife.

Yelling to the room, he sent a note to Devonna and Rafe to come to him. Then he tossed out the doctor and paced the room as he waited. Devonna came alone.

"Saint?" Her soft voice hit him.

"Where is she?" He grabbed her arm and shook her.

"Saint, please. Don't do that." He dropped her arm and looked down at his sister. She was pregnant, and about at the time when she should be going into seclusion. "I don't know where she is. I haven't seen her since the night we went to the opera. That was two months ago."

"You think I don't know that?" he roared.

"What did you want me to come here for?"

"Father thinks that he has been poisoned." He searched her eyes for sympathy and found none.

"Oh. That's too bad. Is that all? I am tired and wish to go home." She nodded her head coolly at her brother and left how she came. Silent.

* * * *

The duke was worsening. It was predawn when the bedroom door swung open to admit a woman dressed in buckskins, accompanied by a black wolf and smelling of fresh air, honey and berries. Ciara. She walked toward the bed, ignoring her husband, and focused on the man lying there.

"You came. I didn't know if you would." The duke's voice was rough from all of his coughing.

"I wasn't sure I was going to." Flicking a glance at Lucien, she spoke, "I need hot water, clean bedding and towels."

Lucien sent the order to the servants waiting then went to stand by his wife. She moved with efficiency stoking up the fire and opening the windows to let the smell of sickness out.

When her items came, she made the duke drink two cups of liquid then had Lucien move him to a lounge in the sunlight, wrapped tight by blankets. While he dozed there, she stripped the bed and remade it quicker than any of his servants could have done. Once that was done, he carried his father back.

"He is very sick. He also lost a lot of blood. Did they bleed him?"

"I think so." Lucien spoke in hushed words as she made sure his father was sleeping.

"He has a fever. I can't promise anything. I will do my best." She settled down into a chair beside the bed, ignoring the fact that her husband, whom she hadn't seen in two months, was in the room.

"Where have you been?" he asked as he pulled up a chair next to her. He would be calm and get his answers.

"Heartstone."

"Why did you leave?"

"You didn't need me here. You have your mistresses here. I hate the city. I tried to tell you that, but all you did was push me to more appointments to meet more people that wanted to stare at me. I left."

"You didn't tell me." His voice grew hard, as was his body from seeing his beautiful wife and being tantalized by her sweet scent.

"Humph. I doubt you even noticed I was gone. Probably just thought I was out in the garden or something like that."

"Damn it. You are my wife. You belong with me. You will stay here after my father is better."

"No. I will stay until your father is better and then I will leave. There is nothing for me here." Slanting him a cool, unfeeling glance, she added, "Bryn is doing fine, thanks for asking."

That hurt. He had forgotten to ask about his son. Only because he had been worried about her and what she had been doing.

"What have you been doing there? Who have you been seeing?"

"I can't believe you are going to act like a jealous husband now."

"You are mine. I won't tolerate anything but faithfulness from you," he spat.

"Leave. Leave me to nurse your father." She rose and checked on Faolan then sat down and stared off into space.

Lucien erupted. He jumped out of the chair then stomped over to where she was sitting and yanked her up to her feet. He pulled her along out of the door, ignoring the word she mumbled to Faolan, and yelled to a servant that they would be back soon.

Shoving her through the door ahead of him, he then slammed it shut. "Damn you. You are my wife. I did you a favor by marrying you. Do you understand that? If I find out that you have not been faithful, there will be hell to pay."

She nodded and moved past him toward the door. "I have not ever been unfaithful to you."

"I did not say you could leave yet." He advanced on her.

"Enough of this. I came for your father, not to fight with you."

"You are mine, and you would do well to remember that." Lucien was angry with himself but taking it out on Ciara. Two months she had just left him alone, by all accounts not caring what he did or whom he did it with. "Don't you even care what I have been doing?" Not that he had done anything.

"I have a good idea, but no, I don't. I saw you that night, you know. The night of the opera." She added at his blank look, "You were all over that woman—Lady Polly was her name, I believe. I don't have to listen to this or you. We have nothing more to say to each other."

She saw me? From what he remembered, he had been kissing and groping Polly in the street. "I didn't say you could leave. Maybe I wish to claim my husbandly rights."

"Perhaps you should go drink some more. I don't think you are quite rude enough yet." Ciara turned back toward the door. "Don't even think about it. I won't stop him this time." Her voice was hard and lethal.

Lucien looked down into the full fury of a raging wolf. Faolan kept himself between him and his mistress. There was no sign of recognition in his gaze. He wanted to hurt the human he was facing. Lucien stopped. What kind of man tried to terrorize his wife? "Go then. I don't need you. There are plenty other women that would like my attentions."

"I am sure there are. Goodbye, Wolf." She and her now silent wolf slipped out of the door and, as it shut, Lucien felt the walls close in on him.

* * * *

Ciara battled the duke's fever for the next seven days. She rarely ventured out of the room, and when she did, she left Faolan to keep watch over him. She made the food herself for him, not trusting anyone else to make it.

On the eighth day, she was sitting looking out of the window when she heard his voice, gravelly and rough. "You did it. You came."

"Aye."

"Will I live?"

"For a while yet. Are you hungry?"

"Yes." He sat with slow movements in bed. "Was it poison?"

"Aye. It was in your drink. I would be more careful who you trust." She set a bowl of broth by him with some soft bread. "Eat slowly."

When he was done, she gave him some water. "Where is my son?"

"Don't know."

"Are you leaving now?" He watched as she gathered up her herb pouches.

"Aye. I did what I came to do. I must return to my son."

"What about my son?"

"What about him?"

"Is he going with you?"

"Don't know." She headed for the door that flew open before she got there. Lucien stumbled in. He was unshaven and unkempt.

"You are all right?" The slurred question was aimed at the duke on the bed.

"Yes. Your wife did it."

"Ah yes. My wife. The one who doesn't care what I do or who I do it with." He leered at her but kept his distance as he spied the wolf. "Who never goes anywhere without her protector."

"You're drunk."

"How nice of you to notice, Father. Yes I am."

"I will leave instructions with your butler. You should be on your feet in a few days." Ciara spoke to the duke, avoiding her husband, and slipped out of the door and left.

"Are you going after her?" The duke's question followed her into the hall.

"What for? She is just going home. I will see her later. I brought her son to town."

Ciara heard the declaration.

Swinging astride Artemis, she headed for his townhome and retrieved her son. She took him with as she headed back to Heartstone. Ciara was the object of many stares as she rode through the streets of London, in pants, astride a horse, with a wolf and mountain lion keeping pace with her.

Lucien found his man Foley, nursing a bump on his head when he returned to the house. Bryn was gone and there was no sign of his wife. Cursing, he spun to go get her, but got sidetracked by Phillip and an invitation to go to Polly's house.

Chapter Twenty-Nine

A few mornings later found him being awakened by a screaming woman. His sister. Devonna was standing in his bedroom raising the dead with her screeches. It was as if she had never been scared of him in her life. She was on the warpath and he was, by some misfortune, in the way.

"Bloody hell, Devonna. Get out of my room and shut your mouth."

"Get your lazy butt out of bed. I can't believe you. I have let this go for too long. Now you have done it. Get up. Get up!"

He stood up, naked as the day he was born, hoping that would send her running from the room, but all she did was arch a brow at him and toss him his robe. Pounding head, sore muscles and in desperate need of a bath, Lucien glared at his sister. "What are you doing here?"

"Trying to keep you from making any more mistakes. Get dressed."

"I need a bath. I need to shave. You need to leave."

"She's gone." Devonna sat her pregnant body on the bed he'd just vacated.

"Who's gone?" The light was so bright. It was too early for this. "Look, I don't know what you are rambling on about. I didn't get in until this morning because I was, well…"

"I know exactly what you were doing. With who and where. What happened to you? I thought you would have changed. She was perfect for you, you know."

"Who, my wife? She left me. Get that through your head, little sister."

"Watch your tone to my wife, Luc." Rafe's deep voice entered the conversation as he stepped forward and moved next to her.

"You too? What do you want?" Could the morning get any worse? Morning? He needed to sleep until late afternoon at the very least.

"Nothing. I wouldn't be here at all if not for my wife's insistence. I think that you are getting everything that you deserve." Disgust laced his tone and his stance.

"What are you talking about?"

"I am supposed to give this to you. It came to me because she said she didn't know where you were staying." Devonna flipped the note on the bed beside her. "She didn't leave you, Saint. You pushed her away." His sister's voice had softened.

"What are you talking about? I'm still here, she's not." He didn't want sympathy from her. That would make him think about *her*.

"You dragged her to London. When you got here, you dumped her to the mercy of the *ton*. She couldn't go riding, she couldn't go for a walk with her son without five people following her.

"You made her an object that people wanted to see. She tried to change. She wore the dresses and other clothes you said she had to wear. She let you take her son away and put him with a governess. You took her freedom from her.

"My god, Saint. Don't tell me you didn't notice it. She wasn't happy. You told me yourself that they called her the 'heart of the mountain.' What did you think was going to happen when you tossed her into town?

"Then you abandoned her. You started hanging around with Phillip. The morning of your wedding breakfast, on our walk, before we came in to see you holding the Lady Levon in your arms, we heard two women bragging about how they had lain with the Black Marquess even though he had been married.

"All she did was try to make you happy by changing for you. All you did was make her life miserable and make her a laughingstock. 'The American heathen that couldn't keep her husband satisfied. The one with all the awful manners, which is why he sent her back out to the country, so she wouldn't embarrass him.'

"I hope you are proud of yourself, brother, for I am ashamed of you. Take me home, Rafe." His sister and her husband left him there in his room.

In an instant he was stone sober. He raked a hand through his hair and looked at the bed where the note lay sealed. It was his seal on it. Hands trembling, he opened it and read.

I have come to the realization that you do not need a wife.

You have an heir and so now you can go about and do that which every other member of your class does. Fine.

I am taking my son somewhere for him to learn about life.

And love. I don't think you will need to reach me, but if for some reason you do, give the note to my Aunt Fiona for she will see that it gets to me. Don't bother them, for they will tell you nothing. I hope the life you are leading brings you happiness.

Take care, Wolf.

The note fell from nerveless fingers as the reality of what he had done came crashing down on him. She was gone. Truly gone. He felt empty in a way he never knew that he could. He cleaned himself up and called for a mount. He had some serious work to do. He had to find a way to win her back. He had lost her twice now and he wasn't about to do so again.

* * * *

Three months later

After he knocked on the door, he straightened his cravat. Potter opened the door and stepped back to admit him. "They are in the library, my lord."

"Thank you, Potter. I know the way." He waved off the butler and walked down the hall. After knocking on the door, he waited until he heard a voice from within.

"Enter."

Lucien pushed open the door and found himself looking at a very somber woman and her husband. For once, Fiona was wearing dark colors. "Lord and Lady Harrington. Thank you for seeing me."

"Come in and sit down, my lord." Trenton spoke. Fiona assessed.

"I came to ask if you would tell me where my wife is?"

"No," Fiona spat. "She said you weren't to be told."

"She is my wife."

"You dishonored her." Green eyes narrowed in challenge.

"Fi, enough. Let him say his piece." Trenton patted his wife on the arm and, although he received a glare for his words, she clamped her mouth shut.

"Look. Since I got the note from her, I have done nothing but worry. I am staying out at Heartstone and haven't drunk a drop. If that matters. I feel horrible about the way I treated her and wish to make it up to both her and our son. I miss my wife. I just—"

"Did you miss her those two months she was here and you were out with your women? Or the ones that she has been gone from here?" Fiona's eyes flashed with fury.

Lucien couldn't meet her gaze. It was embarrassing. He had behaved like his father had, and worse. "I just would like to send her a note. Would you do that for me?" He felt the chasm between him and his wife deepening.

"Yes. We can do that. Leave the note on the table." Trenton spoke before his wife could. "Do you have one ready?"

"Yes. Yes I do." Lucien handed the note over, only to flinch as Trenton dropped it onto the table. The man didn't even want to hold it.

His gaze cut back to Lucien. "Was there anything else?"

"Have you heard from her? Is she all right?"

"Potter." The butler came and took Lucien's note along with one from Fi. When the man had left, Trenton looked back at him. "Yes, I have heard from her. She is well, as well as can be expected. Lucky for us, she is a strong woman."

"I never meant to hurt her." Lucien's voice was low.

"I would have a word with him, Trenton. Leave us."

Lucien was surprised at her tone and even more so when her husband stood.

"Go easy on him, Fiona. He realizes what he did was wrong." Trenton left them alone.

"I was sorry at first that I encouraged the two of you to wed. I should have realized that it would never work. She tried to tell me over and over again. Regardless of her feelings for you, she knew she could never fit into your world. And yet she tried.

"You took everything away from her. How could you do that? You tried to make her into one of the simpering fools that parade around trying to land a rich husband. You hurt her. I warned you not to take her for granted.

"Regardless of the rumors she heard, and the stares that she endured, she stood by you and defended you against those that would slander your name. She is only human. When she saw you with that 'woman', it was too much.

"I don't know why I am telling you this for she didn't want me to. But I will. When she arrived here months ago, she was carrying your baby. When she took care of your father, she was carrying your baby. She was always ready to give you another chance. But you had to blow it. You threatened her.

"I hope you realize what you lost. There will never be another woman like her, for you. She can't be caged. If you had just showed her that you cared after the wedding, she would have tried. You didn't. You pushed her to do things that she didn't want to do. I hope you realize what you have done.

"You killed her spirit. Her heart."

Fiona left the room.

Carrying your baby. She was carrying his baby. What had he done? He had to find her. Ireland. He would head to Ireland.

* * * *

A very tired, very dirty English marquess stood waiting in the great hall of an old castle in Ireland as he waited for the laird three and a half months later than when he had started out.

"Papa! Papa! You came. Mama said you might."

Lucien grabbed his son as he jumped on him. He held him tight as he blinked back tears. God, he had missed holding his boy. He had grown, but his eyes were still the same.

"What brings you here, English?" Conar. The large man strode into the great room. The man still looked larger than life, and he didn't seem too pleased to see Lucien there.

"I am looking for my wife. Is she here?"

"Bryn. Run and find your grandpa." As the boy scampered away, Conar looked at the man standing by the fire. "I thought you would be here sooner, English. Your wife is not here."

"Don't lie to me. I know she is here. Our son is here. Where is she? I just spent three and a half months finding this place." He was rigid with fury.

Conar was also furious. Lucien found that out when he went down with a grunt from the right hook that came at him out of nowhere to hit him in the eye.

Bryn and the laird came into the room. At the sight of Lucien on the floor, the laird grinned.

"Ye're late, lad. She's gone. Come sit, we will eat and drink."

Within moments, Lucien found himself in the middle of a meal with his in-laws. It was unnerving. His eye was swollen and very painful. They were large and staring at him like they would love to rend him limb from limb. The food was good, and the drink warm. Rory Cormac McKay, Ciara's grandpa, didn't seem to be in any hurry to answer his questions.

"Do you know where she is?" he asked her grandfather.

"Nae. I don't know."

"Papa, did you come to take me home?"

"Would you like to come home with me?" He hoped the desire wasn't too plain for his son to hear in his voice.

"Aye. Mama said you may not wish to take me but I could ask. She dinna say I had to wait here for them to return."

"Them?"

"Aye. Mama and my sister."

"Sister? I have a daughter?" Lucien looked at her grandfather, Rory, for confirmation of the news.

"Aye. A daughter. She is like you in every way, except for her eyes. She has her mother's eyes, she does. Keely Lucina St. Martin. That is the name she gave her bairn." Rory let the man digest the news.

Lucien gave a broad smile as he ran the name over in his head. Keely Lucina. She was named after him. A daughter. "Where are they? When are they coming back? How long ago did she leave?"

"I don't know when they will return. There is a note for you. She left it in case you showed up here. She left close to a month ago. Conar, get him the note."

Lucien waited with impatience as Conar retrieved it and handed it over. He ripped open the note and read it.

I must admit I am surprised you cared to make it this far. That must mean something. You have a daughter of which I am sure you have been made aware. I hope you take Bryn with you, he missed you so. I have been doing a lot of thinking and believe that I am ready to try again. I will be back and we can discuss what we are going to do. Take care of my, our son. Go home and spend time with him. For what it's worth, I forgive you.

I forgive you. He could do anything with her beside him. He would make it right.

Lucien looked over at his son who was chatting away with a cousin and nodded. It was time for him to get to know his son. He looked at Rory and watched the old man for a bit. He was proud like his father, but he loved his grandchildren.

"Did she take Faolan and Kosse with her?" He hoped that she had some protection with her.

"Papa, Faolan died. She took Kosse with her, though."

"How did he die?" He winced as he realized that he should have been there to support her during the loss of her friend.

"Protecting her." Conar spoke up, not disguising that he blamed Lucien for that too. "When do you leave, English?"

"In the morning, if there is an invitation to stay the night? My son and I will leave in the morning. Protecting her from what?"

"You are family. Of course you can stay." Rory rose and stopped by the chair that Lucien sat in, completing ignoring his other question. "Don't hurt her again. I won't stand for it." Waving a hand around the room, he added, "None of us will. We love the lass. If she had not made us give our word, you would not be breathing right now for the pain you caused her."

"So do I." As he said it, he realized just how much. He had always loved her, but now he needed her love in return. "Bryn, care to show me around?"

"Sure, Papa. Let's go." He took his father's hand and dragged him off to parts unknown. He realized they weren't planning on speaking of what happened to him.

Lucien ended up staying in Ireland for a week. When he and Bryn left, Rory had given them a pair of wolfhound pups for the siblings to have, named Thor and Loki. With his son riding on Toka, he shook the hand of the Laird of Clan McKay, his grandfather by marriage. His eye was just a little swollen now and he realized how lucky he was that Conar had hit him only once. That man had a fist like a hammer.

"Take care o' my great-granddaughter. And her mother."

"I will." *When I find her.* "Are you sure you don't know where she went? America?"

"I don't know. I would tell you if I did. Safe journey. Be good, lad, mind your father."

"Bye, Grandpa." Bryn waved as they rode off, followed by thirteen members of the clan escorting them to the ship that would take them back to England.

Chapter Thirty

England
Ten months later

A black horse, bearing a hooded figure cloaked in black, trotted up the long drive made of crushed rocks and shells and came to a stop at the large house that sat at the apex of the curve. It was like they had just materialized out of the lingering mist. There were eight horses roped together to follow the one in front. All of them had steam blowing from their nostrils and rising from their burnished coats in the early morning sun that was melting away the last remaining fog. They were an amazing-looking bunch of cattle.

Loping with ease beside the lead horse was a tawny mountain lion and a small gray pup. A silent footman took the reins as the rider and her bundle dismounted, smiling not only to himself but to all those present as he led the horses to the stables. It was promising to be a wonderful day.

Entering the silent house, the cloaked figure nodded at the butler who stood in shock at the sight. It was as if his serious demeanor had never existed for his mouth was hanging open. After hugging and kissing a passing child for a few moments and handing a small bundle to him as well as the care of the two animals, the figure walked down the hall toward the study, steps, sure and yet silent. The person stopped outside the door, then a hand reached out from beneath the folds of the cloak, and knocked sharply on the door.

"Enter." The deep voice streamed through the door and sent ripples of desire and longing through the person hearing it.

Swinging the door open on soundless hinges, the figure stepped into the room, saying nothing, just searching. The man at the desk was facing the window, looking out toward the forest, looking for something lost, something that had gone. A carved statue sat on one corner of the desk—it was the image of a leaping wolf.

"What did you need, Weeks?" He still faced the window but stilled as a familiar scent flowed to his nose.

"Hello, Wolf." The smooth, husky voice made him drop the papers on his lap then hit the floor as he jumped out of his chair and headed toward the vision.

"Ciara. It's you. You're really here?" Lucien moved around the desk but stopped right in front of her.

His movements became hesitant, as if he wasn't sure his touch would be welcome.

As if after thirteen long months, it would just turn out to be another figment of his imagination. "Take off your hood. Let me see your face."

She pushed back the hood with one hand, and raised her gaze to the blue eyes of the man who held the key to her soul. Her heart. Her being. When he reached for her, she stepped back. "Wait."

Lucien didn't want to wait. But he did. His look filled with love and tears. "What?" The agony in his voice was clear to her, and to him. He didn't care.

Ciara reached beneath her cloak and pulled out a carved box. She set it on his desk and stood back. He recognized the box—it was the one from her parents, the one that had been full with the gold and gems in it, the one with the mix of African and Celtic cultures etched on the sides. "This box must adorn the place I call home." She stared without blinking at him as she waited for the meaning to sink in.

His voice shaking with emotion, he asked, "Does this mean what I think it means? Are you coming home to stay?"

"Aye, if you will have me. Us."

Releasing a breath, he enfolded her in his arms. "Always. Oh, always. I love you." He pressed his nose into her hair and inhaled her scent as the tension flowed out of his body after so long. "I love you, and I will never let you go again. I am so sorry for the way I treated you. I never did anything with those women."

"I'm sorry as well." She pulled back and reached up to cup his face. "Would you like to meet your daughter?"

A wide grin split his face and he looked around anxiously. "Where is she?"

"With Bryn, Kosse and Remy." At her words, the study door swung open and admitted his son holding a small bundle, followed by Kosse and the one who must be Remy. It was a gray wolf cub. Lucien chuckled for his home would never be the same. Bryn walked over and placed the babe in his father's arms, stepping back to be held by his mother.

Lucien flipped back the blanket and saw her sleeping. She was beautiful. She had her father's facial features but they fit her. She would grow up to be like her mother, strong and graceful. As he was staring, she opened her eyes. Whiskey gold.

Keely's face wrinkled and her lower lip trembled as she tried to decide whether the man looking down at her was worth crying for. Lucien ran a finger down her soft tan cheek and was rewarded with a smile. It knocked his socks off and made his knees weaken. She had her mother's smile.

Looking over at the woman who had given him two children, he saw her holding her son, speaking to him in her mother's language, which Bryn had begun to teach him. They were speaking way too fast for him to understand. The one thing he did understand as he sat down on the couch, with his daughter in his arms, a mountain lion and a wolf cub lying at his feet, was that he had his family. Completely. And he was going to keep them. They were his heaven.

Lucien watched as his daughter fell back to sleep. He smiled at his son when he sat down by Kosse on the floor, rubbing the thick pelt of the friend he had missed. Ciara sat down beside him and looked at him. "I know that there are things we still need to discuss."

"It is all over. I have you back and that is all that matters to me." He reached out one hand and cupped her face. "I love you, Ciara. I will tell you that every day until you believe me. I am sorry that I was not there for you when you lost Faolan. I know that I killed your spirit and your heart. We will stay here at Heartstone.

If you wish to wear pants, then you will do so. All that matters to me is your happiness. I want the woman from the wilds of America. The wild, untamed princess that I lost my heart to. The woman that taught me how to live life. My wife. My heart."

One of those rare smiles crossed her face, making it light up. "I do believe you. For the longest time they called me 'heart of the mountain.' I found that you are my mountain and if I am not with you I am without my heart. I love you as well, Lucien."

It was a good thing he was sitting down. Lucien. His eyes widened as he looked at her. "Lucien, you called me Lucien."

"Aye, husband. That is your name, is it not?"

"What about Wolf?"

"I don't sense that wildness about you anymore."

"Say it again."

"What? That I don't sense that wildness about you anymore?"

"No, the other. The part before that."

"I love you. Lucien."

He leaned in to kiss her. "Never stop saying my name. I love hearing it upon your lips. Do you think that I can welcome you home in private now?"

"Aye." Turning to their son, he said, "Bryn. Watch your sister for a while. She can be outside in the sun if you wish to go. Nyama is here along with the rest of the herd, Epona as well."

"Okay, Mama." Rising, he took his sister out of his father's arms and left with Kosse and Remy following.

The second he was gone, Lucien stared at his wife with that predatory look in his eyes. He swept her up in his arms and carried her up the stairs, ignoring the staff.

Kicking open the door to his room, he set her on the bed. "Will you stay in here with me?"

"I will stay anywhere with you." She breathed as she tugged his head down for another kiss that scorched him all the way to his soul.

* * * *

Lucien and Ciara came down the stairs for the midday meal. They ate with their children. After dinner, they sat in the large receiving room and watched as their children lay napping on the floor.

Ciara was curled up on a chaise next to him with his arms around her.

"Where did you go?" He broke the silence in the room.

"After I left Ireland, I went back to America. I had to get some things before I came back."

"Like Nyama and Epona?"

"Aye. Among other things. When Faolan died, I realized that there were some things in life that were more important. Letting our daughter grow up with her brother and father was the most important. I kept Bryn from you. I couldn't do that again.

"I took everything from the cabin and what I didn't give to the town I brought. It's all in town and will be delivered here tomorrow. I brought the horses with and came here."

His arms tightened around her. "Why did Faolan die? What happened? How did you get all the horses here?"

"I made an error in judgment. That's all. I paid a large sum for it. It helped that your name was mentioned. Did you mean what you said about staying out here?"

"If that is what you wish. I like it better out here anyway. Besides, I want to challenge you to a race. I want to know what happened to you and Faolan. You will only delay my finding out."

"Not a good idea. I will win." She elbowed him in the stomach, without malice. "You are too big."

"You weren't complaining about my size a little while ago." He nipped her neck as he whispered into her ear.

"Not now either. Just stating a fact. But, I will be glad too. If the wager is worth it."

"Woman. Watch your tongue. I am still the master of the house."

"Uh-huh. Whatever you wish to believe."

Lucien stole a glance over at his son and daughter and saw that they were still sleeping. He slid his hand down the waistband of her pants and flicked his finger over her clit. When she shivered and moaned, he shushed her.

"Shhh. Don't make any noise. You don't want to wake your son up, do you?"

"Stop it. Don't do this here."

"Why? I want it and, from the feel of things, so do you." He probed one finger deep within her and smiled as he watched her stifle a moan. She was hot, wet and tight. Her body was sucking on his finger and he grew hard as stone in response.

Lucien worked his other hand way up under her shirt to cup her full breast. This time a moan did escape. As he glanced over the back of the chaise, he saw his children were still sleeping. Even if Bryn woke, if he stayed on that side, what they were doing was still hidden from his view.

Lucien rubbed her with his thumb as he dipped into her with two fingers. Within moments she was riding his hand and biting her lip to stay silent, her breath coming short and fast.

A knock at the door froze them in place. "Enter." Lucien spoke but didn't remove his hand, just turned his head toward the door. When she tried to pull away, he flickered his fingers deep within her and made her shiver all over again.

Weeks stood in the doorway. "Sorry to disturb you, my lord. There is a man here to see you."

"Who is it, Weeks?" Lucien asked as his fingers brought her to the peak of an orgasm. He kept her hovering on the edge, the danger of being caught adding to the pleasure that was coursing through her.

From their place on the chaise, there was no way that Weeks could see where his hands were. To him, it only looked like they were cuddled up on the couch. He had no way of watching as Lucien's fingers moved within her most private parts as his other hand teased her hardened nipple.

"He is from London, my lord. One of His Grace's men. He has a note from your father that requires a response. Shall I put him in the blue room, sir?"

Faster and faster his wrist moved, making his fingers go deeper and deeper. "Yes. We will be there shortly, just as soon as we wake the children. Give him some food and drink. That will be all."

"Very good, my lord." Weeks pulled the door shut.

Pinching her nipple, he whispered, "What do you want?"

"Please, Lucien. Let me come." Ciara panted and shook with need.

"Very well, princess. You were good. You stayed put even though my fingers didn't give you any rest." He flicked his thumb and sent her flying over the edge. Her back arched and she dug her fingers into his legs.

* * * *

After reading the note, Lucien waved Ciara over. She needed to see this and decide what she wanted to do. As she sat on his knee, she read the note. The duke requested their presence in London. He was giving a party and demanded his son to attend.

"What do you think, Ciara?"

"I think we should go. He wishes you to be there."

"Fine. We won't stay with him but in our townhouse." He penned a response and gave it to the servant, sending him on his way. "Since the party is in two weeks, I will have us go the day before it starts. That way our time in London will be as little as possible."

"Whatever you think best. Come with me, I wish to show you the horses I brought."

Lucien smiled as he followed the swaying hips of his wife out of the door. Once they were in the stable, he spent a good amount of time viewing the horses that she had brought with her. They were hardy stock and would add endurance to his horses.

As he left the stable, he saw his son running around toward the lake with four animals in tow. Kosse, Remy and the two wolfhound pups that had decided that tangling with the full-grown mountain lion would not be wise.

* * * *

For the first time in over a year, the Marquess of Heartstone spent the night holding his wife in his arms. They spent most of the night making passionate love and rediscovering each other's bodies. When Lucien woke the next morning, he was rested in a way that had been long gone from his life. However, he awoke alone.

Dressing, he headed down the stairs and found no sign of his wife or children anywhere in the house. Approaching Weeks, he posed his question. "Have you seen my wife, Weeks?"

"Yes, my lord. She and the children have left to spend some time out of doors."

"Did she say where she was going?"

"No, my lord. Perhaps Lord Harrington could tell you. He is waiting for you in the library."

"Thank you, Weeks." Lucien headed for the library.

"About time you got here. Were you going to sleep the day away?" Rafe asked as soon as he opened the door.

"What are you doing here? Where is Devonna? Is everything all right with your son?"

"Everything is fine. Devonna is out with your wife and the children. I was told to wait for you and direct you to the place for the day's activities. Let's go." Rafe smacked him on the back as they walked out of the door to their mounts that were waiting for them.

Rafe and Devonna had given birth to a son and this was the first time he had seen them since the birth. When his sister had confronted him that day in his room, he had not been welcome in their home. He didn't even know what his nephew looked like.

He had sent a gift, but wasn't sure that it was accepted. His nephew was named James David Carson. Entering the room and seeing the look of contentment on the face of his friend and brother by marriage, he knew that past actions were forgotten and all had been forgiven.

Lucien had not been very social after he had arrived back in England from Ireland. He had spent most of his time with his son and trying to prove something to himself. And to Ciara should she ever return to him. He had vowed not to make the same mistake again. Knowing that he had found the love of his life, he needed just one more chance to prove himself to her. They would not be split apart again.

Riding over a hill, they headed down into the valley that Lucien had seen Ciara jump her horse in. The day she rode up with Phillip behind her. There on the valley floor were his wife, his sister and their children.

His sister was looking beautiful. She was glowing with pride at being a mother and joy at being with the woman that had befriended her despite her past. He swung his gaze to his wife.

Ciara's head fell back as she laughed in response to something that Devonna had said. She still wore her buckskins but looked stunning. His son was running rampant through the meadow, where the horses were grazing and the animals were playing.

Ciara looked up as she saw her husband ride into view. He was so handsome. He could make her heart stop. "You do love him, don't you?" The question from Devonna made her blink.

"Aye. I do."

"I can tell, that look you have on your face."

"You mean one like you get when looking at your husband?" She cut her eyes to her friend.

"Yes," Devonna admitted, laughing. "I would suppose so. I never thought that I would find happiness like this. I thought it was all unattainable for one like me. You know, not right in the head. I know what they all said about me. It just seemed easier for me to play at being dumb rather than fending off unwanted suitors."

With a loving look at her husband as he rode up toward them, she continued. "I have always had an attraction for Rafe. There was just something about him. I just never thought that it would have been returned. And now, with James in my life, well, I just don't know how it could ever get better."

"I am glad that it all worked out for you both. He is a wonderful man and I can see that he loves you. Perhaps it is true what they say about reformed rakes making the best of husbands." Ciara shook her head as she smiled at the look of agreement that crossed Devonna's face.

"I have a confession to tell you." Devonna's voice grew hesitant. "When I found that you had left, I had mixed feelings. The sister in me was angry that you could do such a thing to my brother, but at the same time I realized that he was being a complete idiot. I know that what happened between you two is not any of my business but I want you to know that I still think highly of you, no matter what happened. I am just so glad that you came back. And brought me a little niece. She is so close to James' age, I just can't believe it."

Ciara leaned over and squeezed Devonna's hand. "I am glad that you don't hold anything against me. I am so glad to have you for a sister. Now I have someone to help me stand up to the men in my life. They can be so stubborn."

"Who can be stubborn?" Lucien's voice intruded.

Both women shared a secret smile and answered simultaneously, "No one." Then they burst out laughing, much to the confusion of their husbands.

Devonna rose and embraced her brother, which he returned with gratitude as all was forgotten. "It is past time for you to meet your nephew, big brother. Come say hello." With a tug of her hand, she pulled him over to where James was sleeping next to Keely.

James had fair hair like his father. Lucien reached out to touch the sleeping child. "His eyes are like mine." His sister gazed with love upon her son.

"He is beautiful, Devonna."

"Thank you. Keely is quite impressive herself. She looks a lot like you."

"Do you think so? I think she looks like her mother. Beautiful." Lucien's voice rang with pride as he turned his gaze to his daughter.

Rafe stood next to Ciara as she stroked Kosse on the head. "I'm glad you have returned. He was not the same without you here."

"We both did some things that we should have done different." Ciara looked off toward her horses.

"Thank you." Rafe spoke with sincerity, reaching for her gaze and holding it once he caught it.

"What for?" She raised her eyebrows in confusion.

"Devonna." He didn't need to say any more.

"That was not my doing. There is more strength in her than you realize." She quirked her lips. "For what it's worth, you are welcome. Just remember that when I teach her to ride astride."

Rafe's eyes grew round. "Luc. Your wife is threatening to teach your sister to ride astride. Help me out."

"No way. You are on your own. Besides, I am going to have her teach me to ride better." Lucien's voice was filled with laughter.

The four adults sat on the blanket and caught up on past events. Soon they were ready for some food, when Kosse raised his head to the crest of the hill. It was Phillip riding down toward them with a companion. It was Polly.

Lucien stiffened, as did Rafe and Devonna. Ciara merely looked and took a deep breath. As they rode up, their horses were not very comfortable with the animals around and they dismounted from the rig in a hurry.

"Good day. I stopped by your house and they said you were having a picnic and we hoped there would be enough for us to join you." Phillip spoke as Polly ogled Lucien with her eyes.

"Of course. Please sit down, Lord Edais, and you as well, Lady…?" The question was there—who was she? Ciara spoke with a calm assurance.

"Lady Ward." Polly spoke with a hint of censure in her voice. "I am a very good friend of your husband's." The unspoken meaning was clear.

"Aye. I have heard that you are one of his *oldest* friends." Ciara maintained her calm tone but her words left no doubt that she wouldn't take anything from this woman. Devonna coughed into her hand as she tried not to laugh at the look of horror that crossed Polly's face.

"Well," she snapped, not at all pleased that she was being made the joke, "you know what they say about those that are old friends…"

"Something like when something is so old it should be set aside for something newer"—Ciara gave Polly a scathing once-over before continuing—"younger and firmer. One that can keep up with him."

Even Lucien and Rafe had to fight to hide their smiles this time. She could hold her own. A quick glance at Phillip told the same story. Polly's face was becoming mottled with rage.

Lucien looked at Phillip. "Why did you bring her here? We are not anywhere near London. What are you trying to do? Phillip, I love my wife and want nothing to do with Polly or anyone like her anymore."

"I was coming out here and she just invited herself along. You know how she is. I am sorry. I know that part of your troubles were because of me." He sounded huffy.

Lucien waved off his apology. When had his friend changed so much? "It's over. You are welcome to stay as long as she remains civil to my family." Looking back toward his wife, he noticed that she had served a plate of food to Polly.

"Why don't you have servants to do this?" Polly asked.

"This was just a family picnic." The words were delivered with meaning—that didn't escape her notice. "We have no need of someone to serve us."

"Oh yes, you delightful colonials. Always determined to do something on your own." Polly's eyes narrowed in challenge. She seemed to have forgotten that there was anyone else present.

"When one is capable of doing so, why not?"

"Because work like that shows only one's breeding. A true lady has people wait on her. She would never do menial tasks."

Ciara stared at her like she was looking at a picture and trying to figure it out. "I suppose that would go for how one lived one's life as well. I mean, take someone who sleeps around. Regardless of breeding, that person would be considered a whore—a high-priced whore, but a whore nonetheless. I would rather have someone see me doing a so-called menial task than have them look at me as a whore. I suppose it all depends on the values one was raised with.

"I, for example, was raised to think and do things for myself. And to respect my body. I guess that would be hard for one who is used to sleeping with men to get what they want." The only sign of Ciara's distress was the hardening of her eyes, but Polly didn't even consider that she was treading on thin ice.

"Well, considering—things—I suppose you would be used to hard work. Aren't most *colored* people in your country slaves?"

Collective gasps went up from the surrounding people. Lucien narrowed his eyes and opened his mouth to speak. Ciara beat him to it.

"I suppose you would think that. Most narrow-minded people do. I am not a slave, nor have I ever been one, so that has no bearing on whether I know hard work or not."

"Well, rumor has it you are a freak."

"Polly, enough," Lucien broke in.

She continued as if she'd never heard him. Her eyes were spitting flames and she had risen to stand over Ciara. "They say that you are unnaturally strong. That you can lift a man. That you kicked in a door and tossed some across the room. They say you even carried Saint." Spit flew from her mouth as she spewed her accusations. "What sort of man would want a woman like that? It was no wonder you had to trap him into marriage with that bastard kid of yours."

That did it. That got a rise out of Ciara.

She rose in one fluid movement, before Lucien could. Ciara was taller than the hateful blonde in front of her and she didn't hesitate to use her height to intimidate. "That's it." Her voice was a deadly purr.

She stalked Polly, making the woman back up step by step. "I don't care if you insult me, or where I come from. However, since your foul mouth dared to insult my son, you go too far."

Polly stood still and tried to act unafraid. Ciara circled around her, as if an animal toying with its prey before the final killing stroke is delivered, as she continued, "Tell me something, Polly Ward. If you heard rumors that I was strong enough to throw a grown man across a room, kick open a door and carry Lucien—alone—why would you upset me? Why would you be dumb enough to slander my son in front of me?"

Ciara tilted her head from side to side as she examined the woman in front of her. "I have wild animals as pets, I am, as you say, freakishly strong—why do you do this? Think about it. If I could do that to a man, just imagine what I could do to you." She leaned her head in close to Polly's ear. "If I ever hear that you speak about my children, in any way—good or bad—you will find out firsthand what I can do to you. Leave. Your welcome has been worn out." Ciara stepped back and pinned her glare on Phillip. "You." She stalked toward him and he rose and backed away from her glowering eyes. "You brought her here. You take her away."

Lucien was so angry he was shaking. Rafe had risen and was standing next to him as well, offering his support and desire to throw them out. A glance at Ciara gave him a short shake of her head as she told him without words that it was over. Lucien just about tossed Polly up into the seat of the rig and, without second glances, Phillip had them riding away, fast.

"Ciara." Lucien turned to his wife. "I am sorry about that."

"Don't let them ruin the day. We have a picnic to enjoy." She let loose a whistle that brought Kosse, Remy, the two wolfhounds—Thor and Loki—and her son onto the blanket to have lunch.

They spent the rest of the day having fun and playing games and riding in the meadow. It was a fun day. When the winds began to pick up, they bundled themselves back up and loaded Devonna and the two infants into the wagon along with the food.

"I should ride with my wife and handle the ribbons." Rafe spoke as he looked over at a horse next to Ciara.

"I'll ride with my sister. You go ride with my wife." Lucien grinned as he watched Rafe kiss his wife and head over to Ciara, as giddy as if he were still a school lad. He climbed in and, with a snap of his wrist, he and his sister were headed back to Heartstone.

"I am going to ride back with you and Bryn," Rafe announced as he walked up to her.

"Very well. Where is your horse? Or were you wanting to ride one of mine?"

"I would like to try one of yours." Rafe was gazing at a gelding by Toka.

"Do you ride without a saddle?"

Shock crossed his features as he shook his head. "No. I need one."

They had his gelding stripped and the other one saddled in no time. Before long the rest of them were headed back up as well. Bryn looked at his uncle and asked, "Uncle Rafe, would you like to race?"

"Sure." He paused. "If it's all right with your mother."

"Go right ahead." Ciara smiled, as she knew what was going to happen—Rafe was about to lose to a young boy. "Line up and I will tell you when to go." The males brought their horses head to head. "Both ready?" At their nods, she shook her head. "The race ends at the stables. Ready. Set. Go."

They tore off and were soon heading up the hill. Rafe didn't have a chance. Bryn was lighter and his horse was faster. Nudging Artemis into a gallop, she rode off after them.

There was pandemonium in the stables when she got there. Bryn was running around screaming about how he won while Lucien was making light of his friend's loss to a boy. Devonna was wisely staying out of it but she was sporting a grin on her face.

Ciara swung down into her husband's strong arms. His eyes smoldered with passion as he let her down the length of his hard body. When her feet were steady on the ground, Ciara sucked on her lip, as she did when she was thinking. How she wanted him.

"Thanks for the wonderful day," she said as he picked up their sleeping infant.

"Thank you." Lucien walked toward the house with his daughter in his arms and his son at his side.

Devonna stood with Ciara as her husband carried his son inside. Soon it was just the two women left with the animals.

"It was a wonderful day. Thanks for inviting us."

"It was past time for you and your brother to see each other. Thanks for coming and bringing my nephew."

Ciara put her arm around Devonna and they headed up the steps side by side. "Are you going to the duke's for the party he is throwing?"

Devonna stopped. "I don't know. Part of me doesn't want to see him, but I should."

"I think you should. Regardless of what has transpired between you, he is still your father." They entered the house and joined their family in the sitting room.

Chapter Thirty-One

The night of the party had arrived. Ciara was going to be at the ducal home at the start of the party pulling hostess duties because the duchess had come down with something and was staying in her room.

"I trust all is ready?" the duke asked from behind her.

"Aye. The servants have done a wonderful job. Your house is beautiful." Ciara smiled as she took in the glitz and glamour of the ballroom. They had outdone themselves.

There were chandeliers full of candles waiting to be lit that would cast a brilliant light down onto the guests. Silks covered the walls, making them flutter with the slightest breeze. The colors were a blend of gold and cream. The chandeliers had mirrors around them and cast the light from the candles off in all different directions, making it sparkle.

The house was beautiful. It was warm and welcome, all in all different from the first time that Ciara had crossed the threshold into the cold mausoleum feel the mansion offered.

Turning, she looked at the man that was standing in silence next to her. The duke had recovered from his battle with poison but he still looked saddened. He was dressed in fine clothes and even at his age cut a handsome figure, until the infamous 'duke' scowl crossed his features.

That afternoon he had met his granddaughter for the first time and seen his second grandson for the first time as well. Devonna and Rafe had come with Lucien and Ciara to see how things were going for the party. They had their children with and it had brought tears to his eyes to see them. Not that he would ever admit that to anyone.

The meeting had been a strained one, but it was a start. She knew he wanted to be a part of his children's lives and know his grandchildren.

"I will see you later. I have to go change." Ciara nodded her head at him and walked off.

Ciara stood next to Devonna as the receiving line was at long last dwindling to an end. "Is it always like this?" she whispered to her friend.

"Unfortunately. At least the line is done." Devonna smiled as she looked over at her sister by marriage. She was stunning and handling the hostess job like she had been raised to do such a task.

"Have you seen my husband?"

"No. I thought he would already be here."

"He said that he might be a little late, but I thought that he would be here by now." Ciara had thought that things were better between them. Had believed that differences had been settled.

"Don't give up on him yet. Let's go get a drink." Devonna pulled her off in the direction of the refreshment table.

They were stopped along the way, by many who wanted to offer their congratulations at such a successful party. While they were drinking lemonade, the band struck up the chords signaling the start of the first waltz.

"My dear, would you do me the honor?" the duke asked Ciara as he bowed before her.

Ciara smiled and performed a perfect curtsy before taking the duke's hand and following him. He was a wonderful dancer and made it easy for her to follow. The dance ended and the duke took her back to the place where she had been standing.

Rafe claimed her for the next dance. As she was whirling about the room on his arm, she felt a shiver run up her spine. But she couldn't make out what had caused it.

Lucien was late. He entered his father's house and shook his head at the majordomo when he was going to announce his presence. He wanted the chance to look for his wife first.

He stood semi-hidden in the darkness of a pillar as he watched his wife dance with Rafe. She took his breath away.

Her dress was almost a sapphire blue, though the exact shade couldn't be said, for as she moved the color changed, shimmered. Although it was cut in a more conservative way than the majority of the women's dresses, he found that she was by far the most exquisite woman in the room. It was apparent that other men did as well, for as soon as she was left by Rafe, many single men approached her and sent what he considered leering looks at her. It didn't seem to matter to them that she was the Marchioness of Heartstone. Her husband wasn't in sight.

Her dress showed off her magnificent figure as she moved around the floor with her dance partners. Her hair was swept up in an elegant coiffeur and accentuated her striking facial features. Her eyes were kind as they looked upon the people surrounding her, but her smile was not the blinding smile that he had come to know and love.

The satin reflected the light, making her appear to glow. Magnificent wasn't the right word. He couldn't find one.

Lucien swallowed, a little nervous, and made to step out to greet his wife when he saw his father approach her. He stopped and watched.

"Ciara, would you do the honor of dancing with me again?"

With a small smile, she curtsied and took the duke's hand. "Of course." She followed him out on the floor as her gaze scanned the room. Lucien hoped she looked for him. When the dance was over, she took a seat by Devonna by an open window at one side of the room.

The room fell silent as the band came to a halt. Ciara glanced at Devonna who shrugged in confusion. The conductor of the orchestra stepped forward to the edge of his platform and spoke.

"I am sorry for the interruptions, but we had a request. Someone wanted to make an announcement to all present, so without further ado."

The man bowed, waved his arm, and as if he were Moses parting the Red Sea, he got the people to split and Ciara gazed across the ballroom floor at her husband.

Lucien had dressed in all black—even his intricately tied cravat was black. He presented a very commanding figure. His pants were tight against corded leg muscles and the shirt snug across broad chest and shoulders. The coat fit his body, showing it had been tailored for him and him alone. His hair was cut short and for the first time she could see every expression that moved across his handsome face. There was no more lock of hair falling across his eye, no hair teasing the collar of his shirt. He was clean-shaven and close-cropped. He looked damn good.

Lucien stood tall, feet spread as if he were standing on the bow of a ship as it clipped across the ocean waters. Eyes sharp and assessing. Hands behind his back as he gazed steadily at the woman sitting on a chair on the other side of the room.

"I ask all those present for forgiveness for interrupting this party. Father, your forgiveness." Lucien's voice was strong and deep as it rolled through the hushed crowd. His seductive yet unwavering blue eyes never left his wife's face.

The room was silent as everyone stared at the marquess, once known as the Black Marquess, the man who had cared for naught but his own pleasure, as he was about to set aside his dignity in front of them all. Willingly. Everyone there knew there wasn't anyone else in the world he would humble himself for aside from the woman he'd married.

"As all of you know, I am married. While it has been well over a year, I still feel like a newlywed. What you probably don't know is what type of woman I married. She is amazing. She is intelligent, smart, kind, loving, and the best of mothers to our two children. Unlike any person, man or woman, I have ever had the honor of meeting. I could go on and on."

Lucien moved across the floor toward his wife. His movements smooth, almost predatory but oh so sensual in his own masculine way, it was his own signature walk. No one else had it—no one else could come close to mimicking it. It screamed Lucien.

"Each day when the sun comes up, I thank God that she is in my life. I didn't appreciate her at first. I heard the rumors, *all of them.*" His voice pinned those guilty of spreading those very lies sharper than if his gaze had speared each and every one personally. "The ones of why she went back to the country while I stayed in London. Those are lies. I have heard that people believe her to be less than worthy of marrying a marquess, again lies. If anything, I am not worthy of marrying her. Her lines are impeccable. She hails from royalty on both sides of her family. She is a princess—she is to be a queen someday. Not that what you think matters to me." He stopped in the middle of the floor and resumed his stance, daring each and every person there to defy his words. To defy him.

"There is nothing that this woman could do that could possibly embarrass me. Nothing." His eyes penetrated his meaning straight into her heart. "I know that it is not popular to show that one has a love match. I don't care. I *love* my wife. I tried to get her to fit into this society and it nearly cost me the best thing that has ever happened to me. I will not stand for *anyone* to besmirch her name."

Lucien glanced behind him and the musicians struck up a quiet and haunting love melody that only added more feeling to his words. Swinging his gaze back to

Ciara, he brought one tan strong hand out from behind his back. In it was a flower.

He was holding a single rose, dusky lavender in color. It offered a beautiful combination against his black clothes and sun-darkened skin. Lucien held the rose out toward Ciara, who sat stunned, confident her expression was the one mimicked across the room.

Lucien's mesmerizing voice reached out to her again, ensuring that she couldn't draw away from the lure of his words that caressed her soul. "Ciara, from that amazing day, eight years ago, that I awoke under your care, I have known. I should have married you back then for I loved you at that moment. I can't apologize enough about the way I treated you at the beginning of our marriage. What I did was inexcusable and unacceptable. I am sorry for making you and our family suffer because of my actions."

To the complete and utter astonishment of all present, Lucien St. Martin, the Marquess of Heartstone, heir to the dukedom of Stokley, dropped to his knees in the middle of the ballroom floor and held that single rose aloft.

Man and flower alone under the hundreds of flickering candles were illuminated, making his entreaty all the more poignant to those that were witness. His head stayed bowed, his voice, becoming tortured, reached out to her. "Forgive me. I know that I have done nothing to earn your trust or your love. I offer you everything that I have." He sounded almost desperate.

Ciara rose. Moving forward, she stopped when she stood in front of her prostrating husband. "Lucien, get up." She tugged on the collar of his shirt.

"Forgive me." He wouldn't even look at her, keeping his magnificent blue orbs gazing downward. His shoulders were quivering with each breath he took and the words he spoke.

Ciara's heart broke. He wasn't doing this for himself—he was doing it for her. Under English law, she belonged to him and he could do with her as he wished. Lucien was showing her that he would snub the very fabric of rules that he had been brought up with if that was what it took to make her happy.

"Take the rose. I didn't know what to get the woman who never seemed to want anything I had to offer. I chose a rose because it reminded me of you. Simple. Elegant. Strong. Unparalleled in beauty. I will get anything for you. You are my everything. Please."

That last word, desperate, wanting, pleading, nudged her into motion. Ciara took the rose from his hand and brought it to her nose, inhaling its rich scent. Her eyes closed as she let the fragrant smell inflame her senses. Tucking it behind her ear, she reached down under Lucien's bent chin and nudged his face up to meet her eyes.

When she was looking into his midnight eyes, she smiled. As the tears filled her eyes, she said, "I forgive you. I always had. All I ever wanted was you. I love you, Lucien Remington St. Martin." Tugging again on his collar, she added in a sharper tone, "Now get up off the floor, please."

With one graceful move, Lucien was standing tall over her again. Tan lean fingers cupped the bronze face as lips met. They kissed until the cheering of the gathered crowd penetrated the haze they were surrounded by.

Moving his lips from hers, he drew back so there was a small space between them. "I love you, Ciara Malika St. Martin. I will always love you."

Heedless of the people watching them, she threw herself into his arms, entrusting that he would catch her as he always caught her, with those arms that made her feel so safe, so protected, so loved. Ciara wrapped her arms around his neck and placed a kiss on his lips that would have the whole of London talking for years to come.

When her feet reached the floor, Lucien made a gesture to the musicians and they began to play a waltz.

"Princess." His voice was loud and clear. "Would you do me the honor of a dance?"

Ciara swept a graceful curtsy as she inclined her head in a regal motion. "It would be an honor, my lord."

* * * *

After the party ended and they were back at their own townhouse, Lucien kicked open the door to their bedroom, his wife firm in his grasp. Setting her down on the bed, he once again got on his knees in front of her. "Ciara, I have something for you."

"Lucien, you have given me everything that I could ever want."

"Except a ring." He pulled a box from his pocket and placed it in her hand. "Open it."

"You gave me a ring." She held up her hand that had the plain band on it.

"That was not the one I wanted for you. This one is."

Ciara opened the box. Inside lay a ring that consisted of a wide band holding a topaz surrounded by small diamonds. The band itself had etchings on it, both

African and Celtic. "Ohh, Lucien. It's beautiful." She slipped it on. Perfect fit.

Eyes bright with unshed tears, Ciara reached out for her husband. Lucien moved into her arms and, as they undressed each other with care, they realized that this was what they had searched for.

Chapter Thirty-Two

A few weeks later, back at Heartstone, Lucien worked hard with the colt, Storm, as he half watched his son riding past, going to join his mother and sister.

"Good day, Luc."

Lucien turned to see Phillip standing there. He looked sober and worried. "Phillip, what brings you here?"

"Just stopped by. Thought I should apologize again and see if I was still welcome here."

Lucien smiled. "Of course you're welcome here. How are things in London?"

Phillip leaned on the fence as he watched his friend. "You look well—marriage must agree with you."

Taking a deep breath, he turned the colt loose and walked over to his friend. "It is the best thing that ever happened to me. I am pretty sure that Rafe would also agree. When can we expect you to lose your freedom?"

Before Phillip could say anything, someone else did. "Yes, Phillip. When are you getting married?" It was Rafe.

"Rafe." Phillip smiled as he greeted his friend. "The wife let you out of the house so soon?"

"I am the man. I can do what I want."

"Uh-huh. If you say so. Marriage may work for the two of you, but I have no intention of giving up my freedom. There is not a woman alive out there that can keep me interested for the rest of my life. I like the life of a rake."

Lucien grinned. "I don't look at it that way. I am happy. I have everything that I could want."

"Don't you two ever miss your freedom? I mean going out with different women and not being tied down?"

"Yes, Lucien. Answer his question. Do you ever miss that?" Ciara's voice broke in. As one, the men turned and swallowed when they saw her sitting on her horse. Phillip blanched. Ciara shook her head at the men. With a wink at Phillip and a smile for her husband, she added, "Sorry. I don't mean to intrude. Lunch will be in a few minutes. Lord Edais, will you join us?"

His answer was stammered. "Y-yes. That would be fine. Thank you, Lady Heartstone."

"Call me Ciara. I don't like all that formality stuff. Rafe, I am to tell you that you and your wife will be joining us as well. See you inside." She rode off, disappearing into the stable, leaving the men in both awe and amazement as they watched her graceful movements.

Lucien smiled to himself as he watched the woman he had the privilege to call 'wife.' She was a work of art. Every movement, every motion was beautiful to watch. Sighing deeply, he slapped his friends on their backs. "We should get inside."

Phillip had never felt more like an outsider than he did at lunch that day. Not that the company he kept made him feel bad, or awkward. It was that they seemed so bloody happy with their families. The looks on his friends' faces when they picked up their infant children. The love that was in their gazes as they kissed their wives. It hurt him to think that maybe Rafe and Lucien had a point. For in truth, they didn't seem to be trapped into anything undesirable at all.

Phillip looked around the table and watched his friends smile. They had never been so relaxed-looking before. Rafe was holding his heir and looked content. His wife, Devonna, was bending over a piece of paper that Lucien's eldest, Brenden, had drawn and was showing her.

Ciara sat beside her husband, holding in her arms their daughter, Keely. Lucien was speaking to Rafe about his stables and every now and then would send a secret smile toward his wife as he looked on in wonder at his family. On the floor over by a wall lying sprawled out in complete silence were the rest of the clan, a mountain lion, a wolf cub and two Irish wolfhounds. They were well-behaved despite the conversations going on around them.

Phillip slid his gaze back toward the woman that had snared The Black Marquess. She was intriguing to him. Lucien was right, there was something about her that made a person sit up and take a second look. When he glanced up at her face, he saw that she was staring at him with those unwavering whiskey-colored eyes of hers. It was like she was evaluating him and taking his measure.

Ciara stared at Phillip. The man was a mystery to her. By all outward appearances, he seemed to be one thing, and yet at times he appeared to be completely different. In truth, he seemed to be unhappy. Like his actions were ways for him to avoid the real issue bothering him.

She realized that this quandary of a human male was in fact still nervous around her. Ciara didn't hold a grudge against him. What happened back then was between her and Lucien.

The fact that he'd brought Lady Polly Ward with him that one day had been harder to forgive. She had done it, but it had not by any means been easy.

Ciara turned her attention to the infant she held in her arms. Keely was a miracle. The birth had not been an easy one—she had come way too early. When she came, she hadn't been breathing at all.

Now, she was a strong girl. Growing and smiling at everyone. Bryn looked after and loved his little sister.

There was no jealousy from him. He loved being with her. Keely didn't cry much and she would follow Bryn with her eyes, grinning and drooling when she would see him smiling at her.

The adults spent the rest of the afternoon outside. The nice fall days were coming to an end and Ciara wanted to enjoy them as much as possible.

* * * *

In the weeks preceding Christmas, Lucien was summoned to London. The duke sent the note but no other explanation.

Ciara was lounging in the salon when Devonna stuck her head in the door. "Ciara. Mind some company?"

"Come in, Dev. Did you bring my nephew?"

"I left him with Bryn, Keely and the governess." She shut the door and sat down on a couch.

Ciara had just sat up to ring for tea when Mrs. Ashley knocked and brought in tea and snacks. After she'd left them alone, Ciara smiled at her sister-in-law. "What's the matter, Dev?"

"Rafe was summoned to London by Father."

"Lucien as well. Maybe it means they found Richard."

The door opened and in came Bryn followed by the governess and both babies. "Sorry, my lady. He wouldn't stay in the nursery any longer." Her disapproving tone was clear.

"That's fine." Ciara opened her arms to hug Bryn as Devonna rose to get her son. "I always have time for my son."

"With all due respect, milady, you should be sterner with him. The children ought to be seen, not heard, and only seen at certain times. Left to run loose like this can only bring trouble."

"My son is not causing trouble." Ciara's voice sharpened. "This is his home and if he wishes to leave a room he may do so. I will not allow my son to feel like a prisoner in his own home." She removed her daughter from the dour-faced woman.

"I am doing what I was hired to do." Her words snapped with condescension.

"Your point?"

"That the Marquess of Heartstone hired me. My reputation is well known for dealing with unruly children. If allowed to do this my way and without interruptions, I will have him groomed into a proper child of a marquess."

"Regardless of who hired you, I am his mother."

"My lady, most mothers don't interfere and allow me to do my job. In the end, they are happy with the results. I don't have a biased opinion and can see the children for what they are."

Devonna pulled Bryn down on the seat beside her as she watched the governess sign her own dismissal. "Mama's mad, isn't she, Auntie Dev?"

"I would bet so." She ruffled his hair as they watched the scene unfold in front of them.

"What exactly is my son, really?"

"A child. But one sorely lacking in manners. That's why I was hired."

"Exactly. Was. Not anymore."

The large woman drew herself up to all of her completely unimpressive and stocky height. Her broad shoulders were quivering with indignation as she struggled to regain her composure. She was an extraordinary governess, her services highly sought after by the *crème de la crème* of the ton. She was never prematurely dismissed. This was an outrage. She said as much.

Ciara believed that the teacher could be compared to a fish with her mustached mouth gaping open and shut. "I am relieving you of your position. As you claim there are many who wish for your services, you shouldn't have a problem getting work."

"You can't dismiss me. I was hired by the marquess." The woman shook with rage. "He will hear of this."

"My husband"—Ciara began. Her tone, befitting her station, as regal and pompous as Devonna had ever heard—"may very well have hired you. However, as the case may be, he is in London and I am Bryn's mother. I want you gone. Feel free to send him a note, for you can be sure that I will. Weeks will send some footmen to accompany you to gather your things and take you to the nearest coach. Good day."

Ciara sat there with an expression that dared anyone to contradict her order. Silent footmen stood behind the ex-governess as if summoned by a bell pull and given verbal instructions, when in fact Ciara hadn't touched the rope or called for them.

* * * *

Lucien and Rafe weren't having much more fun in London. Richard had resurfaced and they were trying to figure out a way to make him pay for his heinous crime without dragging Devonna's name into the open.

Richard was being held at the holding center while they figured out what to do with him. Rafe had an idea of what should happen to him but, while Lucien seconded it, they knew they couldn't do that to him.

The duke maintained his calm while he argued with his wife on what to do with her favorite child, the child of hers which could do no wrong in her eyes and therefore shouldn't be punished for the crimes that she believed had been levied against him in some form of injustice.

As tensions were rising in the Stokley household, there were problems at Bow Street holding house number six. An explosion rocked the house, shattering windows and spewing shards of glass. Smoke rolled and billowed as men dressed in the scarlet clothes that had given them their nickname, Robin Redbreasts, scrambled to restore order in the ensuing chaos.

The night progressed as they rounded up the detainees and tended all injuries which had been obtained during the blast. Once things were calmed down and were getting back to what passed for normal around there, prisoners back and accounted for, they discovered one was missing.

Richard Quentin Nidels. The stepson of the Duke of Stokley, Sebastian St. Martin.

Sam Whip, a veteran runner of the Bow Street constables, was sent to deliver the unpleasant news to the St. Martin house.

"What do you mean he escaped?" The roar from the duke reverberated throughout the stone mansion.

Lucien and Rafe watched as Sam tried not to flinch under the fury of the duke. While outraged in equal amounts, the two younger men wanted to hear as much information as they could.

"Luc." Rafe spoke in a subdued voice that allowed only Lucien to hear him. "If he has realized that she's told of what he did to her, and now he has escaped…would he? Do you think?"

"Yes. I think he will go after her. Damn it all. I wanted to spend a nice Christmas with my wife and kids, not worry about Richard." Making his decision, Lucien headed for the door, Rafe right beside him. "Let's go. I will not leave them unprotected. Father, you do what you must here. With him free, our wives are in danger."

"I will join you at Heartstone as soon as I have made some arrangements," Sebastian told his son and son-in-law as he waved them off with a hand. It was time he put his family first and he was not going to fail his beloved first wife again.

* * * *

Lucien and Rafe rode hard and fast into the falling snow. Winter had arrived and it had done so with a vengeance.

The two men had to stop along the way to allow their animals the chance to get warm and dry. As soon as was possible, they headed back out.

The climatic conditions were foul. They couldn't run their horses and, at the speed they were going, neither of them was very happy.

Plodding along at what he considered to be a slower pace than that of a dead turtle, Lucien found himself wishing he had one of the much hardier horses that his wife had brought with her. They could handle this better than his high-stepping, fancy hunter.

* * * *

The upcoming Duke of Stokley rode into Heartstone Manor cold, wet and accompanied by his brother-in-law, a little after the sun had risen. Not that it did much in the way of warming the countryside for it was still snowing and cold.

A footman took their tired mounts as they entered the building, taking the icy steps two at a time. The warmth that hit them stopped them in their tracks as their frozen bodies absorbed as much of the heat as possible.

Once warm, Lucien noticed that the doors were open to the ballroom and there were servants scurrying about with food, drinks and wood to keep the fires going. It sounded like there was a party going on inside.

Scanning the entryway for Weeks, Lucien noticed his home was decorated for Christmas. It was beautiful, warm and inviting. The only thing missing was his family.

"Weeks, where is my wife?" The question slipped from his mouth as he spotted his elusive butler.

"In the ballroom, my lord. Your sister and children are there as well." Weeks allowed himself a rare grin. "Her family has arrived." As he turned away, he stopped. Weeks spoke once again, solemn, "Your brother Lord Richard is there as well."

Those words sent icy chills down both of their spines, eliminating the relief of hearing that the McKay Clan had arrived. Long strides took him to the entrance of the ballroom.

The sight stopped him and brought Rafe to a standstill beside him. The room was full of people. People Lucien didn't know in the slightest. People not of Clan McKay.

The elegant ballroom was full of people dressed in flowing silks of many colors. They were covered with more gold than either man had seen on a member of non-royalty. They looked richer than the king.

They were all striking. Their skin tones varied from a light tan to the darkest coal. His ballroom was full of African royalty.

Richard was in the corner guarded by two men that made even Lucien feel small. They stood with their arms crossed over massive chests and appeared to be carved out of stone. Richard was sitting on the chair, making no trouble.

Ciara was sitting next to a very dignified older couple. The man had dark skin, wrinkled with age. His hair was white, making him appear more striking. Seated next to him was a woman who, despite her years, was incredibly stunning. Her hair was jet black and her skin was the color of rich honey.

They alone had on gold headbands that made Lucien believe that these two were of the highest rank in the room. "Ciara." His voice brought the room to a standstill. Silence descended.

A brilliant smile spread across her face as she rose. "Lucien. Come meet my grandparents." She pressed a kiss on his lips then led him over.

The elder male pinned a gaze on Lucien that had more effect than he would like to admit. "Lucien, meet my grandparents. The reigning king and queen of the kingdom of Shar'al."

Lucien sketched a bow that was reserved for royalty. The queen inclined her head in acknowledgment. The king did nothing except assess with his eyes. "It is an honor to meet you both." Lucien looked up as Bryn came running into the room.

"Papa! You're back." Bryn threw himself at Lucien and, as he was caught by his father, the king allowed himself a smile.

Holding tight to his son, he looked at Ciara. "What is Richard doing over there?"

"He made the mistake of trying to come after Devonna and me in the presence of the king's guard. They are holding him for Rafe to decide his punishment." Ciara grinned at him. "They are here for the Christmas season. They brought some gifts. Two are with Kosse."

He arched an eyebrow. "More animals?" When she nodded, Lucien dropped his head back and laughed. "Then it shall be a wonderful Christmas indeed."

Lucien set down his son and bowed once again to the king and queen. "I am pleased to have you in our home to share this time with us."

Dinner was awesome. There were foods they had never had before and each one was a delicacy that tantalized senses. Rice flavored with rich spices, meats that pretty much fell apart in the mouth—they were so tender and succulent.

When they were enjoying an array of desserts, the door opened, admitting a very flustered duke. A very angry duke. "What is going on here?" He glanced around the room filled with imposing dark-skinned people. The bravado that he had been emitting seemed to wither and die in before those present.

Lucien turned back to his new in-laws. "Your majesties, may I present my father, Sebastian St. Martin, the Duke of Stokley, Marquess of Loqueal, Earl of Antliath, Viscount Tover..."

The king waved away the endless litany with a flick of one impressive, adorned hand. Bestowing a nod upon him, Lucien turned back to his father and spoke to him this time. "These are Ciara's grandparents, their majesties, the King and Queen of the Kingdom of Shar'al."

The night passed in smooth fashion as the families met and mingled with each other. The one, the sole one, in the house who did not was Richard. As the hours of darkness turned to the morn, he knew that his fate had been sealed.

* * * *

Christmas morning came to Heartstone. The grounds were covered with snow, making the whole estate feel pristine and pure. The massive tree that had been taken into the parlor sat covered with candles and surrounded with presents for the children, and a few for some of the adults.

Ciara sat alongside her husband as she watched her eldest child pass out presents to the adults in the room. Bryn's footsteps were dodged by Remy the wolf, Thor and Loki the wolfhounds, and by the newest additions to the family, Arrow, who was a cheetah cub, and Leah, a Serval kitten. Her grandparents had also brought with them a trained black eagle.

Complementing the animals, they had brought lots of silks and other fine woven materials and trinkets of gold. What they brought was nothing to them, but to the English, it was a lot of wealth.

As they opened presents and ate the immense Christmas dinner, Lucien realized that he had everything that he could possibly want, need or desire. He had a family. As his contented gaze centered on the love of his life, she blinked and smiled at him. A smile that reached up to her amber eyes and filled them with love as she smiled a smile that he knew exactly the meaning of. Him alone. The smile was just for him and it rocked him to the core. *I love you.*

Ciara snuggled up closer to her husband and soaked up his warmth. As his strong arm settled around her and tucked her in closer, he placed a kiss on her head. Heedless of the others in the room, Ciara raised her face to Lucien's and meshed her lips upon his. She was home.

Merry Christmas, daughter. We are proud of you. The words echoed in her heart as she leaned up against the man that meant the world to her. Her marquess.

Want to see more from this author? Here's a taster for you to enjoy!

The Monroe Sisters: Need You Now

Aliyah Burke

Excerpt

"Sometimes, you just need some dick."

Eva snorted, the margarita burning her nose as it exited, making her cough and her eyes water. "Did you just—oh, never mind, of course you did." She glared across the table at her sister with the vulgar mouth, Tara, as she accepted the napkin handed to her from the third member of the group. She wiped her lips before she dabbed at the corners of her eyes, hoping this incident hadn't turned her into a damn raccoon with how her makeup was running.

"What?" Tara blinked her almond-shaped black eyes, appearing unconcerned with her statement and how loud she'd made it. "It's true, a good fuck can go a long way." She sipped her Chardonnay and gestured to their other sister, Shai. "Tell her. I mean, she's a doctor. You'd think she would be aware of the benefits." Tara flipped her braid back over her shoulder, the pink streak in it vibrant and outgoing, much like the woman herself.

Shai drained the rest of her extra-dirty martini and put the glass down. "Tara's correct. You need to get laid. All of us do." She gestured for another drink.

Eva shook her head. She was the eldest and these two knew how to test her. "How did we go from my day to talking about a hookup?"

"Because your day didn't include one." Tara toasted her.

She sighed dramatically. *I highly doubt yours did either, Tara.* "That would be your logic. And just for the record, counselor, I'm a surgeon, not a regular doctor."

"Pretty sure there's a fucking MD after your name and I've seen you put DR in front of it. Or so it was the last time I saw you sign something."

Glaring at Shai, she huffed with as much indignation as she could manage to pull off having just choked on a drink moments prior. "No one asked for your opinion, professor."

"That's why I gave it. I am a professor. I interject when all the facts aren't present. I'm an educator." Shai flashed a grin, her white teeth stark against her smooth nut-brown skin.

"Why do I agree to come out with you two?"

"Because we're family and you love us," they responded in tandem.

"Ask me later about the love bit," Eva retorted as she gazed around the table.

Shai, the baby of the family, was the youngest tenured professor at the university. Eva's parents had adopted her when she was only six months old. Tara had joined the family at age two and held the middle-child distinction. All three of them were thick as thieves.

Running a hand over her spike cut, she spied a guy standing by the bar, eyes on the three of them. Her heart kicked up a few notches as recognition set in, but she couldn't pull from her memory banks just where she knew him from.

"Who's McHottie?"

"What?" she asked Shai.

"Which barfly are you staring at?"

"None."

"The witness is becoming hostile. I believe I should press the point," Tara added.

Eva faced her sister and muttered, "Bitch."

"Later," Shai said. "I've been thinking about what was said earlier."

Eva glanced over at her, eyebrows up in silent question.

"You know, about you not getting any cock."

She covered her eyes. "This is the problem—well, one of the problems—with having a professor and an ADA as siblings, you two are used to having to yell. There is something called an inside voice. You know, where you talk quieter, so the entire bar doesn't learn about me not having sex lately?"

"Because that was stated so eloquently and with your inside voice." Shai's tone dripped with humor.

Lord, could the floor just swallow me up? She met the amber gaze of the man across the way.

From the way his bow-shaped lips had kicked up, he'd overheard the embarrassing exchange. He raised his beer in her direction.

"Focus, please."

Professor tone. That's what Eva called it. She'd heard Shai use it numerous times in her classes and it never failed to silence the noise even in an auditorium. However, her sibling had a way with people and could easily get them to listen to her. It was a gift.

"I need a refill for this," Eva groused, waving for another pink-grapefruit margarita. "Especially since the last bit wasn't enjoyed as it exited my nose."

Her sisters exchanged a look and she realized they'd already discussed this and were springing it on her, tag-team style. As they waited, however impatiently, she allowed her gaze to drift back across to where Amber Eyes stood talking with three other men, also good-looking, but none of them rang the bell of recognition for her. His eyes flickered in her direction more than once and she again scrambled to recall where she'd seen him before. He wasn't a random hookup, she didn't do those, but from the way he watched her, there had to be something she was missing.

"Here you go." The waiter set her drink in front of her and took away the empty.

She nodded her thanks and put her attention on her sisters.

Tara with her hot-pink bangs and the long stripe down along the right side of her glossy jet-black hair. Then her gaze flickered to Shai with her purple streak in her dark brown pixie cut. Yep, trouble in their eyes and sass on their lips.

"As I was saying," Shai began again, "we've all been insanely busy. I mean, even for us to get here tonight, we've had to reschedule this three times. Tara and I have already talked about this and we need to step up and take control of our sex lives. Or the lack of them, as the case has proven to be."

"I haven't found a guy I want." Eva rolled her eyes at the lie that poured from her mouth.

Guys led to things like thinking of the future, and that typically meant children, which was where she shut down. She was sterile. Would never have a child of her own the natural way. And while she told herself she'd come to terms with that fact, the truth was she hadn't. Nor was she ready to try to explain this to a man who she'd fallen for only to have him say no and rip her heart out all over again before stomping it into tiny smeared lumps of muscle.

Her siblings sneered in response, yanking her from the depressing dark hole she was falling into as if she'd stepped off a building to embrace gravity.

"It needs to happen for all of us," Tara took over. "We're professional women who are dedicated to our careers and have neglected ourselves. That's unacceptable. We don't have to give it up. Men find a way to do this, which means obviously so can we. This is what we came up with."

Shai nodded. "We each take a week from work. All the same week and pick a beach. We go there, have a room and find some stranger to fuck. A week-long one-night stand, so to speak."

"We're going to the same place?" Eva pushed the instant *no* from her mouth, her body jumping to life, waving its hands, demanding some one-on-one attention from a person of the male variety. Battery-operated machinery wasn't cutting it. Neither was the touch of her own fingers.

"Nope, different ones. If we were together, then we'd be together and wouldn't be getting laid." Tara moved her glass to the side and rested her elbows on the table.

"I can't just take time off," she protested.

Tara glared at her. "Neither can we, but we're planning ahead, so it's not just taking time off. It will be considered a vacation—something we are actually allowed to indulge in. Same week. Different locales. A week of hot, guilt-free, mind-numbing, leg-shaking, can't-move-a-muscle-after, sweaty-all-over kind of sex."

Eva couldn't deny how amazing that sounded. *So long as I can keep my internal commentary shut down about how great he may or may not be with a child.* Damn it, she wasn't supposed to go down this road. She lifted her drink. "Here's to us and our weeks."

"No more arguments?" Shai questioned with a raised eyebrow.

"Nope, you said it perfectly. We've put others before us for too long. Time to take the bull by the horns, so to speak." She drew her phone from her gold clutch. "Where are we each going and when? Different beaches, but same distance of travel? Like we all head to places in Mexico. That way, we can tell Mom and Dad we're taking a vacation together."

"Agreed." Tara's statement was followed within seconds by Shai's succinct one.

They had their phones in their hand moments later as they each picked a location.

* * * *

Puerto Vallarta

Eva shouldered her purse and walked off the plane. The sun shone bright through the airport windows, making even this place seem cheery. As she headed for baggage claim, she withdrew her cell phone and sent a text to her sisters, alerting them she'd landed fine.

She stood with the others and scanned the group waiting for their luggage to come. According to her sisters, all she had to do was pick the guy she wanted and go from there. *God, we should have done this before. I cannot wait to get this vacation started. Now, all I need is to find the right one.* Hell, it was like a candy store. *I pick whichever one I want. No harm, no foul. This is strictly about me and my need to get my world rocked. No strings, no fuss, no muss.*

It didn't take long to secure her luggage or grab a cab to the hotel. Bag on the oversized chair in the corner, she flung open the doors leading out to the balcony. Beyond the railing, the ocean beckoned. The Midwest just didn't have places like this. Not that she had an issue with where she lived...it just wasn't Puerto Vallarta. There were no sandy white beaches with a beautiful blue water outside her window, bringing the sounds of laughter and the scent of the ocean.

Her phone buzzed and she reached for it, smiling as she found a text from Tara.

Glad to hear it. Just pulling up to the gate now. Have fun and ride him hard.

She chuckled and replied with a smiley face. "I would love to ride him hard. Now, I just have to find him first." She opened her suitcase and tossed the phone to the king-sized bed. "That isn't going to happen if I'm keeping to myself in the room." Rooting through her clothing, she found her bikini. "So I need to get down to the sun." Once it lay on the bed spread, she reached for the first button on her white shirt.

After she'd changed, she checked her phone again. Still nothing from Shai, and that worried her, so she sent her another text. According to the itinerary, her sister should have landed already at her destination, and it wasn't like Shai not to send confirmation.

* * * *

The moment she walked into his line of sight, Grant Harrison was mesmerized. Her peach bikini made his dick rock-hard in seconds with how her suit curved around her figure. Tiny waist, toned muscles and a sway to her hips he couldn't manage to tear his gaze from. She carried a small beach bag, not huge and oversized like many of the tourists.

He slid off the stool, grabbed his drink and trailed her to the edge of the hotel bar as she stepped out onto the sand. She turned heads as she walked by to the water. Both men and women took in the view she offered. Drink finished, he followed the same path she took to the beautiful blue water.

His mysterious goddess walked along the edge, the water lapping over her feet. As he watched, she relaxed. He could see the stress in her melting away beneath the warm sun. While not as tan as a lot of the women, strolling practically nude, she still stole his breath.

Heated sand beneath his feet warmed his soles as he navigated to her side. Stopping there, he crossed his arms and glanced down at her. "Beautiful," he commented.

A smile quirked her lips. "Yes, gorgeous. Don't have views like this back home."

He didn't even lift his gaze from her curvaceous form. "Me either."

"I was talking about the ocean."

"Water is water in my opinion. It's what goes with it that makes it beautiful." He had no qualms about being caught staring at her. "Name's Grant."

She angled her body toward him and he dragged his eyes up the front of her bikini, swallowed hard, blinked to see her belly button again and did it once more. High on her hips, the top material dipped low over her chest, teasing him with smooth, pale skin. While not overly huge, her breasts filled out the top in a mouthwatering display of feminine perfection. The dark coral hue smashed into him as if he'd just ingested a plate of oysters and was more than ready to show how good his libido was.

"Eva. And where is home, Grant?"

Yes, her lips mesmerized him as well. "I travel quite a bit for my work, but for the moment, it's in Arizona. For you?"

"Quad Cities." She ran her gaze over him, her hunger spilling free. "An area covering Southeast Iowa and Northwest Illinois."

Christ, it had been a while for him if this was what his small talk amounted to. It shouldn't be this difficult. Not to make his intentions known and find out if she was receptive of them or not. He moved closer, the air between them sparking and charging. "And what do you do there?"

"Work," she said, her tongue flicking out to dampen her lips. She never took her eyes from him. "Too damn much."

He kept his gaze locked with hers. "Nothing more specific?"

She lifted her hand and settled it on his chest. "Are you here with someone?"

"Not other than you." His heart pounded and his dick swelled further. Christ, he was going to puncture his suit if he didn't get some relief soon.

"Wife?"

"Never. Husband?"

"Not yet." She splayed her fingers and moved them through his chest hair. "Are we going to stand here and discuss the ocean or go somewhere else?"

"Somewhere else. My room is right back there."

She never looked to where he pointed.

He snaked his arm around her waist and drew her flush to him, his cock pushing against her. "I've wanted to fuck you ever since I saw you walk by me."

She looped her arms around his neck, tongue peeking out to hit the corner of his mouth. "Don't hear me complaining, do you?"

He lifted her in his arms, wheeled around and strode back to the hotel, staring in her eyes the entire time. Even in the elevator, he didn't put her down. Not until they got into his room did he allow her feet to hit the floor. Then he kissed her.

Grant groaned at her taste, a mixture of coffee and mint. When she backed away, he let her, but he kept staring. Her lips turned up in a small smile as she reached behind her neck and pulled. The top of her bikini fell to the carpeted floor of his hotel room.

Holy shit.

With a sure push, the bottoms were around her ankles and she kicked them away.

He gulped some air as he ran his gaze over her once more. From the sapphire tips of her blonde spiked cut to the exposed creamy skin, she was damn near perfect. A landing strip of hair guided his sight to her core. The lips glistened and he knew she was ready for him and he'd not even touched her yet.

She took a step and closed the distance between them once more. "You seem a bit overdressed for what I have in mind. Let me help you." Bending close to kiss his bare chest, she worked her way down to his belly button.

"Wait." A guttural rasp slid from his mouth seconds before she pulled down his shorts. His cock, long and hard, sprung free, bobbing before her.

"Hello, gorgeous," she purred as she curled her fingers around his shaft.

He widened his stance, breathing faster and shallower. A few cursory pumps prior to when she flicked her tongue over the head.

A moan fell free from between his lips and he sank his hands into her hair. Closing his eyes ever so brief, he tried to control his urge just to thrust deep into her throat. Opening them, he peered down at her to discover she watched him in return with those dark blue eyes.

She never looked away as she blew him. Bobbing on his cock, she didn't allow any part of him to go unattended. From the sensitive head to his balls, she gave each their due.

Grant couldn't pull his gaze from her face. There was something amazing about watching a woman happily give head. When his balls drew tight against him, he lifted her from where she knelt before him and carried her to the bed. "Not yet," he said.

Her response was dragging her tongue along her lower lip.

He placed her down gently. His was cock so hard, it ached. "I don't have much patience right now. I really want to fuck you."

She lay back, legs slightly spread, and he settled beside her. "And we're back to, do you hear me complaining?" A smile. "Although, I have to say, I was enjoying your dick in my mouth."

His cock jerked at her words, then again, when she circled him once more with her touch. "Fuck this." He reached around her to the bedside table and dug in the drawer for a condom.

The moment he found and grabbed one, she took it from him. Eva rose onto her knees as she straddled him.

"Allow me." The rip of the packet was followed by her tossing it to the side. Eva took him in hand and rolled it down his length. She was up and over him, sinking down, taking him deep inside her body. "Oh, shit," she groaned.

Yeah, he was on par with that statement.

Hot. Tight. Wet.

He gulped and grabbed her hips with his hands.

She gazed down at him, bottom lip caught in her teeth. As he stared, she leaned forward and put her hands on his chest.

For a moment in time, they stayed like that, lost in each other's eyes. Connected in the most physically intimate of ways. He swore, there in that second, something more passed between them.

When she moved, any and all thought went out of his head.

Eva rode him. Undulating, rocking, and finding a rhythm she liked as she discovered her own release.

While it wasn't the easiest thing to do, Grant let her set the pace for now. As she fucked him, he swore there would be more. For whatever reason, he could see she needed to get an edge off.

Go ahead, baby, use me. Fuck me as you will, I'm fine with this arrangement, just know that I'll take mine when you're finished.

She closed her eyes and dropped her head back as she continued to guide him along this path she took toward release. Her nails dug into his flesh as she came around him with a cry.

Grant didn't mind the bite of pain, in fact, he rather liked it. But as soon as her slit began pulsing and clenching around him as she came, he rolled them over, putting her on the bottom.

"My turn," he rumbled against her lips.

She kept up with him, never once missing a beat. Hooking her legs behind his back, she drew him in as deep as he could go. He ground his jaw, determined not to give in yet. This was the sweetest pussy he'd been in, ever, and he didn't want to leave.

She didn't make it easy. Not with the way she tightened and flexed her internal muscles around him. She milked him and he couldn't last any longer.

With a low roar, he came hard. Thrusting fast and deep.

Sliding her arms around his shoulders, she pressed her face into him as he went balls-deep inside her. Her entire body shook and shuddered as they both came.

Grant nearly collapsed on her but rolled to the side at the last moment. He gathered Eva in his arms and together, limbs entwined, they let their racing hearts slow, breathing calm, and bodies relax.

"Damn," she muttered against him.

His lips twitched as he smiled. "Couldn't have said it better myself."

She trailed her fingers along his torso. "That took the edge off. I need some more."

A woman after his own heart. "I'm here to serve."

Eva bit at his nipple with light teasing snaps. "Good to hear."

Grant knew this was far from over.

TOTALLY
BOUND
Home of Erotic Romance

About the Author

Aliyah Burke is an avid reader and is never far from pen and paper (or the computer). She is happily married to a career military man. They are owned by six Borzoi. She spends her days at the day job, writing, and working with her dogs.

Aliyah loves to hear from readers. You can find her contact information, website details and author profile page at https://www.totallybound.com

CPSIA information can be obtained
at www.ICGtesting.com
Printed in the USA
LVHW041528191120
672182LV00002B/177